The Evil That We Do

His eyes were open. The clear cornea, normally moistened by tears, was drying out and beginning to shrivel. It was that, more than the blood, that made my stomach contract; it took an effort to keep from retching.

Beyond the body lay a large, pure-white rock that I recognized as a paperweight used in the office. On it were dark red stains. My eyes took in the searing reality of the scene, my mind photographing it in graphic detail. Long after, I could have told you exactly where everything was, could recall that dreadful death-mask stare.

"I'm sure he's dead."

The Evil That We Do

by

Anne Barton

Commonwealth
Publications

A Commonwealth Publications Paperback
THE EVIL THAT WE DO

This edition published 1996
by Commonwealth Publications
9764 - 45th Avenue,
Edmonton, AB, CANADA T6E 5C5
All rights reserved
Copyright © 1995 by Anne Barton

ISBN: 1-55197-086-4

This work is a novel and any similarity to actual persons or events
is purely coincidental.

Designed by: Danielle Monlezun
Cover Illustration by: Jennifer Brolsma

Printed in Canada

*To Mary Mercer, who, were she alive, would say,
"See! I said you could do it!"*

*You created us to love You with
all our heart,
and to love each other as ourselves,
but we rebel against You by the
evil that we do.*

Eucharistic Prayer 5
Book of Alternative Services
Anglican Church of Canada

Prologue

"You never pay any attention to me!" the voice
screamed in tormented fury. "Don't turn your
goddamn back on me. Turn around and listen."

"Don't swear in church." The antagonist spoke
with quiet, acidic disdain and continued to lean
over and shuffle through the pile of papers on the
counter of St. Matthew's Anglican Church office,
as if the complainant's words and presence were
as trifling and insignificant as last week's an-
nouncement in the St. Matthew's Sunday bulletin about a lost earring.

Palpable rage filled the air as a desperate hand
fumbled for a large stone paperweight, lifted and
swung. A skull caved in, a body slumped and
bounced off the counter. As the assailant backed
hastily away, letting the paperweight fall from a
now trembling hand, a fine spray of blood splat-
tered onto clothing.

Stepping across the body, the killer now fled
in panic, footsteps beating a harsh staccato on
the hallway tiles of this usually peaceful place of
worship. Reaching the bolted outer door, the killer

drew back in alarm. Two elderly ladies stood chatting on the sidewalk, blocking any unobtrusive escape.

Another door. On the other side. There had to be another way out.

Racing through the church, the killer stumbled on the step up to the altar, falling on bent knees and raising horrified eyes to see the crucifix bathed in sunlight. Rising again and fleeing across the carpeted chancel of the hushed church, the killer reached the recess of the sacristy, found a door and stepped from the church into the peaceful afternoon light.

For the first time in its ecclesiastical history, blood flowed onto the sacred ground of St. Matthew's.

Chapter 1

Good God, these people must live in a fishbowl!

This thought came to me as I, along with other female members of the Church Executive Committee, made coffee and tea in the plainly furnished meeting room next to the church office and chatted with the wife of a priest who was being interviewed in the office. The Reverend Douglas Forsythe was trying to convince our Selection Committee that he was the man to lead the parish of St. Matthew's Anglican Church in Exeter, a small city in the British Columbia interior. His wife, Betty, ostensibly not involved in the process, must have known full well that the women of the parish would be passing critical judgment on her, and that the impression she made would have an effect on whether her husband got the job.

Betty Forsythe was plump, with an easy smile that dimpled her round face. She made me think of the prairies, with hair the colour of ripened wheat and eyes the deep cerulean blue of the prairie sky. Even her tinkling laugh reminded me of a gust of wind rippling the growing grain.

She told anecdotes of life following her clergyman husband from parish to parish and of raising their three children, now fully grown. The Forsythes had left Douglas' last parish, where he had served for fifteen years, for a year of travel and study. They had helped their youngest son, Ross move into his new apartment in Ottawa, where he would start his first job after graduation from university; had been to visit their older son Stuart, a teacher in Halifax; and were on their way to Prince George to visit their oldest child Claudia, who worked as a surgical nurse. They had seen their newest grandchild, one of Stuart's two, for the first time. They had still not seen Claudia's baby boy.

This was not the first time they had travelled across the country pulling a trailer. Betty's account of moving from the Maritimes to the Yukon in an old station wagon, its roof rack piled high, pulling a small trailer, had us in stitches. There were the three precious young children, all under the age of five, a dog and a mother cat with a litter of kittens. There were diaper bags, toys, games, and snacks, as well as cat litter and pet food. Of course, all the children and pets got hungry, had to go to the bathroom, or got carsick in relays, testing the parents' equanimity and their faith in God. They pulled into a western town late at night only to find a rodeo crowd filling all the motels. Having friends in High Places came in handy, however. Soon the rodeo cowboys, noted for sharing their assets anyway, were doubling up to make room for the Forsythe family. Betty told the tale with wit and charm and I could see all the ladies in the room warming to her unpretentious demeanor. Though I had not yet laid eyes on her husband, I knew I could certainly get along quite well with this lady in the rectory.

The Forsythes had stopped at the cathedral in Georgetown, where they had heard that St. Matthew's was looking for a priest to replace one who had retired due to illness. Our bishop, the Right Reverend Michael Staines, had been a seminary classmate of Douglas Forsythe and was delighted to see him. He had talked Douglas into applying at St. Matthew's. With the bishop's personal recommendation, it would seem that Douglas would be certain of the position, but knowing our intransigent Selection Committee, I had my doubts.

Most people have had the experience of trying to remember, after the event, what they were doing when something especially momentous happened, or to remember their first impression of a person who would become significant in their lives. As we sat in the church meeting room talking to this charming and amusing lady, finding that we could relate to many of her stories and anecdotes, we had no forewarning that the quiet ripples in the placid life of our church were about to break into monstrous waves threatening to swamp us. Nor had I any premonition that the man I was about to meet would change my life forever.

We were a church in transition, floundering after several months without a full-time priest. The part-time priest-in-charge, Philip Eccles, who had been dragged reluctantly out of retirement, had neither the time nor the inclination to put his stamp on our church's affairs. Never knowing when he would be told that his services were no longer needed, and anxious to get back to his quiet gardening, he found his work being extended week after week as we dithered over the replacement of a much-loved priest. The congregation was growing impatient for the Selection Committee to get a move on, but the Reverend Eccles advised caution.

"You will know when the one who is right for this parish comes along. God will guide you."

In the meantime, we had hired a man from outside the church for a job we labeled Programme Director. Frank Corrigan was to administer the non-spiritual part of the rector's job until a new incumbent could take over. Only faint grumbles of discontent were heard, but the quiet consensus was that our temporary director was more hindrance than help. We assumed that with the coming of a new rector, the problem, and Frank Corrigan, would quietly fade away.

Finally, from the church office, a scraping of chairs announced the interview was over, and the interviewers and interviewee appeared at the doorway. Of medium height and build, Douglas Forsythe was still admirably trim for a man in his mid–fifties. His carriage was erect; his brown hair, greying at the temples, was cut short; his face clean-shaven; his clothes good but conservative. He was not wearing his clerical collar. One could mistake him for a successful business or professional man. He had a distinguished face, not handsome, yet attractive, with laugh lines around his warm, chocolate brown eyes. The older parishioners, I was certain, would feel he looked eminently suitable. The younger ones would wonder if he were too establishment to lead the church into the future.

I wondered what the Selection Committee had asked and what answers the Reverend Forsythe had given. I wondered also whether he would like our rather staid community with its high percentage of retirees. We were looking at him and at his credentials, but the selection of a rector is a two-way process.

One of the other applicants our committee had interviewed had informed us that he would not be interested. The committee had not been overly impressed by him, so no one shed any tears. The cuffs of his shirt were frayed and his trouser pockets were patched at the corners. He wore an old sweater that I would have been ashamed to give to the Salvation Army. He seemed to embody the idea of clerical poverty to the extreme. He came from a large city parish, and I'm sure they paid him adequately. Clergy are not paid salaries that match those of people in other professions with similar education and experience. Anglican clergy, I knew, must have a master's degree in theology and a year's experience as a deacon before ordination to the priesthood. But besides their salary, they are provided with a place to live, completely maintained; also with many of the tools of their trade and some fringe benefits. They don't have to live in deprivation, and every other Anglican clergy person I have met has been neatly, if conservatively, dressed. While it is admirable to exercise an unostentatious demeanor, it would be embarrassing if our rector looked as if he got his clothes from the Sally Ann and had to drop into the soup kitchen for lunch.

Only one previous applicant had created a good impression with the committee, but since the vote had to be unanimous, and one member had voted against him, he hadn't gotten the job. I secretly wondered if our resident feminist, Gretchen Schmidt, one of the Selection Committee members, had blackballed him simply because he was a man; if so, would she do the same to Douglas Forsythe? Whether it was she, or someone else on the committee, I now offered my silent thanks. I hadn't been at all impressed and was amazed that the others were so taken by him. I had the impression he would have merely used St. Matthew's as a step up the parochial success ladder and would only have been here until something bigger and better came along.

"I thought the bishop just appointed someone," Myrtle Williamson was saying to Sue Ambler and Gretchen Schmidt. Gretchen sighed, then explained to Myrtle once again how the selection of a new rector was done. I had heard her explain this to Myrtle on at least two previous occasions.

"Remember when Martin resigned, we asked people to be on a selection committee? We sent about a dozen names to the bishop and he chose seven of them to make up the committee. Then we put together a parish profile and advertised the position. Those interested sent their résumés to the bishop who selected several of the most suitable for us to interview. This man has taken leave from his former parish and if we like him and he likes us, he'll be able to start quite soon. Any of the others would have to give notice to their current parishes. How do you like him, by the way?"

Myrtle put her head to one side and frowned, as if weighing her answer carefully. "Oh, he seems nice. He dresses well and he doesn't have a beard, not like Martin had."

"I don't see that a beard has anything to do with his ability to run the parish."

"Hmph! If my husband had ever grown a beard, I'd have thrown him out of the house."

Sue Ambler leaned over toward me and murmured, "No wonder he died young." I giggled.

Douglas Forsythe was being introduced around. Balancing a plate and cup, he adeptly managed to shake hands, make a few remarks and ask questions of each person he met.

"Myrtle Williamson, who has come to us from Fort Watson, and is very active in the Guild," Lew Stern, a young lawyer who chaired the Selection Committee, was saying.

Simpering is the way I would describe Myrtle's response; she nearly curtsied and offered him only the very tips of her fingers to shake. He took the fingertips formally, smiled benignly and made comments about his one trip to Fort Watson. I sipped at my coffee to hide my smile. He was undoubtedly used to such women and knew how to handle them. He dared not get on the bad side of the Women's Guild.

"Gretchen Schmidt, the people's warden, you already know."

They smiled at each other and I was happy to see that Gretchen's smile was warm and welcoming.

"Penny Farnham, a public health nurse." Penny, my best friend, was a young woman of great vitality and a lively sense of humour. She brushed a great mop of brown hair back from her face, extended her hand firmly and grinned at him. I could see his smile extend from his lips to his eyes. He held her hand for a moment while they exchanged a few words. Both of them laughed. He had made a hit with Penny, and she with him. I glanced at his wife, but she seemed totally unconcerned. Straying from the marital fold, it seemed, was not one of his sins. Chalk one up on the plus side!

"This is Jean Givens. She's a real estate agent."

"Sorry," Forsythe joked. "I won't be in the market for a house."

"Too bad. We have some lovely ten-bedroom mansions with sunrooms, saunas and swimming pools." They chatted briefly about houses, then Forsythe and Lew moved on.

"This is Sue Ambler, who is a senior secondary school English and drama teacher."

"You come most carefully upon your hour," she said, smiling.

"It looks as if I'm going to have to brush up on the Bard. What was that quote from?"

"*Hamlet*, Act I. The changing of the guard."

"Ah! Now I remember. Do you have any ghosts here?"

"Not that we know of."

"Too bad. A good ghost would add spice to life." His brown eyes twinkled.

Forsythe and Lew Stern moved on to where I stood. "I'd like you to meet Robin Carruthers. She runs a flying school."

Forsythe took my hand in a firm grip, grinned and said, "Nearer, my God, to Thee."

I burst into laughter. If I hadn't taken to him before, that did it. I had grown up in small rural towns where community churches had Bible-thumping fundamentalist preachers who were as exciting as sliced white bread and as humorous as a basket of dirty laundry. I was only beginning to discover that not all are like that. I think it has to do with your confidence in your faith, whether you can joke about God. Obviously, this man was no sourpuss.

"Did you have a good trip down from Georgetown?" I asked the Forsythes.

They both answered at once, the words tumbling out.

"We had a lovely trip. So much scenery! We started early so we would be in plenty of time, but we kept stopping to take pictures. . ." Betty's eyes sparkled with enthusiasm.

"It was the kind of bright, clear day when all the mountains stand out. . ." her husband interjected.

"There were all these marvelous cloud shadows, making everything look exciting."

"And wind! You could see the clouds scurrying along. You would go from shady patches to brilliant sunshine reflecting off wet pavement where it had just rained."

"It sort of suited our mood. We were so excited about coming down here."

"Typical spring weather," Lew nodded equably.

Penny grimaced. "When it's raining cats and dogs, everyone says that's typical spring weather."

"Typical spring weather is when it changes every five minutes," I offered.

The subject of weather having been exhausted, the conversation lagged while we nibbled on cookies and drank our coffee. Lew shifted to another subject. "What do you think of our little city?" he prompted. All ears perked to their response.

"It's lovely," they replied in unison.

"So neat and attractive with all the spring flowers and the trees just getting their leaves,"Betty went on. "I'm glad that people here like trees. We have been places where men seem to love their chain saws more than they love their wives, and no tree is safe."

"Have you had a chance to see the interior of the church yet?" Jean Givens, the alternate chairman (oops, chairperson!) of the Church Committee asked. Being a real estate agent, she had the building on her mind.

"No, I haven't," Douglas Forsythe answered.

"Oh, then you must," we all chorused. We were proud of our church, which is listed as a heritage building, and were only too happy to show it off. From the exterior, it is a large, impressive stone building surrounded by old, well–cared for maple trees in a park-like setting. Occasionally someone will suggest that we sacrifice some of the lawn and trees to enlarge our parking lot, but that suggestion is invariably vetoed with great vehemence.

But it is the interior that is the most beautiful. We filed from the meeting room through a connecting corridor to a door which opened into the south aisle near the front of the nave. Lew switched on the night lights, providing soft illumination without the full glare of all the lighting.

Stone walls rose to the sloping roof over the aisles, then again higher to surround the nave. An arched ceiling of light-toned wood curved overhead. Through the tinted glass windows along the sides and the clerestory windows above, the reflected lights of the city shone palely. Deep red carpet contrasted with the light-coloured wood of the pews, each with a carving on its central end, the work of a local parishioner back in the twenties when the church was built. His handiwork was present also in the beautifully carved lectern and pulpit and on the overhead rood beam. The carving was interesting, expressing the story of Christ through the use of native Canadian objects and always reminded me of Healy Willan's setting of the Huron Carol. The dim lights highlighted shiny plaques along the walls, commemorating people and events in the church's past.

"You must see the end windows," Lew said and slipped from the church to the lighting panel in the corridor.

Suddenly, the large windows at the east and west ends of the church were illuminated from without and I heard a gasp of joy from Betty Forsythe. Our small city of Exeter was named by immigrants from Devonshire who came here a hundred years ago, prospered, and built a church to commemorate their good fortune. They decided to duplicate, on a smaller scale, the famous stained–glass windows of Exeter Cathedral.

The west window was of roseate design in its upper portion, with several panels depicting biblical persons or scenes at its base. The east window, behind the altar, was made of a series of panels or lights depicting apostles and saints. These were smaller, fewer, and less elaborate than at Exeter Cathedral, but a majestic addition to our modest church. As with that great cathedral, the windows are best seen with sunlight streaming through them, but are nonetheless impressive in artificial light.

For a few moments, no one moved or spoke.

"The organ!" Betty finally exclaimed. The

muted light shone off ranks of bronze pipes. "A real pipe organ."

"Yes," Jean replied. "Quite a good one, too."

"And in a church that was meant for pipe organs," Douglas said. "Did you know that the pipe organ was developed to fill great, tall stone churches with music?"

"Really?"

"Yes. These modern churches don't lose anything by having electronic organs. The sound from the pipes needs the lofty space a church like this provides."

"May I?" Betty asked, tilting her head toward the organ console.

"Of course," Lew replied.

She made her way to the organ loft, genuflecting as she passed the altar, switched on a small lamp and looked around, orienting herself. Soon the motor that pumped air to the pipes could be felt reverberating faintly. Betty poised her hands over the keys, then began to play. Softly, a familiar strain began to fill the church. What was it? Oh yes, Bach's *Sheep May Safely Graze*. The melody floated out beautifully over the watching people, climbed up to the vaulted ceiling and hung there as the last strains died away. For a long moment, we stood motionless, unwilling to break the magic spell. Gradually, clothing rustled, people moved and murmurs of conversation echoed softly in the church.

Penny Farnham had come up beside me. She remarked quietly, "Well, at least we won't have to scramble around for an organist when John Vieth has an attack of his 'lumbago'."

Betty came down from the organ loft and returned to her husband's side. I saw them take each other by the hand, giving a little squeeze and a smile which one could tell was a form of silent communication that spoke volumes.

"What a beautiful church!" Douglas said fervently. From the look on his face, I knew he wasn't going to turn us down if we wanted him, and glancing around at the members of the congregation, I saw by their satisfied expressions that he indeed would be their choice.

The group broke up. The Forsythes left to return to the home of Shirley and Harry Meacham, the church secretary and her husband, where they would spend the night before visiting the next day with our interim priest, Philip Eccles. Jean locked the church and said goodnight, leaving Penny and me in the parking lot.

"Well, what do you think?" Penny prodded.

"About. . .?"

"The rector."

I grinned and gave a thumbs-up sign and Penny broke into peals of laughter.

"See you in Heaven," she called, climbing on her ten-speed and pedaling away.

Chapter 2

On the following Friday, the blustery weather had passed and the sun shone out of a clear blue sky. Lawnmowers and weed-eaters rumbled and snarled. People rushed to the garden stores and newly-planted pansies brightened yards and parks.

I knew that at the Red Robin Flying School, we would be inundated. Our pilots would want to knock the rust off their flying skills after the winter layoff, and new students would be taking advantage of our introductory flight offer. I hoped it would last; I longed for good flying weather through the summer. I'd owned the school for nearly twenty years. It had been a long, hard battle trying to succeed in a highly competitive and marginally profitable industry. A summer of bad weather could be devastating. Long periods of good weather would allow me to bank profits for the future.

I got up early and was at the airport by six, but someone was already there waiting for me. Wendy was a young woman who had received her private pilot's license the previous year, and when the weather turned bad in the fall, had decided to save up in order to fly regularly the next summer. She had been an excellent student, and when I had given her the flight test, had excelled.

"Do you have time to check me out this morning?" she asked anxiously. "I thought you would probably be here early, so I took a chance on coming before work."

"Sure. Let's see which plane is available and you can be pre-flighting it while I open up."

With most pilots, I would have stood over them watching the pre-flight being done, but I knew that this one would do it thoroughly. On occasion, I looked out the window, seeing Wendy move around the red and white Cessna 150 trainer in a systematic fashion, checklist in hand, peering intently at everything. I saw her on a ladder, peeking into the gas tanks, looking at the fuel level. When I got to the plane, she had it pulled out of its tie-down and headed down the taxiway.

"The tanks are full. The oil is down half a litre and everything else is normal, except that there aren't very many spare fuses. There's one of each size, though," Wendy reported. I was pleased that she was so observant. Hardly anyone bothers to check the fuses until they need one, which always occurs at extremely inopportune times.

"That's fine. Let's go."

We climbed into the cramped cockpit and fastened our seat belts and shoulder harnesses. Wendy looked at the fuel selector valve between the seats to make sure it was on, then scanned the panel from left to right, setting the altimeter to field elevation, checking that the primer was locked, the carburetor heat off, and that all the radio and light switches were in the off position. She cracked the throttle, advanced the mixture control to rich, and turned the master switch on. Then looking around, in front, to the sides and behind the plane, called through the open window, "Clear prop," looked again and, seeing that all was clear, turned the key in the ignition. The engine rumbled into life. She watched the oil pressure needle move up into the green arc then turned on the radio, setting it to the ground control frequency.

"Are we going to the practice area?"

"Yes."

She pushed the mike switch. "Exeter Ground, Robin Three, Red Robin ramp, taxi, VFR local."

"Robin Three, Exeter Ground. Taxi runway zero

four; wind calm; altimeter three zero one five; time thirteen twenty-six Universal; taxi via Bravo."

"Robin Three."

At the runup pad, Wendy leaned across the cockpit to look at the engine gauges, tested the mags, checked for carburetor ice, set the trim and the heading indicator, turned on the anti-collision light, moved all the controls and flaps through their full range, and dialed in the tower frequency.

"Robin Three, ready for departure to the practice area."

"Robin Three, Tower. Cleared for take-off. Left turn approved."

We taxied onto the runway, lined up with the centre-line, and Wendy smoothly advanced the throttle to full power. As our speed picked up, she eased back on the control yoke to gently lift the nose wheel off the ground, while feeding in right rudder to counteract torque and keep us going in a straight line. As the plane reached flying speed, she let the nose find the slightly nose-high attitude to which it had been trimmed, and I watched her take a quick look at the oil pressure gauge.

I relaxed, eased my seat back a notch and sighed with satisfaction. Piece of cake! This gal hadn't forgotten anything all winter. As if reading my mind, Wendy remarked, "I've been flying various kinds of flights in my mind all winter, so I wouldn't forget how to do it."

"Good idea! It seems to have worked. I'll have to suggest it to others, if you don't mind."

She gave me a happy smile, then turned her attention back to her flying. She leveled off, set cruising power and re-trimmed, then glanced at me questioningly. "What do you want me to do?"

"Let's follow the road up the valley, and see what we can find. I feel like just playing around."

"I thought you'd want stalls and all that."

"I'm tired of stalls. Let's just have fun. But remember to always have an emergency landing field in mind."

She grinned and pointed to the left. "Right there. That hay field, until we get too far past it."

I knew I should be giving her a thorough checkride, but I also knew from her past performance that she would handle it all right. I had a whole summer of routine training ahead of me, and this lovely morning I wanted to be different, to have fun, and to let this young pilot share in it. I had noticed an extra verve and sparkle about her as soon as the 150 started to roll down the runway. Learning that checkrides could be fun would probably make her more amenable to suggestion that she take advanced training. I wanted my pilots to be competent, but I also wanted them to enjoy flying. They were better pilots that way, and it was good for business.

On our return, Wendy flared out too high on her landing and made a sour face. "I guess I have to practice those a bit more."

"Do that. It wasn't a bad landing, but you can do better. After all, you've had a long lay-off, so you can expect to be a bit rusty on your landings. You'll do all right."

We got out of the plane and I headed back to my office feeling great, but knowing the flights ahead wouldn't all be this easy.

I flew with only one other pilot that day. The president of an engineering firm, Reiner was the typical Type A executive: lean as a greyhound from pushing himself, always on the go, striving to reach the top. I felt that I should fly with him myself because I knew that he was going to be a problem and that my instructors might have to refer him to me anyway.

Reiner was ten minutes late for his scheduled session. He should have had his plane pre-flighted and ready to go, but when he burst into the office he was still talking on his portable phone. He attempted to reach for the clipboard and key for his scheduled airplane while he continued his conversation. Joyce, the dispatcher, hesitated, but I reached over her shoulder and took the clipboard, moving it out of his reach. He looked startled and stopped talking on the phone. "Hey, I need that!"

"Hang up the phone and put it back in your car."

He looked undecided, but my scowl brooked no nonsense. "I'll call you back later," he growled into the phone and hung up with assertive vigour.

"What's the big idea?"

"When you come out here to fly, you need to have your mind on what you're doing. Next time, leave your phone at home."

"Hey, I'm expecting an important call. I gotta take the phone with me."

"Number one, you can't have that phone turned on while you are in an airplane. It interferes with radio communication and navigation signals. Number two, when you fly, you need to have your mind entirely on your flying. You are not to have your phone with you when you fly."

"Oh."

"Is that clear?"

"Yeah. Okay."

He was not a man who willingly took orders from anyone, especially from a woman. Flushing with barely concealed anger, his long strides carried him swiftly out to his car where he flung the phone onto the front seat. It didn't look as if he locked the car after him, but I mentally shrugged off my concern. He was old enough to realize the risk, and if he didn't, it was his own fault. But if he was that cavalier about his own possessions, I would certainly watch him closely when he was handling mine. I silently handed him the clipboard and just as silently he snatched it out of my hand, tucked it under his arm, and strode out to the two-place trainer. This time I would watch very carefully while the pre-flight was being done.

Reiner did not check the fuel in the tanks, so I set a trap for him. Sometimes when I do this, the pilot complains that it's sneaky and unfair, but it is designed to wake him up and make him think. While Reiner was busy doing something else, I unscrewed the cap over the fuse for the fuel gauges, removed the fuse and replaced the cap. I put the fuse in the slot for spares. For the remainder of the pre-flight, I went around behind him with one of our printed checklists, reminding him of everything he missed, making him do it. He grumbled and pouted, but realizing that I meant to have my way, did it.

When we had started up, he asked me, "What's the tower frequency?"

I glared at him. "You're supposed to know that."

Sighing, he reached for an attaché case thrown in the baggage area, rummaged around until he had found a VFR Supplement, and looked up the Exeter Airport listing. I noted that the VFR Supplement was two years out-of-date and had someone else's name on its cover. He was apparently too cheap to buy his own updated version, though we had them for sale in the office. But I knew he would find the correct frequency in it, so I let it go.

Reiner jabbed his thumb at the mike switch. "Tower, this is Robin One, ready to taxi."

"Robin One, Exeter Tower. Contact Ground Control on one two one decimal seven."

"Uh, sorry." He switched frequencies and called the ground controller.

"Ground Control, this is, uh, Robin, uh, One. I'd like to taxi."

"Robin One, Excter Ground. What is your position on the airport?"

"Uh, I'm at the flying school."

"Roger, Robin One. Understand that you are at Red Robin Flying School. What are your intentions?"

"Uh, I'd like to taxi out and take off."

"Roger, Robin One. Will this be a local flight?"

"I guess so."

"Robin One, if you are leaving the local area, you need to use your full call sign rather than the flight school number."

"Uh, yeah, I guess it'll be a local flight."

"Robin One, is there an instructor on board?"

"I pushed my mike switch and replied, "Affirmative. Sorry guys."

"Hello there, Robin." The controller sounded much more cheerful. "Robin One, cleared to runway zero four; wind three six zero at zero five; altimeter three zero two one; time seventeen forty-five; taxi via Bravo."

"Robin One."

We finally managed to get out to the runway. After Reiner had done a half-hearted runup, he switched back to the tower frequency.

"Are you really planning to go flying with empty fuel tanks?" I asked.

He looked at me in surprise, then down at the fuel gauges. The colour drained out of his face; the two needles were sitting on the empty pegs.

"I guess we'd better get some gas," he said weakly.

"Is the engine still running?"

"Uh, yeah."

"What is it running on?"

He sat there, trying to figure it out. "What makes the fuel gauges work?"

"I guess they're electric."

"You guess! Don't you know?"

"Uh, maybe I'd better check the fuse." Looking along the row of fuses until coming to one with the appropriate label, he unscrewed the cap and discovered that the fuse was missing. He pursed his lips, thinking, then tentatively opened the map compartment and seemed pleasantly surprised to find a neat row of spare fuses on the inside of the door.

"What size fuse does it take?" I sighed. He appeared ready to pluck any fuse that seemed handy out of the rack. He cogitated some more and finally remembered to look at the cap, on which was printed the fuse size. Selecting the proper one, he inserted it and the fuel gauges jumped up to full.

"You still don't know for certain whether the tanks are really full of the proper fuel, do you? Well, I do, because I filled them myself. Otherwise I wouldn't take off. Let's go."

He pushed the mike button and said, "Robin One is ready for take-off. We're just going around the circuit once."

"We're going to the practice area," I said firmly.

"But I don't have time. I only want to go around the circuit once, so my insurance will be valid."

"Look, you are going to have to be properly checked out, and I am going to determine what you need in order to do so."

"But I have to get back to the office."

"Then maybe we'd better taxi back. By the way, the tower is calling you."

"Robin One, Tower. How do you read me?"

"Oh, shit!"

"You'd better decide what you want to do."

He shrugged, pressed the mike button and said reluctantly, "Tower, this is Robin One. I guess we'll go out to the practice area."

"Robin One, cleared for take-off. Left turn on course."

The rest of the session fared little better. Some manoeuvers were performed fairly well, others poorly, and on our return, his circuit entry was improper and his landing atrocious. He was hot and high on final, so he dumped the 150's nose down, picking up even more speed, barely leveling off enough so that his touchdown, two thousand feet down the runway, was on all three wheels and not nose wheel first. It should have been on the main gear only. I braced myself for the inevitable bounce, my hand hovering near the yoke and my feet poised over the rudder pedals in case I had to rescue us from complete disaster.

He was still carrying a fair amount of power, which should have been cut long ago, adding impetus to the bounce and carrying us a good three metres into the air. Then, when it was needed, he cut the power, and in the ensuing silence, the wings decided to give up the effort to produce lift and we dropped with all the negative G's of an express elevator plummeting earthward. When we hit, the spring steel gear flattened out, then recoiled like a bungee cord, shooting us high into the air again. The next time we dropped, the 150 shuddered to a stop and sort of squatted there, as if unwilling to take any more punishment.

I checked my neck for whiplash, plucked an aviation chart off the top of the sun visor, and thanked the Cessna company for making such sturdy airplanes. Reiner, who thought of himself as an ace corporate pilot, sat immobilized, then asked tentatively, "What did I do wrong?" His usual golf course-tanned complexion was red with embarrassment, his arrogant demeanor thoroughly humbled. I wanted to howl with laughter, but I hid my face behind the chart I was still holding, not wanting to embarrass him further.

The controller didn't improve Reiner's mood by clearing us off the runway at taxiway Charlie and adding, "I'll record three landings for you."

After taxiing in and shutting down, I told Reiner he would have to fly with an instructor to hone his flying skills. Still thoroughly demoralized by his disastrous landing, he nonetheless tried to assert his dominant personality. He had passed a flight test, he argued. That meant he was qualified to fly. As with many other men, his attitude also implied that he did not expect to take orders about the manly art of flying from a mere woman.

"You haven't flown for six months and your skill level has deteriorated," I explained in a voice that sounded kinder and more controlled than I felt. "That happens with most people in the same situation. It's nothing to be ashamed of. You need to brush up on several things. You don't want to get lost on a cross-country or take passengers along and frighten them. Would you really want to take a potential customer on a business trip and make a landing like that? Flying is more fun, and also more economical, if you do it well. You will feel a lot better about your own abilities if you take some dual instruction. Anyway, those are the rules here. You know that. I can't let you fly, for your sake as well as mine, until you are more competent and safer."

He glared and grumbled, while I stood with arms folded across my chest, my look implacable. Finally, his shoulders sagged in defeat.

"Yeah, I guess you're right. When can I do that?"

"The sooner the better." I forced a smile. He was, after all, helping pay the bills. I didn't want to send him away angry. "Let's go look at the schedule."

* * * *

Since it was Friday and the banks were open late, I left the operation of the school to my capable staff and left early to make a deposit and get change for the till before the weekend. After leaving the bank, my route home took me past the church, and seeing the sedate grey Chrysler of Shirley Meacham, the church secretary, alongside Frank Corrigan's fiery red convertible in the parking lot, I thought I'd stop by to retrieve my copy of the minutes of the last Church Committee meeting.

I was approaching the closed door to the office when I heard a voice raised in argument, and was quite surprised to realize that it was Shirley's. I had never heard her use a tone of voice that was not calm, friendly and gentle. Another voice that I identified as that of Frank Corrigan, the church's programme director, joined in the verbal fracas. I hesitated, not wanting to intrude, yet frankly, I was curious.

"I've been working since nine this morning with no lunch. I'm supposed to leave at two, but there has been so much work to do with no full-time clergy here, I've been working extra every day. I left that item for the newsletter because it won't come out for awhile and I can do it Monday. You don't need to come in here and pick and pick and pick until you find something I haven't done." Shirley's voice rose and became more animated as she spoke.

"You should be able to get your work done in

the time allotted," Frank replied with deadly calm.

"I can do so when all I have to do is *my* work.
You are forgetting that we have no regular clergy
here, so a lot more ends up on my desk."

"If you organized your time better," Frank's
voice assumed a pedantic tone, "you'd be able to
get it done on time."

"You forget that this is a church office and everyone in the parish, and there are several hundred of them, is welcome to come in at any time.
Quite a few things that Martin or the assistant
priest did, I now have to do myself. In fact, you
should be taking some of the load off my shoulders. That's what you were hired for."

"I don't need you to tell me how to do my job,"
Frank snapped.

"And *I* don't need *you* to tell me mine!"

Frank hissed something I couldn't hear, and
Shirley really lost it. "Don't give me lectures about
responsibility. I'm perfectly capable of taking care
of my responsibilities without any help from you.
If you don't like what I do, I have a mind to leave it
all to you and see how you would like *that!*"

With that, she yanked open the door, strode
into the corridor and slammed the door behind
her. She took a couple of steps toward the exit
before she saw me.

"I'm sorry," I stammered. I didn't mean to eaves-
drop, but I couldn't help overhearing."

"Oh, Robin." Shirley flung herself into my arms,
burying her head on my shoulder, sobbing. I'm
not comfortable dealing with anguish in someone
else, and though I put my arms around her, I really didn't know what to do or say. At that inopportune moment, Frank Corrigan came out of the
office, locked the door, and strode past us, trying
to look taller than his five-foot-six, his slight shoul-

ders stiff with anger and a look of contempt distorting his usually cold, impassive features.

He went out the exterior door, closed and deliberately locked it behind him, as if to tell us that we were so insignificant we might as well not exist. The screech of his tires insulted our ears as he gunned his Mazda Miata out of the parking lot.

As the sound of his engine faded into the distance, Shirley's body began to quiver in my arms like a trembling leaf and the volume of her sobs increased. I patted her shoulder, completely nonplussed, wishing I'd forgotten to retrieve those damned minutes, yet feeling compelled to do something to help Shirley in her distress.

"Oh, Robin, I can't keep on. I just can't work here anymore. I can't stand that man and he does nothing but pick on me."

"Don't take him seriously," I counselled inadequately. "Everyone knows how much work you put in."

"It's not just that. It's the way he noses around until he's found some little chink in my armour and then just burrows in."

"He's a creep. Everyone knows it."

"Oh, what shall I do?" She rummaged in her purse and found a tissue. "I've tried to hide it from Harry, but how can you hide something that gets on your nerves every day from your husband? He knows and he's starting to get uptight again. He was doing so well, relaxing and enjoying life. His blood pressure was down and he had so much more energy. My squabbles with Frank aren't doing Harry any good. I can see it. He's getting nervous and not eating well. I can't let it affect him.'

"Talk to Philip," I suggested. "He is, after all, a priest with a lifetime of experience. I'm sure he could help you."

"Yes, I guess I should." She dried her tear-drenched eyes with the equally wet tissue. "I'm sorry to bother you."

"Oh, no bother, "I prevaricated. I was, of course, sympathetic toward Shirley's plight, but felt more comfortable helping a student recover from a mis-handled flight manoeuver than mending a broken heart. "I hope I can be of some help," I added lamely.

"You already have. You don't know how much good it's done to have a shoulder to cry on. I can't go to Harry."

She blew her nose. "Now what did you need?"

I told her.

As she unlocked the door to the office, she asked, "Did you meet the Forsythes?"

"Yes, I did. I liked them."

"They stayed overnight with us, you know. What a lovely couple. We were quite impressed by them."

"I think everyone likes them. I hope the Selection Committee did."

"I can't think of anyone better."

She handed me a copy of the minutes and we left, the clatter of Shirley's high heels contrasting with the soft swish of my Hush Puppies. Shirley's pale forehead under carefully coifed grey hair creased in annoyance as she shot back the deadbolt on the outer door, which Frank had locked behind him in such obvious disdain.

Silent, lips tight with anger, she opened it, let us out, and relocked it.

I wished we weren't in a church; I'd have had some choice words to say.

* * * *

Driving home, I saw Penny Farnham on her bike and flagged her down. "Penny, I've got to talk to you."

"Okay. How about eating at Curly's? I see that they have their patio set up now that the weather's nice."

"Fine. I'll meet you there."

Curly's was an informal place, where Penny, in her shorts and T-shirt, and I, in my usual garb of slacks and short-sleeved polo shirt, would not feel out of place. The flight school shirts were bright red, but since they clashed actively with my carrot-coloured hair, I seldom wore them, usually going in for browns and greens. I had long ago given up on trying to look chic, which is hard to do when you tend to end the day with grease smears on your clothing, deciding to opt for comfort instead. Penny, on the other hand, could have modeled sportswear for the Sears catalog.

We found a table in a corner of the patio and placed our orders. Penny ordered a salad heaped with raw vegetables, topped by alfalfa sprouts, with oil and vinegar dressing on the side. I consider alfalfa to be suitable for rabbits, not humans. Remembering that Curly's fruit salad was a harvest of seasonal offerings-not just a few tinned peaches and pears on a pile of lettuce-I ordered it along with a scoop of cottage cheese. Another battle, if not the constant war, with calories won. While we waited for our salads, Penny frowned and remarked, "You look upset. What's the matter?"

I told her about the argument between Shirley and Frank, and watched storm clouds roll across her face.

"Someone ought to kick his ass."

"How long has it been going on?" I asked.

"Since he came here last fall. You could see

right away that he was going to be one of those types who put on airs and thought he commanded the whole place. He's a male chauvinist who thinks that any woman is inferior and therefore the work she does is insignificant."

"How has Shirley put up with him this long?"

"Patience. It takes a lot to get under Shirley's skin. I'm amazed that she blew up, but on the other hand, I'm amazed she didn't do it sooner."

"I'd never noticed."

"You haven't had as close contact. But since I've been on the Outreach Committee, I've been in the office a lot."

"What do you think will happen?"

Penny shrugged. "Hard to tell. Frank may back off now that Shirley has blown her stack, or—Oh, there's Sue and Jean." Penny left her comments unfinished as she stood up and waved to the two women, who were looking for an empty table on the patio. The popular eating spot was filling up rapidly. Sue Ambler and Jean Givens threaded their way between the tables to our corner.

"Whew! What a day!" Jean slid her bag off her shoulder and plunked it on the floor beside her. She slipped out of her red blazer with her real estate company's logo on it, and hung it on the back of her chair. As always, she looked impeccably neat, not a strand of her short black hair out of place. "Everyone wants to buy houses."

"After they've gone flying." I motioned skyward as a Cessna 150 trainer, probably one of mine, passed overhead.

"You too? Yes, I guess flying would pick up with the nice weather. I've got to get back to work after a bite to eat. Fortunately, Steve is good about taking care of the kids when I have to work late."

Jean and her husband Steve, who was in

charge of the city's water purification plant, lived in a sprawling ranch-style house surrounded by pines and beeches on a hill overlooking the lake. Their twelve-year-old boy and seven-year-old girl were bright, well-behaved children, who answered the phone in a mature, professional manner and who helped the adults serve snacks or ran errands when their parents gave parties. There was also a two-year-old girl.

I didn't know Sue as well, but liked her for her sparkling wit. Several of the teenagers who had taken flying lessons at my school had spoken highly of her as a literature and drama teacher. I knew from newspaper articles that she had a passion for getting kids to like Shakespeare, and had enjoyed considerable success. She appeared to have come directly from school. A stylish brown dress draped a figure most women would die for and went well with her brown eyes and honey-blonde hair that hung in a luxurious cascade over her shoulders. I imagined that many a high school youth had fallen head over heels in love with her!

Jean ordered a BLT and Sue a small chef's salad. I wondered how big the large one was when the waitress brought a bowl of salad that would have fed a small pony.

"Robin has been giving me some bad news," Penny told the other women. "Since we're all on the Church Committee, I think you ought to know."

I told Jean and Sue of the quarrel I had overheard. "In the end, Shirley said she might have to quit."

"Oh, no!" Jean wailed. "She can't do that. The place would fall apart without her."

"What do you think we should do?" Sue thrummed well-manicured fingernails on the tabletop.

We sat there looking uncomfortable, unable to come up with a sensible answer. Penny shifted in her chair, pushing her food around on her plate. "I don't know whether we should do anything at the moment. It may just blow over. I think we should wait and see."

"Probably so, but it worries me."

"However, did Frank get the job anyway?" I asked.

"We advertised and he answered our ad. No one else did, so he got the job."

"But I've heard that he doesn't have a very good reputation, so why did we take him on? I mean, he wasn't even a member of the church."

"I can answer that, I think," Jean said. "It wasn't really much of a job. We were going to call it Administrator, but some of us thought that was too ostentatious, so we dreamed up Programme Director."

"Whatever that means," Penny muttered.

Jean went on, "We might have had more luck advertising for an administrator. We had in mind a retired person who wanted some sort of meaningful activity and didn't need a big paycheck. We thought Harry Meacham might do it, but Shirley didn't want him to take on the extra work and worry, so she vetoed that. She may be sorry now that she did. Also, it was sort of temporary, while Martin was sick and couldn't handle the full work load he used to. Then Martin had to resign and Frank was kept on while we were looking for a new incumbent, especially since the assistant priest was also leaving to become rector of Garrett's Landing down on the Coast, and we would only have Philip on a part-time basis."

"Frank didn't seem to consider it temporary," Sue remarked. "The way he talked, he had a job for life."

"That's Frank," Penny nodded. "Delusions of grandeur."

"Anyway," Jean continued, "no one else was interested, so we got stuck with Frank. He sort of floats around in the real estate world picking up what he can, so he isn't actually working regular hours and has time to do the church work on the side."

"I hear that you and the other realtors aren't too keen on him," Sue said in a tone of good-natured malice.

"We can't stand him." Jean's voice thickened with feeling. "What he does is unethical and borders on illegal, but he manages to get away with it. We can't pin him down on anything outright illegal."

I wondered what exactly it was that Frank did that other realtors considered unethical, but still hadn't gotten an answer to my question. I leaned forward, stabbing the air with my fork.

"If he has this reputation, then how come the Church Committee agreed to employ him?" I hadn't been on the Church Committee the previous year when Frank had been hired, so hadn't been in on the decision.

"I think it is just that when you are meeting in the church, in the presence of the clergy, you don't want to point your finger or pass on gossip or tattle on anyone."

"But this is a business matter, not a theological one. The Church Committee runs the business of the church."

"I know. But I still think people just don't want to speak up. 'Love thy neighbor' and all that."

"It's a business," Penny remarked, spreading her arms, palms up in the manner of a priest and rolling her eyes heavenward as though seeking Divine agreement. "But yet it isn't a business. Because when it comes right down to it, it's a church."

'Lord, what fools these mortals be,' quoth Sue, the teacher of English Lit. We all broke out laughing.

Little did we then realize what an accurate portent the words of Shakespeare's Puck would be.

Chapter 3

Albert Wallace called the meeting of the Church
Executive Committee to order. Smooth, suave, cor-
pulent and well-dressed, with a determined fringe
of grey hair clinging to a head as bald and shiny as
polished brass, Albert managed a large hardware
store. The same characteristics that had gotten him
to the top in business had also propelled him to the
chairmanship of the Church Committee: put up a
good front, mouth the right words, use his good-
old-boy network, and flatter the wives of men with
whom he did business. But when you got to know
him, you realized that after he got beyond the limits of the how-to-succeed-in-business lessons, he
hadn't a clue as to what was going on.

I looked around at the others; a combination of
the well-dressed and the downright sloppy were in
attendance. Layton Nathanson, like Albert, wore
expensive slacks and shirt, while Paul St. Cyr, a
retired journalist who edited our newsletter,
slouched around in a camel-coloured turtleneck and
battered, brown cords. Nick Valutin's broad Slavic
face beamed happily above an old sweatshirt and
well-worn jeans so threadbare and shiny at the
knees and seat that I averted my eyes every time he
bent over. Myrtle Williamson wore a jersey dress
and high-heeled shoes that appeared to hurt her
feet, which were half in and half out of their tight
confines. Jean Givens was still wearing her navy
skirt, white blouse and red blazer with the agency
logo on it. She had probably come straight from
work. The rest of us, men and women, seemed
equally divided between fleece sweat suits and jeans.
Running shoes were the order of the day for both
sexes. We were certainly an informal bunch.

I noticed that everyone's shoelaces were tied. I tend to notice shoelaces. At Red Robin Flying School, I had been forced to install a sort of dress code. Women were told not to wear high heels, and men, both young and old, who favoured basketball shoes with tongues hanging out and laces untied, were told to tie up their shoes. For reasons of safety, I had to insist that no one go onto the aircraft ramp with loose shoelaces. One can't have one's customers falling face first into whirling propellers.

Our meeting room was equally informal. Quite plain, with old lino on the floor, folding chairs and trestle tables, it was not conducive to long meetings, yet we managed to keep our aching posteriors glued to these uncomfortable chairs through many an exceedingly long discussion. If it had been any place but in a church, we would have mutinied.

We opened with prayer, our interim priest, Philip Eccles, asking God to guide our deliberations. This always made me nervous. I was not really a Christian in the true sense of the word. I couldn't bring myself to believe in God, and at times like this, I felt I was an impostor. I joined the church for reasons other than religion, though I had been baptized into it as a baby.

Why had I joined?

I'm a single woman with no immediate family. All my relatives, none closer than cousins, live thousands of kilometers away. My brief marriage had not resulted in any children. As I grew older, though I'm only in my forties, I was faced by the prospect of an old age with no family, no contacts, no one to look after me. In the church, I had acquired a "family", and I knew that if I ever needed them, there would be people to look out for me.

I reasoned also that the Anglican Church had a disproportionate number of professional and executive people who might want to use my charter services, or learn how to fly. I suspected that Albert Wallace made sure he was active in church affairs, as well as the Masons, Rotary, and the Rose Garden Committee for the same reason-business contacts.

But my reasons for joining St. Matthew's were not entirely self-centred. I also realized that the church did many good deeds, and I aspired to be part of its missionary outreach. I was pleased to discover how frequently its members were reminded of and encouraged to fulfill their obligations to the world, and pleased to note the considerable number who did so.

I have made good friends among my fellow church-goers. I think that when folks are in church, they are on their best behaviour so to speak. It is pleasant to share a relaxing morning with a group of people who are, on the whole, doing their best to be at their best. St. Matthew's congregation seemed happy rather than dour in their demeanor, and it once occurred to me that one frequently hears of people having heart attacks at sporting events or parties or in theatres or restaurants, but I've never heard of anyone dropping dead in church. Considering the age of many of our parishioners, that seems amazing.

The Anglican service is participatory. You aren't just sat down and preached at. It has kept up with modern times better than some churches. It doesn't dictate everything you do with your life and it tolerates dissenting opinion. I remember our former rector saying, "The church is a school for sinners, not a hotel for saints." You aren't kicked out for being errant, though your behaviour may not be approved of.

The Anglican Church, I knew, allowed some leeway in how one envisioned God. My trouble was,

I couldn't envision God at all. I'd like to, I often thought, when contemplating matters spiritual. It's a comforting concept having something to look forward to after one's mortal toil is over, an ultimate divine reward. Then again, I'm unusual enough to actually love my mortal toil, and I wondered whether I'd still be able to teach flying in any ponderable heavenly sphere.

I did not subscribe to the idea, frequently expressed by pilots, that they were "in heaven" or "close to God" when flying. The joy I got from flying was a purely temporal pleasure, and I never thought of it in terms of God at all.

So why hadn't I joined the Business and Professional Women's Club or the Association of University Women? I sometimes wondered about that. Thinking back to the time I had first come to St. Matthew's, which was the first time in my adult life I had set foot in a church, I realized that my doing so was no casual decision.

Life was just beginning to treat me well. The business was prospering. My health was good. I was taking advantage of the cultural life the city had to offer, and I felt that I was at the zenith of my ability in my chosen work. I had never been compelled to embrace God when things were going badly or after the deaths of my parents. It was when everything was going well that I vaguely wondered whether there was Someone I ought to thank.

If there is a God, I think He has read the flight instructor manuals. Flight instructors are constantly being told that positive motivations are better than negative ones. God then, must have known that I would not be receptive when things were going badly. I would have said, "God can't be both all-knowing and all-loving if He allows things like this to happen." I would have thought religion a bunch of bunk, a kind of uncritical solace for the ignorant masses.

But God, if He exists, caught me on the upswing. It was when I had vague stirrings of wonder over the source of my good fortune, that I began to think that possibly there was more to it than my own ability and hard work. And if I did need to thank God for it, I felt that I should not leave this obligation undone.

I was not witness to any great revelation. In fact, I found myself just drifting along, *in* the church, but not *of* it. Yet there was indefinably something more to my enjoyment of the church, its services, and the occasional study group I had joined, than just an appreciation of a lovely building or a good show.

It was because I couldn't envision the concrete belief that God was guiding my deliberations in the upcoming meeting that I felt ill at ease and hypocritical during the opening prayer.

When I was asked to let my name stand for election to the Church Committee, I had almost said no. I didn't know that much about the church because I hadn't been in it very long. Then I thought, *What better way to learn?* Since I was to pass judgment on business matters—a field in which I have plenty of experience—not theological ones, I reasoned I could square things with my conscience. So there I was.

Holy fringe benefits, I sometimes thought.

Besides, I love organs and choirs, so church attendance has been very pleasant.

* * * *

"Would anyone like to make a motion for approval of the agenda?" Albert asked.

"I don't see anything in there about Shirley," Gretchen Schmidt remarked.

"That's under the Maintenance Committee."

"Oh?" Gretchen's eyebrows lifted questioningly.

The motion was made, seconded and passed.

"Motion to accept the minutes of the last meeting?"

"I've a correction," Penny Farnham said.

"Yes?"

"I'm not listed as being present, though I see that I made and seconded several motions, and I rode home with the recording secretary." Penny gave me a devilish grin. I flushed brick red and Penny laughed. Penny was my best friend in the congregation. Young and vivacious, a health faddist without imposing her ideas on others, she zipped around town on her bike, which kept her lithesome figure in superb form. Every time I thought of her name, it came out Penny Farthing in my mind and I occasionally let it slip, to Penny's immense enjoyment.

Sue Ambler was acting as secretary at this meeting. "Right," she said. "I'll prick you down as present." Sue generally dropped a Shakespearism or two into the conversation.

"I have a grievance." Myrtle Williamson impaled me with a much less cordial look than Penny had used. "I sent my regrets that I couldn't be here, and I wasn't listed under Regrets. People might just think I forgot to come."

"I'm sorry," I stammered. "I didn't know that's what I was supposed to do."

"Well, you ought to. Haven't you ever been on a committee before?"

Not one that gets picky about such petty things, I thought, then with guilty conscience I glanced at Philip Eccles sitting beside me. I wondered if he could detect the knee-jerk umbrage I felt whenever Myrtle corrected the errors of my sinful ways, but his tolerant smile was reassuring.

"Okay, let's get on with the agenda."

The minutes were accepted, with corrections, and I vowed never again to be talked into acting as recording secretary.

"The Selection Committee is listed last, but I think I'll let Gretchen report right now."

There was a buzz of anticipation.

"The Selection Committee has made a decision," Gretchen stated, smiling. "We have accepted the application of Douglas Forsythe as our new incumbent." A murmur of "Great!" and "He's the right man!" worked its way around the table.

Gretchen went on, "In fact, he can start the middle of June since he doesn't have to give notice."

"How about the rectory?" Jean asked.

Gretchen looked at Nick Valutin, the Rector's Warden and Buildings and Grounds chairman.

"It's in good shape. There are just a couple of minor repairs that need doing and the Forsythes say that since the interior was just recently painted, they don't want us to bother redecorating. Martin left it in good shape. His sons did a lot of work there when he and Mary were living in it. They were really handy at such things."

Big shoes to fill. Everything the new rector did would be measured against the extremely popular previous one, even against Martin's handy sons.

"Also a bit out of order," Albert continued, "Anders Olafson wants to talk to us about security, and he's waiting outside."

Nick hoisted himself out of his chair and lumbered off to fetch Olafson. Frank Corrigan slipped in the door behind Olafson, and I noticed some raised eyebrows among the committee members.

Frank was not a member of the Church Committee, but since meetings were theoretically open to
anyone who wished to attend (no one ever did
unless they had to), Frank was within his rights
to be there. Dressed simply in navy slacks, white
shirt and blue quilted jacket, Frank was a small
man with wavy black hair tinged with grey, and
dark eyes. His usually expressionless face was now
furrowed into a frown, and he looked edgy. His
eyes darted restlessly about the room, alighting
on no one in particular, as he jingled the change
in his trouser pocket.

Olafson engulfed the doorway as he entered,
actually ducking, though his head would just have
cleared the door's lintel. His large frame seemed to
fill the room. Even taller than Albert's six-foot-two,
with thinning blond-grey hair, blue eyes and a
friendly smile, he was no stranger to me. He looked
after our security at the flying school, and I knew
him to be capable, thorough, and utterly reliable.

"This is Anders Olafson, owner of Sentinel Security, who wants to speak to us about our security problems," Albert explained.

"Do we have problems?" Frank Corrigan
challenged.

A small shock wave of surprise travelled around
the room. We were unused to outsiders even putting
in an appearance, much less entering our discussions, unless specifically asked. It just wasn't done!
I saw Myrtle's mouth open and close like a fish as
she tried to find words to register her displeasure.

"That depends on how you look at it." Olafson's
deep bass voice was equable.

"Yeah?" Frank needed convincing that on a
sunny day, the sky was blue.

"I'd like to explain that out of all the buildings
we do security checks on, this one gives us the
most trouble."

"Trouble?" Frank asked. How could, his dubious tone implied, there be trouble under his directorship?

"We find more breaches of security here than in any other building. Let me explain what we do. We come around sometime between ten and eleven every night. If we find a meeting in progress, we come back again later.

"We enter the building, check all the lights, ensure that the heat is turned down, that the office door is locked, and that all the exterior doors and windows are closed and secured. Once we found water running in the wash basin, so we check that also. We make sure all the night lights are on, inside and out, and leave you a note if any bulbs are burned out. We exit the door out here," he motioned toward the door outside the room we were meeting in, "lock it and enter the security code into the alarm to set it. We return early in the morning to check again, and we come at other times if we think it necessary, like on summer long weekends when lots of kids are partying in town."

"You're supposed to do all those things. I wonder if you really do?" Frank, who usually gave a good imitation of a hibernating groundhog when you wanted him to get something done, continued to challenge Olafson's presentation.

"We also give you detailed reports."

"Anyone can write a report."

"I wonder what Frank has against Anders?" I whispered to Penny. She shrugged and pulled a face.

"To continue, we find more breaches of security in this church than in any other building in town. We've found lights left on, the heat not turned down, the office not locked, the alarm not set and, as I have said, we have even found water running. Of greatest concern is that we find that everyone has left the church without locking it.

"I have some suggestions to make." Anders paused and looked at our now worried faces. "First, I wonder how many of you have keys?"

Everyone exchanged glances and shrugged.

"Shirley still has a key," Frank remarked.

"How many keys are there altogether?" Albert asked. "I have three."

"There are seven," Philip Eccles replied. "The church, the outside door, the office, the hall, the kitchen, that big storage cupboard, and an extra one for the sacristy. I don't know why it is keyed differently than the rest of the church. Does anyone here know?"

Nick had the information. "Several years ago, someone tried to break in there because it's on the side of the church away from the street and is shielded by shrubs. They broke the lock, which was an old one and easily damaged, but got scared away when the alarm went off and never actually got in. All the church locks are old and it couldn't be matched, so a new one was put on."

"Do you need seven keys?" Anders asked. "Don't you think that one master key for the outside doors, which would fit all the locks but the office, would do? I know you keep valuables in the office, so it needs to be locked separately."

"We also keep confidential material in the office," Gretchen asserted.

Philip said, "The church itself needs a separate key. There is a lot of very valuable material in the church. We need at least three keys: one for the church, one for the office, and one for the rest of the doors. The sacristy should be keyed the same as the other church doors."

"We'd have to change all the locks," Nick stated.

"Exactly," Anders nodded. "Do you know how

many people have keys to the outer doors?"

Albert shrugged and looked at Nick, who shook his head. "I think they give out keys to every group that has meetings here."

"How many groups?"

"I don't know. Martin took care of that."

"Shirley should have," Frank stated.

"Actually, I think she did," Sue replied. "She did most of the things that got done around here," she added pointedly, spearing Frank with a piercing glance.

"Well, anyway," Anders went on, "I suggest that you change all the locks. Key all the church doors the same and all the other doors except the office the same. Have a different lock for the office and give keys only to people who have business in the office on a regular basis. Ditto for the church itself. Make only the number of keys for the outside door and the hall that you know you will need. Number them and sign them out. Have only one key for people who rent the hall. Have them pick it up the day of their meeting, sign it out to them, and have them bring it back the next morning."

"I have a suggestion," I said.

"Yes?"

"On the key that we give out, have a large tag on it, so people will be more apt to remember it if they put it in their pocket or purse. Don't have the church name on it, for security reasons, but have in large block letters, a sort of checklist like, 'Turn down heat; turn off lights; lock door'."

"Good idea," Anders grinned at me. "Like the checklists for your planes."

"Right."

"I think that's an excellent idea", Nick said. "We'll follow up on it."

Anders Olafson continued, "Then get your

alarm security code changed and give it only to people who need to open up in the morning."

"Why should we do all this?" Myrtle Williamson asked. "We haven't had anything stolen."

"You haven't yet. If you don't tighten your security, you will."

"It sounds like a lot of expense and we have an overdraft at the bank already. Up in Fort Watson....."

"Let's get on, shall we?" Albert interrupted hastily. Even he was learning not to let Myrtle get going on the subject of Fort Watson, the Perfect Parish. Whenever we had a problem, we would get a long lecture from her on how wonderfully well the parish in Fort Watson, which seemingly was peopled only with saints and angels, had handled similar problems.

"Thank you," Albert said formally to Anders. "We appreciate your concern. Thanks for coming in and giving us your advice. We'll let you know what we decide."

Anders left, but Frank remained, exuding an aggressive determination to be included in the decision-making.

"I still think. . . "Myrtle started.

But Albert ignored her and asked Nick, "Would you find out how much it would cost to get the locks changed?"

"All right. I'll get a couple of estimates."

But Frank wasn't satisfied. "I wonder if Olafson really does all the things he says? We only have his word for it."

That was too much for me. "I use Sentinel Security," I said. "I have found them very thorough. They don't miss a thing. They check every one of our planes and if they find one unlocked, they call me and stay there until someone comes. You have to lock planes with keys. They're not like cars."

"They do that just for a little airplane like yours?" Layton asked.

"Our 'little' airplanes have several thousand dollars worth of radios in each one, to say nothing of their basic cost. Anyway, Sentinel has an excellent reputation. If they say they check everything, I'm willing to accept that they have done so."

"I wonder," Frank mused, "if our righteous redhead doesn't deliberately leave one of her precious little airplanes unlocked so her big hunk will have an excuse to call her out in the middle of the night."

I sprang to my feet and leaned across the table, glaring directly into Frank's beady little eyes. "Frank, that's enough out of you. Shut your dirty mouth and get out of here." Frank leaned back in his chair in an attempt to get out of my range.

"Frank," Philip said firmly but quietly, "there is no call for remarks like that and I suggest you apologize to Robin."

Frank had the decency to look ashamed, but he didn't apologize. He made himself small and kept his mouth shut, his lips a thin, tight line. Philip reached out and laid his hand on my arm. "Let it go until later," he said gently. Still hot with anger, I subsided into my chair.

After an embarrassed pause during which no one looked my way, Frank changed the subject. "How about the janitors? Has anyone ever checked to see if they locked up? I wouldn't be surprised if they walked out without bothering to lock the doors."

Nick shook his head. "No way. They only come on Fridays, to get the church cleaned up before the weekend. They do the church itself first, then the office, because they don't have keys to them. Whoever is in the office locks the church after they're done in there. Then they do the hall, before the Highland dancing class starts. Then they do whatever is left over, the washrooms and kitchen and stuff. They lock this door out here when they leave, but the Highland dancers have to lock the hall. Anyway, we've found doors left unlocked on other nights than Fridays."

"What do you know about the janitors, though? That French fellow is a surly bastard."

"Guy LaRoche is hot-tempered, I'll admit, and he has a rough way of speaking. But we haven't had any cause for complaint. His company came with good references. The Roman Catholic church uses them and said they were quite reliable."

"I still think that if anything came up missing, I'd wonder if he'd picked it up."

"Frank, will you cool it!" Paul St. Cyr complained. "I don't know what's got into you, but you don't need to go around bashing everyone, eh. Take it easy."

Frank didn't respond, but sat hunched over, a sulky look on his face. He showed no inclination to leave, though I, and I suspect everyone else, wished he would.

"Okay, now let's get on with the agenda. Maintenance Committee meeting minutes. Anyone want to move that we approve the Maintenance Committee's actions?"

"I so move," Layton Nathanson, the treasurer stated.

"You can't," Gretchen declared. "You're on the committee."

"Yes, but. . . .."

"Robert's Rules," Gretchen stated with finality?

"Okay, anyone else?"

"I so move," Jean Givens murmured.

"Second." This from Paul St. Cyr.

sisted. "It would all come out the same."

Paul nodded toward Sue. "Let's hear what Portia would have us do."

But Albert cut the discussion short and called for the vote. I was dismayed to see seven or eight hands raised in the affirmative. Sue, Paul and I were the only nay-sayers, with Penny and a couple of others abstaining.

"Carried. Now let's get on to Old Business."

Humph, I thought, now in a thorough mental pique. Even St. Matthew's isn't entirely free of fools. Couldn't they see the consequences of glossing over this error? Didn't they realize that Frank's purpose in being at this meeting was to defend his position if need be?

Once again, Sue's earlier quote rang in my mind with the persistent peal of a church bell. "Lord, what fools these mortals be. . . ."

Looking at Frank's pouting countenance, and wondering what kind of a game he was playing, I had the gut-tightening feeling that all was not holy in this House of the Lord.

Chapter 4

I arrived at the church about ten minutes before the ten-thirty Eucharist and found a pew. I had to be careful where I settled myself, having learned that there were elderly parishioners who always sat in the same place; if one had the temerity to appropriate one of these pews, one would be told politely but firmly to remove oneself. Respecting the pleasures of these obdurate oldsters, I had mapped out the nave and had learned, after having suffered a few mental bruises, where it was safe to sit.

To get myself into the right mood for the service, which I enjoyed and thought probably to be good for my practical-minded and success-oriented character, but which gave me twinges of guilt because of my skepticism, I tried to focus on some architectural or symbolic object in the church, concentrating my attention in the hopes of distilling some essence of the Christian experience. I focused on the intricately carved rood beam, but found in its bears, geese and beavers no spark of Divine inspiration.

A woman I knew only slightly came up to me. Marcia Chancellor was a saleslady at a very chic dress shop on Main Street. It was the kind of shop I never frequented. They sold nothing that suited my style of wardrobe, and their prices certainly did not fit my budget.

"Would you come to the meeting room after the service?" she asked.

"All right. What. . .?" But Marcia was gone, moving with surprising speed considering that she wore three-inch heels and a sheath skirt that limited her stride to a few inches. She paused to speak briefly to Penny, who then hurried over to sit beside me. I asked her if she knew what the meeting was about. She shrugged.

"I'd guess it's about Shirley's resignation. She and Marcia are good friends." Penny slid to her knees on the padded kneeler in front of us, her shapely bum still planted firmly on the edge of the pew. I had noticed the pious ancients in the congregation, at least those whose arthritic joints had not totally petrified, had knelt properly with backs straight, hands folded, heads bowed in uncompromising dignity. No half-sitting, half-kneeling for them!

After the service, we made our way toward the meeting room. Sue Ambler joined us, as puzzled about the occasion for such an unusual meeting as we were. In the room were Marcia, Albert, the two wardens, and Dr. Alan Gotfriedson, who wore a fierce scowl. Jean, Paul and Layton soon arrived, as did several other parishioners who were not Church Committee members. I recognized them as friends of Shirley. We waited for Philip Eccles, who would come as soon as he finished greeting parishioners at the door of the church. When Philip arrived, in the act of removing his alb and stole, Albert cleared his throat portentously.

"Let's get the ball rolling here. Dr. Godfrey, you asked for this meeting. Go ahead and state your case."

"Right." Alan Gotfriedson, after wincing at the shortening of his name, sat forward in his chair, clasped his hands, leaned his forearms on his knees, and looked around the room belligerently. His spiky grey hair bristled even more than normal and his owl-like eyes peered out of horn-rimmed glasses perched militantly on the bridge of his prominent nose.

"I am appalled at what people are saying

around town about Shirley Meacham. I had to be
told by my receptionist, who certainly isn't a church
member, that Shirley no longer has her job that
she has held for twenty years. Also, my wife met
Keith McNabney, the minister of the Presbyterian
church, at the golf course, and he asked her what
was going on in our church. I haven't heard a word
about it here at St. Matthew's, but the gossip is all
over town."

"Oh, you're exaggerating!" Albert exclaimed,
waving his hand as if brushing away the doctor's
claim.

"No, he's not," Marcia asserted. "I've been hearing it in the shop and you wouldn't believe what
people are saying. Someone even suggested she
might have been caught stealing from the collection plate."

"That's ridiculous," Sue voiced her indignation.
"Who could possibly think anything like that?"

"The woman who runs that Alternative Lifestyle store next to our shop does, or at least pre-
tends to. She'd love to do the church some dirt."

"What do you mean by 'Alternate Lifestyle?'"
Albert seemed never to have heard the term, not a
rare situation with him. Most of what went on
around him flowed by without registering, his mind
a courseless stream.

Penny responded with a moue of displeasure.
"It means alternative to any kind of authority or
establishment. She's what I call an againster. She's
against everything normal. She sells books on al-
ternatives to standard medical care and pamphlets
on kinds of spirituality that are anti-religious and
downright spooky."

"And she dresses atrociously," Marcia added.
"The owner of our shop hates to see her come in
for fear the customers will be offended and leave."

"Is she that string-bean of a woman who wears long, gauzy dresses and droopy, loose-weave cardigans and three or four earrings in each ear?" Jean's thin lips tightened to a slit.

"Yes, and several chains of beads and dozens of jangly bracelets. That's her."

"Does this phenomenon have a name?" Paul roused himself to inquire.

"She calls herself Tuonela." Marcia's voice was tinged with scorn. "I doubt if it's really her name."

"Her last name isn't Swan, by any chance, is it?" Paul asked musingly, humming a bar of music.

"As a matter of fact, I think it is. Why?"

"Swan of Tuonela. Tone poem by Jean Sibelius."

Penny snickered. "I think we can assume it's not her name."

"Actually, I think these alternate remedies have some merit," Layton essayed tentatively. "My sister-in-law. . ."

I glanced at Alan Gotfriedson. His mouth was puckered in distaste, as if he had sucked on a lemon.

"I think we had better get back to the subject at hand," Philip said with unusual vigour. A frown creased his brow, a rare occurrence for him, as he contemplated his bickering flock.

Marcia went on, "Shirley had to find out from her hairdresser that she was fired. Nobody at the church told her."

"Wait a minute. Wait a minute." Albert held up his large, pink hand, palm thrust forward, as if to push away the words being hurled at him. "She wasn't fired. She resigned. And furthermore, she was told that her resignation was accepted. We sent her a letter."

"Who did?" Dr. Gotfriedson demanded.

"I did."

"Shirley hasn't gotten any such letter. She's totally up in the air about what's going on."

"That's not true."

"Yes, it is true. May I say something?" Philip forced his way into the conversation. Everyone fell silent, their heads swiveling in his direction. "I went to visit Shirley and Harry and found them all confused. It is true that she has not received the letter from Albert, and it is also true that she was told by her hairdresser that she had been fired. I had gone there to help, if I could, with the trauma of leaving after all those years, and to assure her that everyone hoped that she and Harry would continue to attend church. They haven't been coming lately, you may have noticed."

Dr. Gotfriedson took over again. "I asked for this meeting because of my concern, first for the well-being of the Meachams, and secondly for the reputation of the church. Somehow the letter you sent to Shirley hasn't reached her, but the news is all over town and we are in for a first-class scandal if this continues.

"Also, as you know, Harry Meacham sold his interest in Lakeside Lumber three years ago and retired because he was becoming a prime candidate for a heart attack. His blood pressure was sky high. He was anxious and easily angered. He was about to blow up. At Shirley's and my urging, he retired. He started gardening, taking his grandkids fishing and to hockey games, and enjoying life. Now he is a wreck again, and I'm worried about him. Also, Shirley is getting migraines."

He looked around at each of us, as if to imprint his anger in all our minds. "You might think that I shouldn't be talking about my patients, but the Meachams have told me I may, and I'm not telling you anything you don't already know. What I want is to get this whole thing out in the open and resolved. Shirley needs to know whether to come to work or to hand in her keys. The gossip in this town needs to be silenced, and our policies toward our employees need to be clarified. I can't see how we can just toss a loyal employee on the trash heap like this."

A chorus of dissent at this last remark ricocheted around the room like a racquet ball, and a discordant discussion ensued. The members of the Maintenance Committee felt put upon, needing to justify themselves. Sue and I found ourselves repeating over and over, "You don't understand. . ." without being able to finish our explanation. Albert, Layton, Nick, Gretchen and Philip, trying to defend themselves, were all talking at once. Jean, an anguished look marring her attractive features, seemed caught in the middle. Alan and Marcia wore belligerent scowls. Shirley's friends joined the mêlée.

As the fur flew, I could see a chasm widening between those who had voted to approve the Maintenance Committee's action in accepting Shirley's resignation and those who felt that the former were siding with Frank and were incensed by it. Some committee members found that in defending themselves, they were labeled pro-Frank, when their sympathies actually lay with Shirley; but because they were being castigated by the pro-Shirley forces, they found themselves defending the pro-Frank camp.

Sue tried several times to make herself heard. "You've got the wrong idea," she kept repeating. Finally she got the attention of the meeting by pounding on the table with a large ring she wore on the middle finger of her right hand.

"When I brought up the subject of Canon Law, it wasn't to tell you that Shirley was right and Frank was wrong. It was to say that the Maintenance Committee didn't have jurisdiction and the whole Church Committee needed to decide the issue."

"Well, you sure embarrassed us," Albert complained.

"I didn't mean to. I just wanted to point out that in an important matter like that, the whole Church Committee should make the decision."

"I don't see what difference it would make. Everyone knows that Shirley resigned voluntarily. Why make a big deal out of it?"

"Because we don't want to set a precedent. We need to do things right."

"It would all have come out the same way in the end, so why can't we drop the whole thing?" Nick Valutin asked. His almost perpetual smile was sadly lacking.

We were getting nowhere.

"Alan," I boomed in a voice that can drown out the sound of an airplane engine on take-off. Everyone stopped gabbling and stared at me. "What do you want us to do?"

"I want a special meeting called, at which any parishioners who so wish may state their case. Then I want the Church Committee to reopen its discussion and decide who should go-Shirley or Frank."

"I don't think we have any reason to ask Frank to resign," Albert said tentatively.

"I think you have *every* reason."

"All right. All right." Albert raised his hands in surrender. "I'll see about setting up a meeting. Paul can put it in the newsletter."

Paul nodded. "I can do an editorial if you want."

"I don't think that would be a good idea," I said.

"Let's be calm and mediate this rather than being confrontational. Enough of you have your backs up already."

"Okay. I'll just put in the date and time, what it's about, and invite people to come and say their piece."

"And let's be sure it isn't just a big squabble," I suggested. "Give everyone a time limit, and let's hear them one at a time."

"Okay, I'll set it up," Albert agreed, sighing resignedly.

"Let's get it done before the new rector comes," Jean Givens urged. "I'd hate to hand him this problem when he first sets his foot in the door."

* * * *

The special meeting was held ten days later. About a dozen people, with prepared speeches, delivered their opinions. We gave them five minutes each. None were allowed to stay in the room while the others spoke.

No one had thought to invite either Shirley or Frank.

I couldn't see that the exercise accomplished anything. As Jean had said about meetings in the church, no one was willing to express a controversial opinion on either side of the issue. They spoke in platitudes and circumlocutions and it was sometimes difficult to relate the remarks to the subject at hand. Maybe a good squabble would have accomplished more after all. Perhaps it was a democratic rite, but it left me with the feeling that we had wasted an hour and a half of our time. Church Committee meetings often seemed to last until the cock crowed, anyway.

After the speeches, we thanked the people and

saw them off, then got down to business. Jean tried to explain to Albert, "If we're going to reconsider our acceptance of the actions of the Maintenance Committee, we have to have a motion from one of the members who voted in favour of it."

"Why's that?"

"Because people who voted against it, when it was passed, can't ask for another vote. Only those who voted in favour can do so."

Albert threw up his hands. "You have me totally confused."

"I have a suggestion." This from Sue. "Jean is assistant chairman. . ."

"Chairperson," Gretchen corrected.

"Chairperson then. Albert, why don't you hand over the running of the meeting to her this time?"

"Gladly," Albert sighed, rising from his chair with a gesture of shoving all his papers in Jean's direction. "Jean, it's all yours."

Jean moved to Albert's place at the head of the table, carefully moved Albert's materials aside, and replaced them with a small note pad. "What we need is a motion from one of the people who, at the last meeting, voted in favour of accepting the actions of the Maintenance Committee, that we reconsider our acceptance."

Gretchen made the motion, with some prompting on the wording from Sue. It was seconded by Philip.

"All in favour?"

Most of the hands went up.

"Opposed?"

No hands, but a couple of abstainers shifted uncomfortably.

"Carried. Now we need a motion on acceptance of the actions of the Maintenance Committee."

"But we just voted on that," Albert complained.

"No we didn't. We voted to reconsider it. We are now back to where we were before we ever voted on it in the first place. We have to have a motion on the floor before we can discuss it."

Albert, looking confused, shrugged.

"Anyone like to make a motion?"

"How should it be worded?" Philip asked.

"The same as at the last meeting; a motion to accept the actions of the Maintenance Committee."

"All right. I so move."

"Second," from Layton. No one bothered to tell him this time that he couldn't make or second the motion because he was on the committee in question.

"Discussion?"

Boy, was there ever discussion! We rehashed everything we had been wrangling about for the last ten days. Voices were raised, everyone talked at once, and Jean's attempt to mold the proceedings into an orderly discussion went for naught. Feeding time at the turkey farm, I thought.

Finally, Jean raised her hand for quiet. "I think that's enough. Does anyone have anything that hasn't already been said three times?"

Silence.

"Now, when we vote, if you think the committee did the right thing, you vote Aye. If you don't, you vote Nay."

Nods all around.

"All in favour?"

None of the hands went up.

"Opposed?"

A dozen or so hands shot up and waved briskly.

"The motion is defeated."

"I still don't understand what we're doing," Myrtle Williamson whined plaintively. She had not voted on either motion. "Up in Fort Watson. . ."

Firmly Jean cut in. "We are voting on whether to approve the actions of the Maintenance Committee. We just voted not to. So now we have to vote on each of the things they did in their meeting. Let's get the expenditures out of the way first."

We quickly decided that the committee had been correct in paying our bills and replacing the glass in the rectory, which was just as well, since these things had already been done.

"Now to the sending of the letter to Shirley accepting her resignation."

Dead silence. We had already said all there was to say.

"I move we table that until the new rector comes," Layton suggested. "After all, he's going to have to work with them."

"Yeah, that's right," said Nick. "I'll second that."

"Any discussion?"

I said, "I thought that in our meeting Sunday before last, we decided we wanted to get the matter over and done with and not hand it on to the new incumbent."

Jean gave me a rueful smile and held out her hands in a gesture of helplessness. Another silence followed.

"All in favour?"

Most of the hands went up.

"Carried."

Oh, hell, I thought. Here we go again! If Douglas Forsythe knew what he was getting himself into, he'd probably make tracks for his son's place in Halifax and put the maximum distance he could between himself and the problems at St. Matthew's.

Chapter 5

The church was packed. There were almost as many people at the service as had attended Martin's last one, after which we had held a party for him. Our miserable attendance figures were going to get a boost as everyone was out to see the new rector. I had heard people say that Martin's first service in this church was on a summer holiday long weekend and hardly anyone had come, but this Sunday, with school not yet out, people had not departed on their summer holidays. And after several months without an incumbent, parishioners were anxious and excited to see what we had gotten, especially since no one except those present on the night of his interview had ever met him. He represented mystery and salvation, and hope also that his presence would not be a comedown. Could he overcome the legacy of the departed Martin, or would he fall flat on his face?

John Vieth played the organ with unusual verve as I looked around for a place to sit. Jean Givens lifted two-year-old Sarah onto her lap to make room for me.

The organ music died away. An anticipatory hush fell over the crowd. Then we rose to our feet as the organ thundered out and the procession began to move toward the altar. In the lead, the crucifer, twelve-year-old Jeremy Givens, held the cross aloft, his dark eyes turned upward and a look of intense concentration on his face. He was followed by the gowned choir, in a double row; then came the communion assistants in their white linen albs and an elderly priest who had retired to Exeter and often assisted in the services. He was small, thin-faced and white-haired. He wore his green stole crossed at the waist underneath the cincture that held in the folds of his alb. In the rear came Douglas Forsythe wearing a green chasuble, embroidered in purple and gold.

The choir sang out and the congregation joined them:

> "All hail the power of Jesus'
> name;
> Let angels prostrate fall;
> Bring forth the royal diadem
> And crown Him Lord of all."

The choir members and communion assistants made their way to their seats and the elderly priest took his place on the south side of the altar, facing it. Douglas Forsythe reached the altar, genuflected, turned to face the congregation, raising his arms, palms upward, the rich fabric of his green chasuble falling in graceful folds at his sides. In a vibrant baritone voice, he intoned:

> "The grace of our Lord Jesus Christ,
> And the love of God,
> And the fellowship of the Holy Spirit,
> Be with you all."

"And also with you," the massed congregation chorused in response.

The first service of the new rector of St. Matthew's Church, Exeter, was underway.

When we had sung the Gloria and Douglas had recited the Collect, we settled into our seats to listen to the readings. Little old Eleanor Ware made her way to the lectern and disappeared behind it. For a long moment, she was lost from sight. Then her grey head bobbed up, barely visible above the lectern as she stepped up onto a stool. The congregation collectively let out its breath, as one might when a swimmer has disappeared under the water and then has surfaced again. Eleanor read a passage from the Old Testament in a clear, firm voice that carried well on the sound system. We recited the Psalm, then Sue Ambler, speaking with scholarly diction, read the Epistle, a reading from the New Testament.

We rose to sing. The hymn was in a section of the book entitled *Missionary Hymns*, which puzzled me. Was this going to be relevant in some way? The hymn was, as I would soon find out. I liked the hymn, with its repeated reference to flight.

> "Thou whose almighty word
> Chaos and darkness heard,
> And took their flight,
> Hear us, we humbly pray,
> And, where the gospel-day
> Sheds not its glorious ray,
> Let there be light."

Hmmm. This was the bad guys taking flight. But it got better in Verse three:

> "Spirit of truth and love,
> Life-giver from above,
> Speed forth Thy flight:
> Move on the waters' face,
> Bearing the lamp of grace,
> And in earth's darkest place
> Let there be light."

More light than flight, I'm afraid. Flight is probably only in there to rhyme with light, as the last line of every verse was, "Let there be light." Oh well. There are many images of flight in the *Bible*, some very beautiful, as in what I think of as the nature psalm, Psalm 104. It contains radiant imagery of God in nature, and contains the lines,

"You make the clouds Your chariot, You ride on the wings of the wind. . ."

The elderly priest read the gospel from the floor between the pews as we stood and faced him, then kissed the gospel book and held it aloft. I gathered that this was an outmoded custom, as I had never seen anyone else kiss the book.

"The gospel of Christ."

"Praise to You, Lord Jesus Christ," we chanted.

Douglas came down from his seat beside the altar, turned to face the altar as he asked for God's guidance, then made his way to the pulpit. In his rich and vibrant voice, he proclaimed, "You are the light of the world!" He paused for a moment, surveying the faces of the packed throng. "*You* are the light of the world. Let your light so shine before others, that they may see your good works and give glory to your Father in Heaven."

Again he paused, then in a quieter tone, continued. "Is this the voice of a disciple talking to Jesus? No, it isn't. This is the voice of Jesus talking to His disciples. Let *your* light so shine before others, that they may see your good works. He speaks to us down through the ages, as He spoke on that day in His Sermon on the Mount. *We* are called to be His disciples. *We* are called to let *our* light shine by doing good works in His name."

As we sat, entranced, straining to hear his every word, watching his every gesture with intensity, this ordinary-looking man unleashed on us the power of his oratory. We'd gotten ourselves a good one! His vision for us was bold and ambitious, but not unreachable. We could make a difference, he told us, in our parish, our community, our nation, and the world. But he cut our commitment into bite-sized chunks that we could, as one single parish, handle in periods of time by which we could measure our progress.

"Each of you should try to be that which God desires you to be, and by so being, to reflect the light of Christ in your lives, to be a light unto others. That was the message of Christ to His disciples. That is the message of Christ for us today."

We sat in stunned silence as Douglas descended from the pulpit, walked to the altar, bowed, turned, and said, "Shall we stand and recite together the Apostle's Creed?" As if released from our trance, we rose in unison.

After the Creed, we were led through the Prayers of the People by Leah Gotfriedson, Alan's wife. Then came the Confession. Even in our new *Book of Alternative Services*, which has stirred up so much controversy, there are quaint phrases you would find nowhere else.

Silence is kept, the rubrics tell us. But three-year-old Billy Stern couldn't read the rubrics, and filled the silence with his childish version of "Vroom, vroom", as he crashed his toy truck into the end of the pew.

"We confess that we have sinned against You in thought, word, and deed, by what we have done, and by what we have left undone," we said. Whether you believe in God or not, I don't think it's a bad idea to pause once a week and ponder what you have been doing, asking yourself whether you could have done better.

Then the Peace. We turned to our neighbors in the pews, shook hands and greeted one another with the phrase, "Peace be with you". Douglas made his way from the altar to the back, shaking hands and greeting people. In the back of the church, he edged through the throng to where Harry and Shirley Meacham stood, having come in late, deliberately, no doubt. He gave Shirley a hug and clasped Harry's hand between both of his, and all the people in the church could see that he was signaling to them that they were welcome.

During the offertory hymn, while the collection plates were being passed, one of the sidespersons stopped at a pew where two children, a girl and a boy, were sitting and invited them to carry the bread and wine to the altar. They clutched the vessels tightly, lest they drop or spill them, and seriously handed them to the elderly priest in front of the altar. Their eyes shone as they rushed back to their seats. They could hardly contain their excitement.

The organ sounded a note and Douglas chanted, "The Lord be with you."

"And also with you," we chanted in reply.

"Lift up your hearts."

"We lift them to the Lord."

And so it went, through the Eucharistic Prayer while Douglas and the communion assistants prepared the gifts of bread and wine.

After we had chanted the last "Glory to God for ever and ever," and had sung the Lord's Prayer, we subsided into our seats and joined the choir as they chanted, "Oh Lamb of God that takest away the sin of the world: have mercy on us."

The communion hymns were different. From the new hymn book, they were strong on nature and mild in tone. I took communion, though I could not bring myself to believe in it as the body and blood of Jesus Christ. Still, I found something that one might call spiritual in the ceremony. Perhaps it was an affirmation of being part of something important. I would have felt left out if I did not partake.

The Prayer after Communion, the Doxology, a blessing from Douglas, and then the recessional hymn rang out. "Rejoice, the Lord is King, Your

Lord and King adore," we sang while the procession made its way from the altar to the back of the church.

"Go in peace to love and serve the Lord."

"Thanks be to God."

The service was over.

*   *   *   *

I shuffled along with the crowd that was slowly spilling out of the church. Inside the door leading to the porch, Betty Forsythe had cornered a young man whom I had seen in church but did not know. "I was sitting in front of you and noticed your wonderful tenor voice. We would love it if you would join the choir."

"I've never had any choral training," he countered hesitantly. "I haven't sung since I was in school."

"Have no worry. Elspeth Dodderington, our choir director, is a former music teacher from the local schools. She can teach anyone to sing. Besides, you sounded right on key."

"Well. . ."

"Good. Come meet Elspeth."

The stream of people exiting the church eddied as Betty, with her captive in tow, moved across it. I could see her in earnest conversation with Elspeth. The tenor looked hesitant, but eager.

In the porch, near the outer door, Douglas had hooked a fish of his own.

"I hear that you and your wife used to lead the Journey in Faith sessions," he was saying as he clasped the hand of a middle-aged man who replied in the affirmative. "Good," said Douglas. "We must get those started again. Come see me soon, and we'll work out a schedule." The man agreed with enthusiasm.

This congregation isn't going to know what hit it, I thought. I remembered an old slogan I had heard about army life: I need three volunteers; you, you and you.

In the days that followed, the calendar in the church office began to fill up with meetings, and every time Douglas talked to anyone, he had in his hand a small, black appointment book in which he was always writing.

Our days of aimless drifting were a thing of the past.

Chapter 6

After a week of cloud and intermittent rain, on Tuesday the weather cleared. Wednesday morning was bright and calm-a good day for the young student who was scheduled for his private pilot flight test. As I drove to the airport for my nine a.m. appointment with this student, I reflected that I had come a long way since I had met and married a good-looking pilot; when our brief marriage had broken up, I had received a flight school in the division of our assets.

Dale Carruthers had taught me how to fly. He had been a good instructor and always remained a good pilot. He was the kind of demanding perfectionist who pushed students to exceed what they thought were their limits. He had been trained in the military, and my experience with military pilots is that they receive topnotch training and have instilled in them a pride in doing their best that lasts long after they have left military service. Dale was never satisfied until the person he was teaching showed the same kind of dedication that he did. He lost a few students as a result of his uncompromising attitude, but those who stuck with him became exceptionally capable pilots, a living tribute to his skill as an instructor. Even though he had not been associated with the school for years, his legacy lived on in the way I taught the next generation of pilots. Dale's talents as a businessman, however, left a great deal to be desired.

He was tall, straight and lean, with sandy hair that clung to his head in tight waves; grey eyes that always seemed to have a faraway look, as though he were perpetually in the clouds; and a ruddy complexion. He had a gravelly voice and a slightly lopsided smile, which he bestowed lavishly on anything female. He took his flying very seriously; unfortunately he didn't show the same attitude toward his marriage.

I had always wanted to fly. When I had scraped up enough money to start taking flying lessons, Dale was the only instructor around. He had a Cessna 150 for training and a 206 for charter work. My flight training was often interrupted by Dale flying off on a charter when I had a lesson scheduled. This infuriated me, and I let him know it, but he would always apologize very contritely and give me extra attention-until the next time.

The flying bug had bitten me. Wanting to continue my training and go into a career in aviation, I was a pushover when Dale proposed marriage. After a whirlwind courtship and a weekend honeymoon spent flying, we settled down to run the business. I realized later that Dale thought, when he married me, that he was getting free office help, but instead I worked hard toward my commercial and flight instructor licenses. Soon Carruthers Aviation had two instructors. For a while, we settled into an unplanned division of labour. I taught students; Dale flew charters. It was then that the marital waters began to get rough and choppy.

Our home life was almost non-existent. We lived in a small basement apartment near the airport, ate meals on the fly, and while Dale was often away, I spent most of my waking hours at the airport.

Dale would do anything for a buck, but he would cancel regular customers to fly his fishing buddies into remote northern lakes, having put floats on the Cessna 206 for the summer. When his buddies paid him, if they did, he shoved the money into his pocket. He was a free spender, and often came back from trips that had tied up an expensive airplane and an experienced pilot for a week, with only a couple of crumpled twenties in his pocket.

He stole other people's customers. Aviation around this part of the country was pretty much a cutthroat business anyway, but Dale was known as the most brazen of the pirates. I have spent years trying to overcome the distrust and dislike that this particular trait of Dale's had engendered in other people in the aviation world.

Reflecting on my own experiences and listening to the complaints of others, I felt that our business would be more successful if it were based on honesty and trust. Dale, with perfect chauvinism, let me know that my feminine instincts were useless for running a flying business, and I shouldn't bother my pretty little red head over it. I, on the other hand, was trying to balance the books and pay the bills. I had nurtured a small core of loyal students, and since Dale spurned the little 150 for his charter work, I usually managed to meet my commitments. The problem came whenever the 150 needed repairs or its annual inspection. We could never afford it, according to Dale, or the 206 had to be done first. "Just fly it anyway," he would say. "The feds never get out here to look at our books." When I would complain that I didn't want the students to fly a plane with a defective compass or a cracked cowling, he would belittle my concerns and tell me about all the times he had flown planes that were less than perfect." But not when you were an inexperienced student, "I would argue.

"Didn't have to. The friendly taxpayers just bought me another airplane." He would grin, sidestepping the real issue. His perfectionist ideals did not extend to maintenance, since bush flying, which he had done a lot of, required a good deal of deviation from manufactures' recommendations. You couldn't just call someone to fix it. You either fixed it yourself before flying it, or flew it to a place you could get it repaired, and damn the consequences. Dale did teach me a lot about compensating for inoperative equipment, from flying without an airspeed indicator to taking off and landing with a flat nose wheel tire.

Then we picked up Rod O'Donnell, an aircraft maintenance engineer looking for a job and a place to raise his burgeoning family. Maintenance problems suddenly dissolved, as Rod not only knew his stuff, he knew where to get parts at a discount, and was willing to take some of his pay in the form of a place to live, an old house Dale owned. We added aircraft repairs to our services.

It was nerve-racking trying to keep the airplanes flying, the students happy, the tax man at bay, the bill collectors from the door, and my wandering husband at home long enough to at least keep the business going. But things were running reasonably well. The bust-up came totally unexpectedly.

A man who was working toward his instrument rating wanted Dale to go on an overnight business trip with him. It would be a two-hour instrument flight into busy Calgary International, with its layers of air traffic control to deal with. Dale flew the 206 to Pine Hill to pick up the instrument student. He also arranged to pick up a young woman student who I was teaching, but who also liked to schedule with Dale on my days off. I was too busy and too naive to notice that there was anything unusual about this. I know that people must have been laughing behind my back.

When Dale's businessman student arrived with his flight plan, aviation gear and overnight bag, he found Dale's girl getting into the back seat of the plane. Since he had been driven to the airport by his wife, who looked the girl over from head to toe like a racehorse trainer appraising a foundered nag, he lost his temper. He had hired Dale to give him flight instruction and not to provide Dale with a night out with his tart, he said. Dale didn't like the tone of voice the man used and said that who he took along was his own business.

"Not when I'm paying for it," the man said, glancing warily at his wife.

The result was that the student marched back to his car and took his righteous anger to the other end of the field where he scheduled a Cessna 182 from our arch-rival, Garth Hughes.

I heard about it. Oh, how I heard about it. Scandal travels faster than a Lear Jet in a hurry. Actually, I was relieved. I couldn't explain to family and friends that I wanted a divorce because my husband wanted to protect me (prevent me?) from having to contend with the running of the business. Plain old adultery they could understand just fine.

Dale had put the initial investment into the business, which he had started on a shoestring, and hadn't progressed much farther. Most of the glimmerings of success that we had achieved had been in my flight school end; most of our liabilities resulted from the charter flying. So our lawyers decided that the best way to divide things was to do it in the way partnerships are dissolved. One partner sets a price on the business. The other decides whether to buy or sell. Dale got to set the price, and I got to make the decision.

I gathered what resources I could, made a plan for operating and expanding, and with shaking knees, took it to the bank. I waited, hardly daring to breathe, while the bankers examined my proposal and asked innumerable questions. I tried to project a positive image. I had drawn my hair back into a bun to try to make myself look older than the twenty-something I really was, and had dressed myself in a conservatively cut suit, medium heels, and nylons, attire that I was not used to wearing. The bankers phoned people who had flown with me and companies we bought supplies from. Cautiously they decided they would give me a loan of an amount that I knew would not cover the cost. I would have to come up with some additional cash in order to swing it. I decided I'd cross that bridge when I came to it. It felt sort of like flying across the mountains of British Columbia—it is better if you don't let your thoughts dwell too long on the jagged peaks so close below you.

Years later, I found out that the bankers didn't really think a woman could successfully run an aviation business and had offered me less than I would need thinking to discourage me. It still makes me angry thinking about it.

With the shaky promise of a loan, I set out to raise the additional capital I would need. Then I got the little boost that sent my confidence soaring. I had heard that since the marital breakup, Rod had been looking for another job. Now Rod said he'd stick with me if I bought Dale out. Rod's wife would handle the office while I was out flying. Suddenly, I knew that I would choose to buy the business even if the price Dale set was on the high side. My lawyer counselled caution, but there was no way to calm my exuberant mood.

What happened is a perfect example of both Dale's lack of business sense and his misunderstanding of career-oriented women. Assuming that because I was a woman, I would not want to buy the business, he deliberately set the price low so he wouldn't have to pay me much for it. It took me only about two minutes to decide to buy him out, and most of that time was spent in trying to get my jaw back in place after it had dropped halfway to the floor in amazement.

Dale never could understand where he went wrong. After it finally dawned on him that he no longer owned Carruthers Aviation, he took himself off up north where he flies firebombers in the summer and is a bush pilot the rest of the time. We've met at airports a few times since, and have had lunch together, but all the old spark has gone from our relationship, though I can think of him without rancor.

Recently, Penny Farnham found a bookmark in a store and bought it for me. On it is the statement, *Behind every successful woman is a man who tried to stop her.* Yeah, that's Dale and me.

* * * *

If you had left the airport when I first became sole owner of the flying school and then came back today, you wouldn't recognize it. From a motley collection of old hangars and shacks, it has become a vast expanse of large hangars, offices, fuel pumps, and aircraft ramps. There used to be a small passenger terminal on our side of the field, but now there is a big new one, surrounded by landscaped parking lots, over on the other side, next to the new control tower. That's their side of the field. This side now is all ours, all general aviation.

I changed the name of the business to Red Robin Flying School, using a nickname people had occasionally hung on me. We have a new hangar, with office space next to it. My office overlooks our ramp, and we also control the ramp next door, beside the new motel. That gives us some transient tie-down space. We fuel airplanes for pilots who use our tie-downs, as well as fueling our own, but we don't advertise that we sell fuel. There is a big fuel dealer at the other end of the field.

We have a roomy pilot's lounge with comfortable couches and large tables to spread charts on. One wall is papered with aeronautical charts that cover all of Canada and the northern States. On another wall is a framed copy of the favourite of all aviation poems, *High Flight*, by John Gillespie Magee. There is a cork board on which are pinned the shirt tails of students who have soloed, and of course bulletin boards with many and varied announcements and bits of advice, such as, *Safety is no Accident* or *If you think safety is expensive, try having an accident.* The rest of the space is pretty well covered with pictures of aircraft of bewildering variety.

The school has six planes now: three Cessna 150's, two 172's, and one Beech A36 Bonanza, a six-place retractable used mainly for charters but also for advanced training. I'd had my heart in my mouth when I'd signed the papers to buy the Bonanza. The price was right, though it was six figures, and Rod passed it as fit; but it took a big chunk of cash and I would get next to nothing for the old 206. The Beech is gradually paying for itself and I am just getting to the point where I don't wake up in the middle of the night in a cold sweat, worrying about the next payment.

We get students from all over, mainly by word of mouth, but we also use our planes as mobile billboards. The planes are all painted red and white. I devised a chirpy little red bird as a logo, and all our planes proudly proclaim that they belong to Red Robin Flying School. We wouldn't have done that in Dale's day. He often wanted to sneak in and out of airports unnoticed.

I have also become a pilot examiner, giving flight tests to aspiring pilots at the end of their training. I test pilots from my school and from others in the area: for private, commercial, instrument, multi-engine, and seaplane licenses. I'm the only pilot examiner in this part of the province.

Each of our planes has a number, from one to six, much easier than using their full call signs, so the first plane to attract my attention that morning was referred to just by number. It attracted my attention because it wasn't there.

"Where's Two?" I asked, dropping my attaché case on my desk.

"It's not back yet," Joyce, the morning dispatcher replied. "I called flight service over in Pine Hill to see if Lance had filed a flight plan. He hadn't, but the man at Flight Service said the plane was sitting there on the ramp at Pine Hill."

"Lance knew I needed that plane this morning for a flight test." I could see the nervous student, a young man named Peter Trask, pacing around outside.

"I know. I told Pine Hill that if Lance showed up to tell him to get his butt back over here on the double. By the way, Employment Canada called. Here's the number and the person to ask for."

"What do they want?"

Joyce shrugged. "She didn't say."

"Okay. I'll call. Tell me if you hear from Lance. I want to talk to him. And tell Peter to hang in there for awhile. No chance of shifting him to One or Three?"

"No. They're booked solid."

I sat down and reached for the phone, dialing the number Joyce had given me.

"We need you to fill out a Record of Employment for one of your former employees. You haven't done it yet," she said accusingly, giving me the name of a teen-age boy who, like others before him, had come out to the field begging for work in exchange for flying time. I gave them odd jobs and set them to washing airplanes. I kept their time in a notebook and when they had accumulated enough for a chunk of air time, I scheduled their lesson. Several have gone on to complete their training, and one is now an instructor at the school.

"Record of Employment? Isn't that for people who are laid off?"

"That's right."

"He isn't laid off. He's never been laid on."

"Oh? He reported that he had worked for you in the past. Since he is not working for you now, he wants to be sure he does not lose any of his unemployment compensation."

"What the. . .Look here, he's a kid who came out here looking for airplane rides and offering to work in exchange for flying time. He worked two days the week before last, for a total of three and a half hours. Last week, things were slow and I didn't have any jobs for him. If he thinks I'm going to spend half an hour filling out a bunch of government forms every time he doesn't work for a few days, he can go fly a kite."

There was silence on the other end of the line.

"Tell him to get out here and we'll have it out."

"You *will* fill out the form?"

"I will *not*. If you see him, tell him that if he wants a job, he'd better quit saddling me with a bunch of red tape."

I slammed the phone into its cradle. Damn! It

was going to be one of those days! How the hell could a kid living on unemployment compensation afford flying lessons anyway?

The 150 wasn't back yet, so I corralled one of the instructors in the lounge. "If he's not back by ten, take another pilot over to Pine Hill and ferry it back. Take Five. It's not scheduled until noon. Lance can just take the bus home."

Joyce and I examined the schedule and with some shifting, found that we could schedule the flight test later in the day. I sent Peter home, told him not to get uptight, have a good lunch and try to relax.

"Remember, you're not going to be killed. You're only going to take a test."

Peter gave me a wry grin and obediently trotted off.

It was midmorning before Lance Brock got back with the plane and I called him into my office. He sidled through the door, leaving it ajar and standing close to it, one hand on the doorknob. He gave weather as the reason he hadn't gotten back the previous night and couldn't take off this morning, knowing that weather was the one excuse I would accept. I cocked an eye at the clear, blue sky and he replied that there had been fog over the lake at the end of the Pine Hill runway and he didn't know how extensive it was. I let him go.

Like weather, events can be deceptive. My day settled down into its normal routine, giving no hint of events to come. I forgot my premonition that things were destined to go wrong. Looking back, it was like being in the eye of the storm-calm, with the worst yet to hit.

Chapter 7

Toward noon, a provincial air ambulance taxied up and parked near the motel. They had called us on our radio frequency and asked for tie-down space for the night. As the two nurses headed for the motel, the pilots remained behind to secure the plane. They had ordered fuel from the dealer at the other end of the field since we didn't have the jet fuel required for their pressurized, turbo-prop Cessna 441. While they waited for the fuel truck, they gave us a guided tour of the plane.

The province has several air ambulances, from helicopters to jets. The jets are for long-range flights; the helos for backwoods areas; and the mid-sized, twin-engine 441's for short trips from regular airports.

Ambulance is hardly the word. These planes are flying intensive care wards, and we were awed by the equipment they carried. I was especially impressed by the positive pressure breathing apparatus; that would keep a patient oxygenated even if pressurization was lost. Pilots should be so lucky! If this plane lost its pressurization, the patient would be the last person on board to pass out. I wasn't sure whether that was good or bad. Seriously, it showed the extreme care that was taken so that the flight itself would not make the patient's condition worse.

The pilots told us they had been on several trips lately, had used up their legally mandated flying time, and had been told that after delivering a patient to our regional hospital, they were to stay at Exeter, relax, go to the beach, and sleep. They wouldn't even fly back to base until the next day. They were a relaxed, cheerful pair, pilots who knew they were the best in the business, and who enjoyed the feeling of having done something of value for others.

* * * *

In the afternoon, Peter Trask presented himself for his test. I gave him a short oral exam and set him to plotting a cross-country flight. His scheduled airplane had been returned from another flight and fueled, ready for him to use. We went out to the plane. He stood hesitantly in front of it.

"Should I do a pre-flight?"

"Would you if you were going on a trip in it?"

"Yes."

"Well then, do it."

I knew all the students at the school and knew Peter was shy and diffident, hesitant to take command when in the presence of a higher authority. For most students, their flight instructor is the next thing to God, and the fear of the Lord has nothing on their fear of the pilot examiner. I felt he needed some bracing up. He had flown with Jan, the female instructor on my staff, and I knew that he would be well-prepared and capable.

Peter took out his pre-flight checklist and carefully examined the airplane. He pulled the chocks, moved the plane onto the taxiway, and we climbed in, he in the left seat, I in the right. Meticulously, he went through the pre-start checklist, yelled, "Clear prop!" and looked around, started the engine and checked the gauges and instruments. Turning the radio on, he tuned it to ground control and set the VOR, a radio navigation aid, to the frequency of a station he would use on his cross-country flight. He arranged his flight log and aeronautical chart carefully on his lap and glanced my way as if asking my permission to start moving. I sat there impassively.

Peter adjusted the mike on his headset, squirmed in his seat as if to make himself more comfortable, cleared his throat, and having exhausted all useful delaying tactics, hesitantly asked ground control for taxi clearance. We taxied out, and he remembered to do a brake check and noted that the turn indicator and heading indicator were working. He did a careful runup, checked the heading for his initial cross-country leg, and switched over to tower frequency. I let him make a normal takeoff and get on course, trying to be as inconspicuous as possible, offering no help and no hindrance. I felt that this was a very important part of the test; the applicant should be allowed to do his thing without any interference. I would give him a lot of problems later on.

Peter leveled off at his planned altitude and trimmed the plane while busying himself with his navigation. I could see him industriously checking landmarks against their depiction on his chart. He noted the time over a checkpoint and entered it on his flight log. A few minutes later, I asked, "Where are we?"

"Right here." He pointed to a spot on the chart. Right on, I thought.

"Give me a ground speed check."

He flew on to his next checkpoint, noted the time and figured how long it had taken to fly from his previous one. Since he had the distance already noted on his flight log, he took out his flight computer, twisted the dial and gave me an answer. Right on, again.

Now the fun began!

"You are flying along and note that the clouds

are lowering ahead. How far below them do you have to be?"

"Five hundred feet."

"Okay, descend to stay legally under a three thousand foot ceiling. That's three thousand ASL".

The ground below us was over two thousand feet above sea level. We were in a valley, with hills rising steeply on either side. Peter started his descent, looking apprehensively to either side and down at his chart.

"I won't be able to keep to my course. There's terrain higher than this ahead."

"What are you going to do?"

"I could go around here." He traced a course on his chart with his fingertip.

"What's the weather like on the other side?"

"Today?"

"On this hypothetical day when you are descending to stay under the weather."

"I don't know." He was silent for a moment and when I made no comment, he continued, "I'd call for a briefing, but I don't think there's any weather reporting station up there." I was still silent. "I guess I'd have to go back," he said, lamely.

"Okay, suppose the weather is closing in and you don't think you can make it to your destination. You call Pine Hill Radio and the weather seems better over there, so you decide to divert. Take me to Pine Hill." I sat back, folded my arms and stared out the side window.

Out of the corner of my eye, I could see him draw a rough line on his chart, estimate a bearing, and turn the plane to the new course. He busily scanned the terrain and matched it to his chart. After a while, he made a course correction, glancing at me with a worried expression. Far from faulting him on his slightly inaccurate first heading, I gave him full marks for promptly realizing it and making a correction.

"I'll have to climb to cross those hills."

"The ceiling is still three thousand ASL."

"Then I'll have to go around over here."

I said nothing. Peter turned left, skirted the higher terrain, and made another course correction to take us toward Pine Hill.

"Tell me when you see the airport."

After a couple of minutes, he said tentatively, "I think I see it."

"Well, *do* you?"

A pause while he leaned forward as if the extra six inches closer to the airport, still miles away, would allow him to see it better.

"Yes, I do."

"Okay. The weather has cleared a bit and the ceiling is higher. Let's go up to circuit height. We don't want to fly across the town at this altitude."

"Are we going to land there?" Peter asked as he advanced the throttle to full power.

"Would you if the weather was closing in behind you?"

"Yes."

I turned and gazed out the side window, and Peter, in his indecision over what to do next, overshot his altitude, hastily pulled back the throttle and dumped the nose down. He leveled off somewhat uncertainly at the proper altitude. He already had the Flight Service frequency dialed in. "Pine Hill Radio, this is Cessna 150, Foxtrot Lima Quebec Sierra, ten miles west for landing."

The FSS specialist replied with the weather, wind and altimeter setting and suggested that we use runway three four, a runway with a heading of 340°, so that we would land into the mild northerly wind.

"Uh, this is Lima Quebec Sierra. I didn't get the altimeter setting. Would you repeat it?"

"Stand by," the FSS specialist said as he made a radio call to another aircraft.

I scrunched down in my seat and hid my face in my hands. As Peter gave me a startled look, I said, "I don't want anyone to know I'm in this plane if you're going to put on this kind of amateur act. I know Jan has taught you proper terminology and procedure. Use them!"

Peter frowned, but when the FSS man called, "Lima Quebec Sierra, go ahead," he pressed the transmitter button and said in a firm voice, "Pine Hill Radio, this is Lima Quebec Sierra. Say again altimeter setting. Over."

"Pine Hill altimeter three zero zero two."

"Roger. Lima Quebec Sierra."

We joined the circuit, and on downwind for runway 34, flying parallel to it but in the opposite direction, I said, "See the first taxiway from the threshold?" Peter nodded. "That is the end of the runway," I went on. "Just beyond it is a stone fence."

Peter licked his lips as he mentally reviewed the short field landing procedure. He pulled on carburetor heat, retarded the throttle until only a soft purr came from the engine, and letting the nose of the plane drop slightly, he reached for the elevator trim wheel and trimmed the back elevator pressure off. His head was swiveling as he looked for traffic. He put the flaps down halfway, letting the nose drop to a new attitude as the plane slowed. I could see his intense concentration as he judged the point at which he should turn to his base leg. This is the art of flying. No two landings are ever the same.

From base, we turned to final, after a look back

along the final approach course for other traffic and a radio call to announce our position. On final, he lowered the flaps the rest of the way. We could feel the braking effect as the big flaps moved down into the airstream. The nose assumed a new lower position. We were slightly above the speed for a short field approach and Peter eased the nose up and retrimmed. Now we were flying only slightly above stall speed, the speed at which the wings stop producing lift. We were on a steep-angled approach to the runway, which seemed to be moving toward us. Too high. Peter reduced power further and the plane settled onto an approach path that would bring us right to the threshold of the runway. The approach was over the lake. Beyond were the beach, a road, the boundary fence, and a short section of pavement before the marked runway threshold. As we got close to the water, its chill temperature caused a downdraft. Peter added a little power and in a moment, we were in the updraft over the beach and the road.

He was sweating now as he pulled the throttle back to counter the updraft. We skimmed across the threshold. Peter cut the power completely and pulled the nose up. The wings lost their lift and we sank onto the runway on the main wheels. He firmly lowered the nose wheel, flipping the flap switch to the up position. As the flaps retracted, we lost the aerodynamic braking but the airplane's weight settled firmly onto its wheels. He stomped on the brakes and we shuddered to a stop well short of the taxiway and the imaginary stone fence I had erected in front of us.

"Good," I said and Peter's tension relaxed.

As we taxied off the runway, the FSS specialist called, "Hello there, Robin." I'm the only person who ever makes landings like that on his four thousand foot runway, so he knew I was giving a flight test.

"Hello, Bill," I replied.

"Flight test?"

"Affirmative."

"Well, I wish him good luck."

Peter grinned, thumbed the mike switch and answered, "Thanks."

We did some takeoffs and landings, using the parallel grass strip where the glider club operates for our soft field work, then went out to a practice area for some manoeuvers. After that, I had Peter put on an instrument flying hood. This device allowed him to see the instrument panel without being able to see outside the airplane. I became his safety pilot, with the responsibility of watching for traffic. Then it was back home again. Soon the familiar terrain around Exeter was passing under our wings, and I experienced that increasingly frequent feeling that the world was treating me pretty well and there was nowhere I'd rather be on this early summer day than up here with an aspiring pilot who was doing quite nicely on his flight test. Peter's landing on the sixty-four hundred foot runway was not his best, and was farther down the runway than I would have liked, but it was passable. I'd have to speak to him about complacency when landing on a big runway with plenty of room to spare.

As we taxied off the runway and got ground control clearance to taxi to our ramp, Peter asked, "Did I pass?"

"I have no idea," I told him, making the tone of my voice deliberately vague. He gave me a perplexed look and I added, "The flight is not over yet, not until we are parked and shut down."

Peter taxied to the proper tie-down spot and

turned the plane so that we could push it directly back, carefully straightening the nose wheel before we stopped. He went through the shut down checklist, calling out, "Radios and lights off. Mixture, master, mags." He took the key out of the ignition and put it on top of the cowling. If the key is on the cowling, it can't be in the ignition switch. If it isn't there, the mags can't be on, and theoretically the prop can't turn over. All my pilots, however, have had drilled into them the possibility of a hot mag, one that isn't grounded, and must always treat the prop as if the engine might start at any minute. There is no more lethal weapon than an airplane propeller.

We got out, pushed the plane back and Peter chocked and tied it. He put the control lock in place, moved the propeller to the vertical position to indicate that the plane was to be fueled, standing carefully to the side in case it kicked over. He folded the seat belt neatly across the seat, reached across to lock the right-hand door from the inside, and gathered up his gear. He took out the journey log, noted the time on the hour meter and made the entries in the log; then, taking the key from the cowling, closed and locked the near door.

He looked at me questioningly. I held out my hand, grinned at him and said, "Congratulations. You are now a private pilot."

In the office, I called out loudly to Gayla, the dispatcher on duty, so that any pilots in the lounge could hear, "Would you make out the paperwork for this man's private pilot license?"

Immediately, a small crowd erupted from the lounge, Peter's girlfriend, Lisa, in the lead. Someone shoved a glass of bubbly into his hand, and they bore him off to the lounge where a large cake rested on a tabletop. I got caught up in the merriment and soon found myself with champagne in one hand and cake in the other.

Peter caught Lisa in one free arm, pulled her to him and planted a long, passionate kiss on her lips to the oohs and aahs of the crowd. Good for them. Maybe *their* marriage would turn out all right.

I edged toward the door. While walking back from the plane, I had noticed something that bothered me. A Cherokee Arrow, a small four place retractable, was parked where it was blocking the Medevac 441. I peered out the window. It was still there. I went into the hangar, told Rod to join the party, and asked him about the Arrow. "We can't have it there. If the Medevac has to go out, it's blocking their way."

"They shouldn't be going 'til tomorrow," Rod countered.

"Still, if there's an emergency here or somewhere nearby, they might send another crew over. See that it gets moved."

"I tried, but it's locked and the brakes are on. I think the pilot is going to be back pretty soon. Ask Gayla."

Gayla confirmed that this was her impression. The pilot had asked about transportation into town and she had told him that if he went out where the entrance road turned into the airport at thirty-five minutes after the hour, he could catch a bus into town. It was twenty after, so he said he'd get fuel when he came back, and left to catch the bus. He hadn't said anything about staying overnight, and he didn't have any bags with him.

Grumbling, I put it down to one more irritant for the day, cancelling the buoyant mood of a few minutes before. But the worst was yet to come.

The phone rang. Gayla answered it, looked up

and said, "It's Garth Hughes. He didn't say what he wanted." That boded ill; if he had merely wanted to lease a plane for a day or two, as he sometimes did, he would have made his request to Gayla.

I went into my office and shut the door. "Hello, Garth. What's up?"

"Hello, Robin." Garth's voice was surprisingly refined and musical, and seemed at odds with his appearance. A large, heavy-set man, with white hair, weather-beaten countenance and a limp from an old war injury, he dressed like a lumberjack and was noted as a skilled bush pilot. "Saw you and your victim over here at Pine Hill. He pass?"

"Yes, he did."

"Good. I just wanted to tell you I saw one of your planes over here last night. I live by the airport, you know, and can't miss your planes. This one had the number 2 on the tail."

"Yeah, I know. He was supposed to be back last night, but he didn't get in until after ten this morning. He fouled up the schedule pretty badly."

"That so? Well, the reason I called you was that he landed about eleven o'clock, after the airport was closed for the night, on an unlighted runway."

I groaned inwardly. Red Robin Flying School has never had an accident or a violation of the regs. I wanted to keep it that way. I supposed that Garth had already called the Ministry of Transport before he called me, and feared that we would have sour minions of that federal agency descending upon us. Of all the people to notice one of my pilots breaking the regs, it would have to be Garth.

Garth let me stew for a few moments, then I heard his chuckle coming over the line. "I thought I'd tell you about it, Robin, instead of calling Transport Canada. I figured you'd like to know and that you'd do something useful about it."

"Thanks, Garth. That's good of you." My surprise must have showed in my voice. He chuckled again.

"If it had been Dale's business, I'd have been on the phone to the MOT first thing this morning. But you've been decent to me, Robin. You've always played fair."

"You don't know how welcome those words are, Garth. By the way, what was your weather like this morning?"

"Severe clear. We've been flying steady since six a.m."

As I hung up the phone, I was calling the unfortunate Lance all kinds of names. Tardy about getting back, he had not notified me, he had broken the regs, and when questioned, he had lied to me. I'd have to call him on the carpet. I would also have to devise some sort of remedial training for him. I debated what I would want to have him do. Ground school on the regs, that was for sure, and a flight check. I'd have him sweat it out through the whole book of regs. I didn't want him ever to have the excuse that he didn't know he was doing wrong. I found my most experienced instructor, told him what had happened and what I wanted. I pulled Lance's card from the file of pilots who were cleared to fly solo, and put it in the file of those who had to have an instructor checkout before they could do so. It was five minutes after five. Lance didn't answer the phone when I called.

In a decidedly grouchy frame of mind, I found Rod and told him, "Before you go, move that Arrow. I don't care what you have to do, but move it." Then I went back into the office and reached for the phone. This time, Lance answered.

Chapter 8

That evening, I picked up Penny and we arrived at the church about fifteen minutes early for the seven o'clock Church Committee meeting. Jean Givens was just pulling into the parking lot in her blue Ford Taurus with the agency logo on the door. She explained that Albert would be a few minutes late and had asked her to open up and get the necessary papers from the office. We met in the spartan meeting room next to the office.

Jean unlocked the exterior door and the three of us trooped in. "Oh, dear," Jean said, "someone left the office unlocked again. We really have to do something about the locks." She walked to the door, opened it, and entered, then bounced back as if she had hit a rubber wall, screaming.

I pushed past her, handing her shaking body into the arms of Penny, the nurse. I backed out just as abruptly.

Frank Corrigan was lying on the floor at an angle to the counter, his feet near it, his head near a bank of filing cabinets. His legs were bent and he was lying on his left side with his right shoulder rolled toward the door, his head lying flat on its side, unseeing eyes staring in our direction, arms flung at awkward angles. Under his head a dark red stain of blood had clotted and dried, showing vividly on the light-coloured vinyl flooring. Someone had stepped in the edge of the pool of blood and had slipped backward. The resulting smear was indistinct in size and outline and was on the far side of the body.

His eyes were open. The clear cornea, normally moistened by tears, was drying out and beginning to shrivel. It was that, more than the blood, that made my stomach contract; it took an effort to keep from retching.

Beyond the body lay a large, pure-white rock that I recognized as a paperweight used in the office. On it were dark red stains. My eyes took in the searing reality of the scene, my mind photographing it in graphic detail. Long after, I could have told you exactly where everything was, could recall that dreadful death-mask stare.

"I'm sure he's dead," I said to Penny, who was looking over my shoulder. My voice was shaky, my throat dry. "You're the expert. What do you think?"

"Here, hang onto Jean." Penny advanced to a position near the body but outside the rim of blood spatters, squatted and reached out to touch it. She backed up to where Jean and I stood. "He's dead, all right. For some time. He's getting stiff. Here, I'll take Jean into the meeting room. There's a phone in the hall, isn't there? You dial 911 and report it."

"I'll call the RCMP direct. I know the number."

At the flying school, we dealt with the police on occasion. They chartered planes to look for people, to fly personnel to places the airlines didn't go, and to take aerial photographs. When I dialed, I was relieved to hear the voice of Grace DeBerg, the person who usually called to arrange flights, and who lived across the street from me.

"Hello, Grace. This is Robin Carruthers." I hesitated, words sticking in my throat. "I'm afraid I have to report a murder."

"A murder? Are you sure, Robin?" Grace, as always, sounded very calm and competent.

"Yes. His head is bashed in."

"Where is this?"

"At the church. St. Matthew's Anglican Church. Actually, in the church office."

"Are you sure the victim is dead?"

"Yes."

"Do you know who he is?"

"His name is Frank Corrigan. He's a church member."

"Okay, I'll send someone right out. Don't disturb the body and if you can stay completely out of the room where he is, do so."

"Don't worry. We nearly tossed our cookies the first time we went in. We're not anxious to go back."

I hung up, went into the meeting room, and seeing that Penny had Jean lying on a couch, said I would go to the outer door and steer people away from the office. Already we could hear the wail of a siren gaining in intensity.

In minutes, a blue and white police car swerved into the parking lot and two young constables pelted up the few steps to the door. I motioned toward the office. They went, looked, conferred, and one rushed back out to the car, where I could see him talking on the radio. The other turned to me and asked, "Are you the person who found him?"

"One of them. Three of us came in together. One of the others went into the office first, but we were all pretty much together."

"Where are they?"

I indicated the meeting room and he took a look inside. He came back to me.

"Names?"

I gave all our names.

"What are you doing here?"

"We have a Church Executive Committee meeting scheduled here. Here come some more Church Committee members." The door opened and several others came in, all goggle-eyed at the presence of the police. The constable told them to go into the meeting room and stood in the office doorway, blocking their view. They moved meekly along. I left it to Penny to give them the news.

"Was the door locked or unlocked when you came?"

"Locked. At least I think so. Wait a minute. Let me think." I cast my mind back to our arrival and could visualize Jean inserting the key in the lock, twisting it unhesitatingly and pushing the door open. I could hear the single thunk as the deadbolt shot back.

"Yes. The outer door was locked. The office door wasn't though, and it should have been. Jean re-marked about it."

"Who had the key?"

"Jean Givens. She's the alternate chairman," I replied with total disregard for Gretchen's sensi-tivity in referring to the office.

"Do the rest of you have keys?"

"No, except for the chairman, the wardens and the incumbent." I noted the young man's glazed expression at the unfamiliar titles.

"Are any of them here?"

"One of the wardens, Nick Valutin, was in that group that just came in."

Another car roared up, and two more men, in plain clothes this time, rushed in. The taller of the two seemed to take charge, issuing orders in a terse, quiet voice. They went into the office and carefully, without touching the knob, pulled the door shut behind them.

The next figure to run up the steps was that of Douglas Forsythe, clad, on this warm summer evening, in a white clerical shirt. In the dim light of the corridor, his clerical collar blended with the shirt and made it look like a turtleneck. The con-stable did not seem to recognize him as a clergy-man, challenged him, and was about to direct him into the meeting room.

"What happened?" He divided the question between me and the young Mountie, anxiety evident in his voice.

"Frank Corrigan is dead. Someone hit him on the head with that big white rock we use as a paperweight."

I heard his gasping intake of breath and noted his stunned expression. He turned to the policeman. "I must go in to him."

The Mountie barred his way. "We can't let anyone in there now."

"But he is one of my parishioners. I must insist. . ."

The door opened and the tall plainclothesman stood in it. "Who are you?"

"Douglas Forsythe, the incumbent."

"Incumbent?"

"Rector. Priest."

The man eyed Douglas but, meeting a steely gaze, said, "It's not a pleasant sight."

"I have been a priest in parishes serving fishing, mining and lumbering communities. I am not unfamiliar with violent death."

"Let him in." He moved aside and Douglas entered the office. "Don't touch anything."

By now, all the Church Committee members had arrived and had been herded into the meeting room. Most were subdued. Albert tried to assert his authority but found it exceeded even by that of the very young constable at the door. He subsided into a chair. Myrtle seemed to think that murder and policemen were a personal affront. I thought that if she even once started to tell us how they would have handled a murder in the church in Fort Watson, I'd strangle her with my bare hands. Jean had gotten hold of herself and was sitting up, looking pale but composed. Penny abandoned her patient and moved over to where I stood by the door. She brushed her hair back from her face, then seemed not to know what to do with her hands, clenching them, then fiddling with a ring on the middle finger of her right hand, then running her hand through her hair.

"Whoever killed him must have had a key," she murmured.

"Yeah, maybe. There are other doors."

"That's right, but if he bolted, he'd probably run out this door."

"Don't let Gretchen hear you say he or she'll give you a lecture on how women are just as good at committing murder as men are."

Penny suppressed a giggle. "I shouldn't be laughing, but I can just picture it."

We stood restlessly, and after awhile Douglas came out of the office, his face a grim mask. He entered the meeting room, stood for a moment, then said, "Let us pray."

We huddled together, holding hands, and Douglas said a prayer for the soul of Frank Corrigan, for strength for the rest of us to get through the difficult times, for understanding when the results of the investigation were known, and for guidance for the police as they did their work. During the prayer, a constable had bustled into the room, paused and backed out, considerately waiting until we had finished before coming in again.

"Sergeant Jameson wants to know about the dead man's relatives and where he lived."

Douglas stepped forward. "His personnel file is in the office. I can show you."

"Just tell us where to find it."

Douglas did. "You will find his home address

there. He lived alone. His next of kin is a son in Georgetown. The son's address and phone number are in the file. His name is Brett Corrigan."

"An adult son?"

"I assume so."

"Thanks. None here in town?"

"None that I know of." Douglas looked around the group. Several people shook their heads. "I didn't know him well. I've only been here a week."

Long enough, I thought, to have become thoroughly familiar with the personnel files. No moss was going to grow on this man.

After a while, a constable came into the room and spoke to Douglas. "The sergeant would like to see you."

Douglas went out. I took up my previous position by the door, which was open. The tall plainclothesman came out of the office, handed Douglas a card and identified himself as RCMP Sergeant Bruce Jameson. Douglas glanced at the card, then dropped it into his shirt pocket. Jameson was tall and slender with sleek, dark hair. He was neatly dressed in blue slacks, blue-and-grey checked jacket, white shirt, and blue-striped tie. He moved gracefully. His face was alert and his grey eyes darted around, missing nothing. Not a person to fool with, I thought.

The outer door opened and a group of men with cases of gear entered. Jameson paid scant attention to them. They were presumably the technical people, and he acted as if he knew they would get on with their job with no supervision from him. Through the glass in the outer door, I could see people beginning to gather. Across the street were cars with the signs, *Exeter Chronicle* and *Lakeside Cable, Channel 11* displayed on them. I groaned, but thought back to Douglas prayer. He had no doubt handled intense media coverage before and knew what to expect.

"You're new here?" Jameson asked.

"Yes, I only started on the fifteenth."

"You came from where?"

Douglas told him.

"Then you didn't know the dead man very well?"

"No. I only met him twice. Once when he came into the church office on business and once when I made an appointment to talk to him to become acquainted."

"I understand that he was some kind of director. I'd think he would have worked a lot closer with you."

"It was a temporary, part-time job, and would soon have been terminated."

Oh ho! So our new rector had already solved our problem for us!

"Oh? What did he think of that?"

"He had hoped to stay on."

"Was he angry?"

"He seemed disappointed."

"What did he seem like to you? As a person?"

Douglas considered. "I can't say. I had not had the opportunity to get to know him that well."

I could tell that Jameson thought Douglas was stonewalling. He bored in.

"What did other people think of him?"

"That is not for me to say."

"You must know whether there was any bad blood between members of your staff."

Douglas frowned and looked stubborn.

"Oh, come on!" Jameson exclaimed. "It's all over town that you have a knock-down drag-out feud going on here."

"That is gossip," Douglas stated firmly. "One employee had an argument with him and resigned her position. That's all."

"Harry Meacham's wife, wasn't it?"

"Shirley Meacham. Yes."

"So at least one church member had it in for him and I'm sure a lot of the others probably sided with her."

"That is not a motive for murder."

"You'd be surprised at the motives people have for bumping each other off."

"Not these people."

"Oh, holier than thou, are they?"

Douglas refused to be stampeded. "The disagreement between them was just that. Furthermore, now that I have arrived, Frank's position was to be terminated. That was in the job description that was written for him when he started. The secretary who resigned would have been able to apply for the position again. I know her and her husband, and they are quiet, loving deeply religious people and would not have committed murder, if that's what you are implying."

"You say you know them, but only for a week."

"No. I was acquainted with them before. I have stayed in their home."

"I've known lots of people who swore on Bibles that they didn't do something we caught them redhanded at."

"That's different."

"Well, you're welcome to your rose-coloured view of the human race, but we see the other side."

Jameson lounged against the wall, a good head taller than Douglas, a look just short of arrogance on his face. Douglas stood erect, feet together, shoulders squared, back rigid, his hands clasping a file folder of papers in front of him. His head was tilted back in order to look up at the tall policeman, his jaw was set. Their eyes met. Each at a similar stage in their respective careers; knowledgeable, confident, self-assured; each refusing to be intimidated by the other.

Jameson dropped his eyes first, glancing down at a notebook in his hand. "I'll want to talk to everyone here. Is there another room?"

"A table and chairs could be set up in the hall." Douglas gestured toward a door.

"Right." Jameson summoned a constable, who went off to set up the interview room. "I'll want to see the three ladies who found him first. We'll let you know when we're ready."

As Douglas returned to our room, a policeman came out of the office and shut the door, closing us in.

"How dare they lock us in!" Myrtle complained.

Douglas went to her and laid a hand over hers. "I expect that it is because they are taking the body out now," he explained gently.

"Oh!" she gasped and clasped a hand to her breast.

Douglas sat down beside her, providing a comforting presence. No one spoke. We could hear considerable activity next door, accompanied by muted voices. After a while, a constable re-entered the room.

"Mrs. Givens, would you come with me?"

Jean rose shakily, but walked firmly out of the room with the policeman, her eyes staring straight ahead, her hands clasped in front of her. Albert began to grumble, complaining that as Frank had obviously surprised a burglar in the office, he did not see any reason why the important people of the Church Committee should be kept cooped up like common criminals.

"It's not as simple as that," Douglas said. "I doubt if it was a burglar."

"Who else would do such a thing?"

"That is for the police to decide." In a louder voice, glancing around the room, he said, "We should give the police our full cooperation. They have a job to do, whether we like it or not, and they can do it much better if we give them all the help we can." Albert grumbled, Myrtle whined, but several others murmured in assent.

Soon Jean returned and I was summoned. Jameson motioned me to a chair on the side of the table opposite him.

"You're the one who called us?"

"Yes." I described our arrival and the discovery of the body.

"Did anyone touch anything?"

"The door jamb, I'm sure. We didn't go far into the room except for Penny Farnham, who is a nurse, to check that he was dead. She didn't go close enough to get into the blood on the floor and she didn't touch anything else."

"Were you watching her?" Jameson's tone insinuated doubt.

"Yes. I was." I didn't like my veracity challenged.

"Did any of you step across the body?"

"No."

"You're sure?"

"Absolutely. We all left the office and came in here." I was responding to his doubting tone by speaking more sharply and emphatically than I normally do. The guy was rubbing my fur the wrong way, and he had hardly started.

"I understand that the dead man and the church secretary, one Shirley Meacham, had a feud going."

"No."

Jameson raised his eyebrows. "No?"

"No. They had one argument. I doubt if they've even seen each other for over a month."

"Maybe they met again today." The detective leaned back in his chair, fiddled with his pen, and let a sneer creep into his voice.

"No. That is, if they did meet, nothing would have come of it. Shirley would have used her social skills to avoid a confrontation."

"But if they were alone together, they might have had another argument."

"If you think Shirley Meacham would have lost her temper enough to bash in Frank's skull, you're out of your mind."

"What makes you think his skull was bashed in?"

"I have eyes. I saw a pool of blood under his head and a blood-stained rock lying near it."

"Do you know where the rock came from?"

"It's a paperweight used in the office. Someone found it and thought it was pretty, so they picked it up. I think it was one of the former incumbent's children."

"Why did the former, uh, incumbent leave?"

"He had cancer of the colon and is at the University Hospital undergoing treatment."

"Did he get on well with the dead man?"

"I don't know whether he ever met Frank. Frank wasn't a church member before he was hired."

"How about the secretary?"

"She was his right arm. They worked very well together for years."

"So she might have resented his being replaced by this director."

"He was not replaced by Frank. He was replaced by an interim priest named Philip Eccles, and now by Douglas Forsythe."

"You like this Shirley Meacham, don't you?"

"Of course I like her. She is a wonderful, caring person."

"And her husband?"

"He is also. They are the salt of the earth." I hardly knew Harry Meacham, but I wasn't about to let that get in the way of giving him a glowing recommendation.

Jameson sighed, as if having to question blind idiots like me was almost more than he could bear. Then he asked, "Did the dead man have any other enemies?"

"I don't know whether he had any enemies. Not in the church, at any rate. He annoyed several people, but I say again, these people don't go around bashing in skulls just because they don't see eye to eye."

"People sometimes do."

"Not *these* people."

"Where were you this afternoon?"

"At work."

"Which is?"

"I own the Red Robin Flying School."

Jameson brightened. "Oh, yes. I've gone up with one of your pilots. Specifically, what were you doing?"

"During what time period?"

"Oh, say from two o'clock on."

"I was at the airport, doing things in and around my office early in the afternoon. That can be verified by my employees as well as several pilots and students. At three, I went out on a flight test with an applicant. Do you want his name?"

Jameson nodded and I gave it to him.

"This flight test was done in an airplane?"

"Most *flight* tests are."

Jameson disregarded the sarcasm. "How long did that take?"

"We got back about four-forty-five and Peter's girlfriend had a party for him, so I joined in. I did a few things around the office, talked to my maintenance engineer and my chief flight instructor, and went home about five-fifteen or five-twenty, had something to eat, picked up Penny Farnham and came here. We arrived about six-forty-five." I deliberately omitted giving Lance Brock's name as a reference. After the tongue-lashing I had given him this evening, I doubted if he'd want to confirm an alibi for me.

"We'll be out to your office to talk to your employees tomorrow. Before you go back to the other room, we'd like to look at the soles of your shoes."

I lifted one foot and then the other, while a policeman examined my shoes closely. I knew that the slightly rippled composition soles would not show any bloodstains.

As I left and Penny was being summoned, I heard a familiar bass voice and turned to see Anders Olafson at the outer door.

"What's the trouble here?" he asked, identifying himself. A constable went to get Jameson, and Anders, seeing me, smiled and said, "I saw all the cop cars and I thought I'd better stop and see what was happening."

"I guess I'd better let them tell you," I said. Penny and I were left standing in the corridor while Jameson talked to Anders. We heard the word locks used several times.

"The cops seem pretty deferential to your hunk," Penny said mischievously.

"Penny!"

"Oh, don't worry, Robin. No one believed that. Though I must say," she sighed wistfully, "he does have sex appeal."

"He probably also has a perfectly nice wife."

"He probably has, at that. Don't worry, Robin. I won't spill the beans to the cops."

I made a face at her and as Jameson returned

from his talk with Anders and motioned Penny to follow him, I whispered in her ear, "And I won't tell them about your washing the blood off your hands."

She held them out and said, "'Out, damn spot!' No, that's Sue's line."

* * * *

Several of the Church Committee members seemed puzzled at having the police ask to see the soles of their shoes. Albert, of course, tried to throw his weight around, and Myrtle was distressed. We could hear her shrill voice through the wall.

I said in a low voice to Douglas, "Surely, whoever stepped in that blood would have changed shoes."

"So you saw that. It's possible that the person didn't realize that he, or she, had stepped in it."

"Did they ask to see the soles of your shoes?" I asked.

"No. But I daresay they took a good look while I was kneeling by the body."

After the interviews were over, Jameson entered the meeting room with a technician who carried a small case. "I'll have to ask for your cooperation and I hope you will understand. We need to take your fingerprints in order to get prints of as many people as possible who have been in the office recently. We will be asking other members of the congregation to give us their prints also." He turned to Douglas. "We would like to ask you to help solicit their cooperation."

"Certainly."

Douglas stepped forward first and let himself be printed. I followed him. I had always imagined that you just stuck your fingers onto an ink pad and then onto some paper. Instead, the technician, who wore a corporal's chevrons, placed an ink pad and some specially marked cards side by side on the table. He grasped my hand, pressing one finger at a time onto the ink, then onto the card with a rolling motion that produced a print of the full width of the finger. After the ten prints were neatly pressed onto the card, he gave me a moistened towelette to wipe my fingers. I was surprised that all of the black ink readily came off. There were complaints from several people, but the corporal assured us that all prints that were not relevant to the case would be destroyed. People showed various degrees of concern, interest or compliance as the pile of prints mounted up.

* * * *

When the police let us go, I dropped Penny off and drove out to the airport. All the planes but one were sitting neatly on their tie-downs. The hangar door was up and in its brightly lit interior I could see Rod, lying on a creeper, working on the underside of a 172, a small four-place airplane.

He saw me, grinned, and said, "Hi. No problem. Just a loose antenna. This baby will be back on the line in the morning."

"You'd better get home, Rod. It's late."

"I'll be done in a jiff."

"I see that the Arrow is gone. That's good."

"Yeah. The guy skipped out without paying the parking fee."

"How did that happen?"

"I was down at the other end of the line fueling the insurance company's twin when I heard him start up. He just sneaked out and got in and never even did a pre-flight. He didn't do a run-up, ei-

ther, just took off, the little cheat. I got his regis-
tration, though. I put it on the desk."

"Joyce can look up the owner tomorrow and
send him a bill. No action with the Medevac, I see."

"S'right. Everything else is okay. You go on
home, Robin, and get a good night's sleep."

"Not very likely."

Rod caught the change in my tone and looked
at me quizzically.

"We had a murder at the church and I'm one
of the suspects."

Rod shot out from under the plane on his
creeper, and sat up so fast he hit his head on the
strut.

"Holy shit!" he exclaimed.

Chapter 9

In the morning, I was irritable when I went to work. It was one of those times when something I should be doing was nagging at my mind and I couldn't place it. I made sure Joyce had billed the transient pilot who had sneaked off without paying, but the amount was only a few dollars and didn't really seem significant when compared to murder. The Medevac 441 was gone, and all the school's planes were sitting on the ramp, ready to go.

We were having an open house on Saturday night and I should have been attending to the myriad last minute details. When I could bring my attention back to the job at hand, I found that I couldn't remember things I had done only a day or two before.

"Do we have enough VCR's and TV's for all the videos?"

"Yes, we do, "Joyce assured me patiently. "Everyone who is bringing a video is also bringing their own setup. We can use our own for the school's material."

"How about electric cords and outlets for all this stuff?"

Joyce, a long-suffering look on her face, responded, "Rod has it all taken care of, remember?"

I didn't remember. I passed a damp hand across my forehead. I couldn't think of any time in the past when I had been so completely disconnected from the world I was working in. I'd have to get hold of myself. I couldn't keep on like this.

I asked other inane questions and received reassuring answers. I didn't feel I was as on top of the situation as I should have been. It was a big event-our annual awards night and open house-designed to make students feel good about their accomplishments—and to bring in new customers.

The police arrived shortly after eight. Jameson and another plainclothes officer made themselves comfortable in my office as if they had a lot to discuss with me. Jameson leaned back in the comfortable visitor's chair and crossed his legs. His sharp, grey eyes gave the room a thorough and systematic going-over. The other man opened a notebook.

"We would like the names of all the people who were here yesterday and can vouch for your whereabouts," Jameson began.

I mentioned as many as I could think of and told the policemen that those people might remember others who had been there.

"And you were with this Peter Trask from three o'clock to four-forty-five?" Jameson had the habit of using the word this to precede the names of people he had not yet met, almost as if they were not real to him until he could see them face-to-face. I wondered if it was a mannerism, or a way of mentally categorizing the many individuals he must have to deal with in his work. He seemed to be distancing them from himself until he met them. I had the idle thought that in Douglas' work, if he did that with all the parishioners he had not met personally, it would be disastrous. This led me to the speculation that priests must automatically love everyone they meet, while police must automatically suspect them. They were two groups who dealt with the well-being of humanity, but what a different approach they had to take!

"Yes. I can give you his home and work addresses and phone numbers. Actually, he can probably vouch for me until at least five o'clock, and for awhile before three. There were quite a few people who talked to me between the time I got back from the flight test and the time I went home. Also before the flight test. I was here all day. I didn't even leave for lunch."

I still didn't tell them about Lance. I mentioned Rod and the instructor I had detailed to fly with Lance.

"Also, I didn't think to tell you last night, but the government of Canada can verify my alibi, and they have it on tape."

"How can they verify it?"

"When I went out with Trask on his flight test, I talked briefly to the controller on duty in the tower, to let him know that our flight was a flight test. All the controllers here know my voice. Also, all the radio transmissions are taped. We flew into Pine Hill, where there is a Flight Service Station, and the specialist on duty there is a friend of mine. We exchanged some chitchat and that will be on tape. I also forgot to tell you that another flight school operator who had seen us at Pine Hill, called here a few minutes before five and I talked to him."

The second policeman busily wrote down names and times.

Jameson seemed satisfied. "All right. We'll check all this out."

I relaxed, thinking that the police would now leave and I would be through with them. Then Jameson said in a quiet voice, "You forgot to tell us something else, too, didn't you?"

I stared at him blankly.

"Come on. Stop holding back on me. You forgot to tell me about the violent quarrel you overheard between Mrs. Meacham and Mr. Corrigan."

Taken aback, I was momentarily at a loss for words. Then I felt anger flooding over me and could feel my face redden. I said in a barely controlled voice, between clenched teeth, "I didn't tell you any such thing because it didn't happen."

"It did happen and you know it. You were right outside the church office listening in."

"I overheard a disagreement between them because I happened, at the time, to be going into the office. It was *not* violent."

"No?"

"No!"

"I heard otherwise."

"Then you heard wrong. Shirley got annoyed because Frank was picking on her." Instantly I regretted my choice of words, but I had used the ones Shirley had used in telling me. I went on. "If everyone committed murder after having an argument like that, there would be no one left alive."

"Why do you think she quit, then?"

"Because she found her work environment less pleasant than it had been, and until Frank left, which would have been in a month or two, she chose to avoid him, not to murder him."

"It upset her husband, though."

"I wouldn't know."

"His doctor thinks so. Furthermore, the doctor told you all about it at a meeting."

"He may have been exaggerating, but even if he wasn't, that was a month ago, and since Shirley had left the office, there was no more reason for Harry to be upset."

"Except that Corrigan had forced his wife to leave her job."

"Which she would have gotten back in a very short time."

"You hadn't decided on that, though. You were having a big disagreement in your meetings about it."

"No, we weren't. We had a disagreement over

the way her resignation was handled, but that was over whether proper procedure under Canon Law was followed. So we wanted to do everything else by the book."

"Canon Law?"

"Church law. The rules by which the Church operates."

"Oh." Jameson stared thoughtfully off into space. Then he impaled me with his penetrating eyes and asked, "What was the threat Mrs. Meacham made during this argument she had with Corrigan?"

The effect on me was one of such a letdown, I had to laugh. "She threatened to quit and leave him with all the work. Has someone said she threatened him?"

"No other threats?"

"Not at all."

Jameson got to his feet and moved toward the door. "We will check all these statements. Thank you for your time."

"Do that. You're welcome."

I watched them leave, my mind whirling with the implications of his questions. Someone had given the RCMP an earful. No one had said anything last night, while we were together, to indicate who it might be. It might even have been someone who wasn't there last night. I thought back to that meeting where Alan Gotfriedson and Marcia Chancellor had been decrying the spreading of rumours about Shirley. Someone was being a very busy little rumour-monger. I hadn't the faintest idea who.

I also had the feeling that Jameson would have loved to believe that I had done it. I was extremely thankful for my well-documented alibi.

I couldn't settle down to do any useful work,

despite the fact that my interview with Jameson had served to focus my mind and sharpen my senses. I paced around, making everyone nervous, going over and over everything in my mind. Then it dawned on me why I had a feeling of having left something undone. I should be over at the church, doing something, helping in some way, to straighten out the twisted threads of rumour and accusation that seemed to be entangling us. I felt it imperative that I do so; it was far more important even than the upcoming open house at the school. I was useless here, anyway. I was needed at the church.

"I'm leaving," I told Joyce as I strode past her on my way out the door. "I don't know when I'll be back." I saw her watch me leave, a perplexed, concerned look on her face.

* * * *

At the church, I was stopped at the outer door by the constable on duty. There was still a small crowd outside, and reporters were in evidence, shoving through the crowd to interview people, sticking microphones under the nose of anyone who seemed to have any role in the investigation. I managed to get through the crowd unscathed. I told the cop I was a member of the Church Executive Committee and needed to see the rector. I was directed to the meeting room and was told that no one could go into the office.

I seemed to have developed a habit of walking in unannounced on other people's discussions. I could hear Betty Forsythe talking in the meeting room and could see Douglas through the open door. His back was toward me. He was dressed that morning in black clerical garb, and was absentmindedly patting the pockets of his coat as if looking for something.

I heard Betty say rather sharply, "You're not going to start smoking again, are you?"

"Oh, sorry," Douglas replied, stopping his search. "It's just that old habits linger. I don't have any cigarettes on me, anyway."

"Well, don't go borrowing them from someone else. It's been quite awhile since I've seen you reaching for a smoke when you were upset. I thought you were over it."

"I am. I promise, I won't start again." His answer was quick and defensive. "I made the decision to quit and I'm not going to go back on it."

Betty's voice became more relaxed. "Good. You had me worried."

Then Douglas made the remark that raised my own anxiety to the level where I could feel the tightness in my stomach.

"There's something else I think I'd like to go back on, though," he said.

"Yes?"

"I'm not sure I should have taken this position. I had no idea. . ."

"Nonsense. You had no way of knowing and no one will blame you."

"It still means that I have to start out on the wrong foot. I can't just carry on with my agenda in the midst of a murder investigation."

"It will all work out. The police will probably solve the case in a day or two and things will get back to normal."

"I hope so. It depends on who committed the murder, though. If it was someone in the church, I expect that the repercussions could last forever."

"It will come out all right. Remember how fortunate we felt to have found this place. *I* want to stay. You can't back out. Don't worry about it, please."

"All right, love." I could hear the tenderness in his voice.

He couldn't leave! I don't know whether my reaction at that time was merely a result of the feeling of rootlessness from when we were looking for a new rector, or whether this particular man had already made a positive impression with his powerful sermon, his organizational ability and his aura of being fully in charge. I couldn't bear the thought of having to start the quest all over again.

I backed up to the outer door, opened it, closed it again as loudly as I reasonably could, and walked firmly back toward the room. As I entered, Douglas, who was sitting beside Betty, rose and came toward me, hands outstretched.

"Come in, Robin. I've been expecting you."

"You have?" I asked, surprised.

"Yes. Everyone else has come or called this morning after the police have been to see them. They are not used to being investigated in connection with murder and are in various stages of concern or anger over it. You are the only one who hadn't contacted me yet."

"Oh, that. They came to see me, but I can account for my whereabouts, and I even have the federal government to back me up. That's not why I came."

"You look upset."

"I am upset. It's about Shirley and Harry. I think the police are latching onto them as their prime suspects, and they are the last people on earth to have committed a murder."

"I agree, but what makes you think the police are singling them out? Everyone else who has called has felt that he or she is the one being accused." Douglas seated himself beside Betty again, and motioned me to a chair, but I didn't want to sit down.

I told him about Jameson's questions concerning the quarrel, and of my suspicion that someone in the congregation was deliberately, even maliciously, spreading rumours. I was still angry and it must have showed. I stood there, my wind-blown hair standing out from my head, my face reddening as it did when I became angry, feeling taut, wired, on edge.

"What are we going to do about it?" I demanded.

Douglas leaned back, smiled and shook his head. "I know that God will want me to come to the aid of my parishioners, but I didn't expect Him to send an avenging angel to help me."

I was rendered speechless. I stared at him with his bland, amused smile. He was looking at a tall, middle-aged woman beginning to put on a little extra weight around the waist and hips, with flaming red hair, green eyes and a ruddy complexion, wearing tan slacks, a light green polo shirt and brown, moccasin-toed shoes. Someone less like an angel, avenging or otherwise, I could scarcely imagine.

"You're right. I've been thinking about what I should do and have been asking for God's guidance. I have to be careful, you see."

I groaned inwardly. Don't be a wishy-washy fence-sitter, I willed him. Don't you dare say it would be unseemly to get involved in a murder. I thought better of you than that.

"People expect their clergy to come to their aid in many ways. But I can also see that many members of the congregation would think it unseemly if I made an issue of protecting my parishioners from the law. I have to walk a narrow line."

I frowned, waiting for him to continue.

"So, I have been asking for God's guidance. My feeling is that, yes, I should become involved. I realize that this will net me some criticism, possibly even from the same people who would criticize me if I don't. So I have decided that I must do something, but have not figured out what."

I felt I had received a blow. Douglas was saying *he* had to do something. Was I, a woman, going to be pushed aside again, while this man went out and wrestled with whatever devil lay in wait out there?

Betty Forsythe now spoke. "Yes, I agree. Not only for the sake of the people who are being investigated, but also for the sake of the church. We have already seen what harm rumour can do. This is going to do far worse, unless we can stop it."

I watched Douglas' face soften and one of those looks pass between them that expressed love and understanding, thanks and praise, and heaven knew what else, and I felt the first twinges of envy that I had never experienced anything like that.

Douglas looked from Betty to me and back. "What do you think we should do?"

We! Glorious we. I was going to be included after all. But I also was at a loss to suggest a way to proceed.

Betty, who seemed to be a practical, common-sense sort of woman, said, "I think you should talk to everyone and get their stories. Then you can quash any wild rumours that get started."

"Also, people will talk to you in a more relaxed manner than to the police, and may remember things they had forgotten," I added. "I know that I didn't remember half the sources of my alibi when the police questioned me last night."

"Yes, of course. Obviously, we can't duplicate

the work of the police, so we shouldn't try."

"You seem to have more faith in the cops than I do at the moment," I growled.

"Don't underestimate them, Robin. They are very competent at this type of investigation and I have faith that they will come up with the answer."

"Well, I don't like the way they're going about it."

"Don't let that bother you. It's an act."

"You're kidding!"

Douglas shook his head. "No, Robin. I've seen them at work a number of times before. What Sergeant Jameson is doing is using a technique which he feels will be useful in this particular case. You must realize that when he arrived here last night, he was faced with a group of people who were banded together, holding hands, and saying a prayer, and who had one single thought in mind, the thought that no one in the church should be suspected. He needed to use a technique that would break the solid front we presented, and open up a crack somewhere."

"Well, he found someone."

"So it would seem. Believe me, that bothers me."

"Who all have they questioned?" I asked.

"Let's see." He sat back and thought through the calls he had received that morning. "Your friend, Penny Farnham called just before you got here. She said she usually talked her problems over with you, but your receptionist told her you had left." I nodded and Douglas continued, "She was more annoyed than worried, annoyed for the same reason you are, by the method of questioning the police are using. She does not seem concerned for her own sake, but was also worried about the Meachams. However, she was questioned about her whereabouts and seemed to feel that she had come under suspicion because she is one of the ones who had spoken out against Frank. Sue Ambler and Paul St. Cyr are suspect because, along with you, they voted against Frank."

"We didn't vote against Frank. We voted against the actions of the Maintenance Committee in accepting Shirley's resignation, because they didn't have the authority to do that."

Douglas held up his hand. "I know that, but a lot of others still don't. That was the gist of Sue Ambler's complaint, also."

"But if that were a motive for murder, it should have been Frank bumping one of us off."

"I believe the thinking of the police is that if one of you had gotten in a quarrel with Frank over it, the grievance may initially have been his, but an altercation could have ensued in which his antagonist hit him."

"That's stretching things."

"Maybe. I talked to Sergeant Jameson this morning, and he confirms my impression that it looks like a spur-of-the-moment crime, with the perpetrator just picking up a weapon that happened to be handy."

I nodded. "It looked like it, didn't it? That rock isn't even on the counter all the time. It could have been on the desk, and anyone planning to use it would have had to walk around the counter, get the rock and walk back around again."

"And by that time, Frank would have been out the door, making tracks."

"You are in the office a lot more than I. Do you remember where the rock was?"

"I've been thinking about that. I'm pretty sure it was on the counter. Even if the killer had known it would be there, why go over on the other side of Frank and have to step over the body to get out?"

After a moment's silence, I said, "That doesn't

necessarily mean that he didn't bring a weapon. He may have had a gun or a knife, but decided to use the rock because it was handy."

"Yes. The police are considering that possibility. By the way, Jameson said there were no prints on the rock because of its rough surface, but they have matched nearly all our prints to ones found in the office. They have also found some quite fresh prints, on top of others, that they haven't identified, so they still want to print everyone who was in the office in the last day or two. Because of the timing, they don't think it's the janitors, but will ask them because one or more of them has a key."

"I don't suppose they suspect Anders Olafson?"

"No, apparently not, though I understand that all his employees' prints are on file because of the nature of their job."

"I can't imagine Anders doing it anyway. He is a really gentle person."

"He's big enough, though," Betty commented.

"That's one reason why I can't imagine him bashing in someone's skull," I answered. "I can see him picking up Frank by the front of his shirt and shaking him like a dog with a stuffed toy, but I can't see him sneaking up behind him like that."

Douglas and Betty both chuckled at my description.

"The police are quite interested in the situation of the locks and keys," Douglas went on.

"I remember them questioning Anders about it last night."

"Anyway, it seems that all the outside doors were locked. All have deadbolts except one. That would mean that anyone going out would have to have a key to lock the door behind him—or her. They wanted to know whether it was likely that Frank would have locked the door again when he came in."

"I wouldn't know."

"They thought it odd that he did. His key was in his pocket, by the way."

"You said that there is one door without a deadbolt."

"Yes, a small door leading out of the sacristy."

I frowned and found that I could not picture it. "Where does it lead?"

"Nowhere, really. Onto some lawn and shrubs. It must have had a purpose when the church was built, but I don't think anyone uses it much now."

"That's way over on the other side of the church. It seems farfetched that anyone would go out there. Why not just leave the door unlocked if you didn't have a key?"

"The police thought it unlikely that the killer left by that door. They think it more likely he had a key. Personally, I'm appalled at the laxity in handing out keys."

"We discussed it at the last Church Committee meeting."

"Yes, I know. I talked to Nick Valutin. He had some information he was going to bring up at the meeting last night. At any rate, it seems that there could be dozens of keys floating around the community and it could be quite easy for people with no right to have them to get hold of one."

"Right. That was the impression I got at the meeting."

"So you see, Sergeant Jameson isn't intent on pinning it on one of the parishioners."

I thought it over and, realizing the logic in Douglas attitude toward the police, admitted grudgingly, "I guess you're right."

Betty asked, "What reasons did the police give other people for suspecting them?"

"Let's see. Albert Wallace was questioned as to

whether Frank may have picked a fight with him because he let the Church Committee question his actions. Albert would have had ready access to the church and could have had legitimate business here, so he might not even have been noticed when he came out."

"Jean said he called her to get materials out of the office. If he was in there, why didn't he take them?"

"Possibly because he committed a murder first and fled. When did he ask Jean to get the papers?"

"I don't know. Jean didn't say. But that was why she was there early to open up."

Douglas stroked his chin. "Hmm. The police might think that he asked her to do that so she would be the one to discover the body. Yes, I think we must talk to Albert and find out just what he was doing up to the time of the meeting."

"Who else?"

"Paul St. Cyr came to see me at the rectory this morning. It seems that when he worked at the *Chronicle*, he wrote an article about shady real estate practices and one of the shady operators he listed was Frank Corrigan, though to avoid libel, he didn't use Frank's name. Again, it would seem that Frank had the motive to strike out at Paul, but the same reasoning goes. If they had an argument, it might have gotten out of hand."

"All these motives seem pretty farfetched, don't they?" I asked. "I mean, they are really stretching to come up with one."

"That's my impression, too, but with Jean Givens, things are different. She seems to have the strongest motive of all."

"Real estate?"

"Yes. Every time she mentions Frank, she lets annoyance creep into her voice. I don't know whether there is anything specific, but he must have had some effect on her business, and might have cost her a sale at some time. It's the only motive outside the church, and the only one aside from the Meachams' that isn't stretching things."

"They may as well suspect Sue because Frank didn't appreciate Shakespeare."

We all laughed.

"Or Gretchen because Frank referred to Albert as chairman of the Church Committee. She always corrects us on that."

"As a matter of fact," Douglas remarked, "that did have something to do with Gretchen's complaint. The police evidently gave her the impression they suspect her because Frank was a male chauvinist and Gretchen is so obviously a feminist. I gather that she told the police what kind of chauvinists she thought they were as well."

I chuckled. "She would".

There was silence for a moment. I had finally consented to sit down, and we all sat silently, wrapped in our private thoughts. Betty sat in the corner of the couch, her legs crossed at the ankles, looking relaxed. Douglas leaned back, his hands folded, staring upward, seeming to be in deep thought. I sat nervously on the edge of a chair, unable to relax.

Douglas continued, "Layton Nathanson is suspect because a couple of years ago, when he worked for Revenue Canada, he caught Frank in a minor income tax fiddle."

"Oh, oh."

"However, according to Layton, Frank would not have known he was the one who caught him. Nick Valutin came here this morning to talk about the locks and keys. He has keys, of course, but is off the hook because he was having a beer in his backyard at the critical time with his next door neighbour who happens to be the Inspector in charge of the local RCMP detachment."

"Now there's an alibi for you!" Betty declared.

"And I thought I had such a good one" I added with mock dejection. "So, where do we start?"

"I had thought the Meachams are the ones in most need of the assurance of the church that they are in our prayers and we are standing up for them."

"Absolutely," Betty remarked. "No matter what, we should visit them."

"I think you should come along, Betty."

"Of course. I haven't visited them since we stayed there, and I certainly should."

"What about me? May I come along?" I asked, suddenly hesitant.

Douglas grinned. "By all means. Officially to represent the congregation, and personally because your flaming passion may do a lot of good."

I hadn't seen the Forsythe's four-wheel-drive Jeep Cherokee, which they had gotten for the purpose of pulling their trailer across the country, and asked if they wanted to ride with me.

"Ours is here," Betty said. "I had to park several blocks away because of the congestion. Douglas walks down here every morning."

I visualized where the rectory was in relation to the church and estimated that it was a good one and a half kilometers away. No wonder he stayed so trim. He might need all that athletic vigour in the days to come. I had the feeling that this investigation was going to put a strain on all of us, but on Douglas in particular. He might, after all, decide to leave, and the thought gave me another bout of anxiety, another sick feeling in the pit of my stomach.

Chapter 10

The Meachams lived in an old area of town known as Victoria Hill. The houses, all built in the early part of the century, had been well-preserved or lovingly restored. Large old sycamores shaded the streets, the pavement sometimes detouring around them. The houses were set well back from the street, each with its well-tended front lawn. Considering how crowded the rest of the city was becoming, it was relaxing to come into this oasis of spacious luxury. It was a four-block area that had resisted the trend in the central core toward subdividing old houses into warrens of cheap apartments.

The Meachams' large, two-storied house, of wood construction recently painted white with dark green shutters and trim, had a porch across the front. Large picture windows and a solarium were recent additions.

The police certainly would have no cause to think that Shirley needed the low-paying job of church secretary in order to make ends meet!

Shirley and Harry welcomed us with obvious pleasure. Shirley and Betty hugged each other and the rest of us shook hands all around. Harry did not look like the beleaguered candidate for a heart attack that I had been led to believe. He was spry, with crinkly grey hair and humourous blue eyes. His smile would have melted an Arctic lake. They had every appearance of an ordinary retired couple welcoming their man of God into their home. Shirley bustled off to make tea while the rest of us engaged in idle chitchat.

When Shirley had poured the tea and taken a seat beside Harry on the couch, the conversation took on a serious tone.

"Have the police been to see you this morning?" Douglas asked.

"Oh, yes," Shirley replied. "We were quite appalled. We didn't care much for Frank, but it is dreadful that *anyone* should be murdered."

"Did they question you about the quarrel you had with Frank? Robin says they are making quite an issue of it."

"Oh, dear. I hope they didn't bother you because of that, Robin. It was such an imposition on you in the first place." Trust Shirley to think first of the other person.

"That's not what's bothering me," I told her. "What I don't like is their coming to me and trying to get me to say something that would implicate my friends. It seems that there is someone in the congregation who has been spilling all our secrets to the RCMP."

"How terrible! I wonder who would do something like that?"

"We haven't the foggiest."

Harry leaned forward. "They asked us where we were yesterday afternoon. Is that when it happened?"

"Apparently," Douglas answered.

"We couldn't tell them very much. We were at home. Paul called early in the afternoon to get us to renew our subscription to the Georgetown Symphony, but otherwise we were here alone."

"Paul St. Cyr?"

"Yes. He is one of the local workers for the Symphony."

"What time was that?"

"Umm. Let's see. It must have been before three. Bob Kerr and *Off the Record* were on—CBC Stereo, you know. At three, there's the news and I remember *Disc Drive* just starting when I went upstairs for my nap. I like that Jurgen Gothe. He's a character."

"Harry has been taking an afternoon nap since he retired. It's done wonders," Shirley explained, patting Harry's hand and glancing at him affectionately.

"Yes," Harry smiled. "Couldn't do that while I was working. Makes me feel lazy, but I enjoy it."

Douglas turned to Shirley. "Did you see anyone or talk to anyone?"

"No. Not that I can remember. I'm rather vague about it, but I think I spent the afternoon in the kitchen. I put a roast in the oven and made a gelatin salad with vegetables in it. That's good on warm days like we've been having. I know I puttered around the kitchen doing this or that until Harry came down."

"Which was when the delicious aroma of roast beef wafted up the stairs to my nostrils. I think it was around five."

"Then we went out on the patio, sat there and drank iced tea until the roast was nearly done. I'm not supposed to indulge in any before-dinner cocktails because of my stomach problem." Shirley made a face. "Harry won't have one unless I do."

"I dare say it's better for me as well."

"Really, it was quite an ordinary day. I suppose one or two of our neighbors might have seen us on the patio, but otherwise we were by ourselves."

My heart sank. They were not just home together, but were home separately in the latter part of the afternoon. Looking at them, I knew that Shirley did not suspect Harry of feigning his normal nap and sneaking out to do murder, nor did Harry doubt that Shirley had indeed been in the kitchen all the time. The more I looked at them, the less like a pair of desperate murderers they seemed. But would the police believe it? And that was not the worst.

Harry remarked quite casually, "They took our fingerprints the first time they were here."

"The first time?" I exclaimed. I couldn't keep the alarm out of my voice.

"Yes. They came back later," Shirley replied unconcernedly. "They had found our fresh prints in the church office."

Douglas, Betty and I stared in dumbfounded silence.

"You see, we went in to get a book that I had left there. I called Ethel Fuller, who is doing the secretarial work temporarily, to see if I had left it there. She said I had, so we went by the church on our way to do our grocery shopping yesterday morning. I'd forgotten that Ethel doesn't work the same hours that I did. She comes in at ten, not at nine." Shirley looked at Douglas. "I guess you had left after morning prayer. I noticed that the home communion kit was gone."

Douglas nodded. "Yes. I visited two patients at the extended care facility."

"Anyway, I still had my key, so we went into the office. I had to hunt a bit for the book before I found it."

"And I leaned on the counter while she looked." Harry showed no alarm.

I couldn't believe it! These people were the prime suspects in a murder, they had no alibi, and their fingerprints were all over the murder scene. Surely they must have known the danger they were in, yet they sat there, relaxed and smiling, as if we were discussing flower arranging or fly tying or something else pleasant and noncontroversial. If it had been me, I'd have been in either a rage or a panic. Most people would have shown some form of alarm or anxiety.

"I can't believe you're taking it so calmly!" I blurted out. "I'd be climbing the walls."

I could see a similar look of anxiety on Betty's face. Douglas, more used to maintaining his cool in all manner of situations, nevertheless was frowning. The Meachams, sitting side by side, quietly enjoying the social occasion, seemed like a cut-out picture imposed on a background that did not fit.

"Well, you see, it's like this," Shirley said calmly. "After I left my job, Harry and I decided that we couldn't let the events of the last few months get us down. We prayed, we read scripture, we focused on the terrible injustices that Jesus had suffered, and realized that our own were very minor in comparison, and we decided to give ourselves over to Jesus. We prayed for Frank, and for the congregation, as well as for ourselves."

Harry took up the story. "Since we made this decision, we have felt God's grace resting upon us, and we know that whatever happens, it will be all right. I know you think we should be concerned, but we know that justice will be done and that since we are blameless, we have nothing to worry about."

Douglas got up, went to them and took them by the hand. "God bless you, both of you. It is wonderful for me to meet people with such abiding faith."

It might be wonderful to him, but it certainly didn't hit me that way! I could imagine the police talking to these dear old folks and thinking they were loony and just the religious types who felt they ought to take God's work into their own hands and eliminate a few sinners. I viewed with anguish the possibility that these truly pious people might be completely misunderstood by the rational, secular world. If I didn't know Shirley, I might have had doubts about them myself.

Douglas said a prayer for them and they were obviously deeply moved. We all rose from our chairs.

I don't know why the line popped into my mind and couldn't exactly remember where it came from, but I heard myself saying, "Strength for today. Bright hope for tomorrow."

Shirley threw herself into my arms, for the second time.

"Oh, Robin. How wonderful. That is just what we need. Thank you so much."

I stood there, embarrassed, but when Shirley had let go of me, Harry came over, put an arm around my shoulder, and said, "You have been so kind and thoughtful. We really appreciate it."

I wasn't sure what all they perceived that I had done, but I guess my concern for them showed more than I realized.

* * * *

We took our leave. On the sidewalk, Betty said, "I have to go to a Guild meeting at Myrtle's house. I can drop you off at the church first if you'd like."

"No thanks. We'll walk." Douglas gave me a questioning glance as he said this. I nodded.

We walked along tree-lined streets and across the lawns of the city government complex. The sun was bright but not hot and a gentle breeze ruffled our hair. The spreading maple trees, scattered across the lawn in alternating red and green, cast dappled shadows on the carefully tended grass. Neat displays of flowers flanked the buildings.

Douglas brow was furrowed in thought. After

we had walked a ways in silence, I commented, "I wish they had an alibi."

"Yes. That would make things easier."

"It seems a shame that nice people like that should be suspected of murder."

"Do you seriously think the police are targeting them as murderers?"

"They certainly act like it."

"No, actually, they don't. Not yet. They are skeptical, and they have to investigate every facet of the case, but I don't think they're committed to any one, or two, suspects."

"I remember last night that sergeant accusing you of looking at the world through rose-coloured glasses."

Douglas smiled. "Perhaps I do. But I don't seriously think they will arrest those two, and I don't think Shirley and Harry are worried about it, either."

"They didn't seem to be, did they?"

"They have a deep, abiding faith in God, and I think that faith will carry them through. I hope I'm right."

"I hope so, too. Still, it's a shame that they have to go through such an ordeal."

Douglas looked at me sharply. "Did they look to you like people suffering an ordeal?"

I thought for a moment. A vision of the Meachams' placid faces came to my mind. "No, they didn't." Then I added, "Not yet."

"They are not the ones undergoing an ordeal. The person who is suffering an ordeal is the person who killed Frank."

"Oh! Yes, I suppose so."

Again we walked in silence for awhile, passing from the springy turf to the firm surface of interlocking paving stones as we rounded the corner of the library building. Then I asked, "You said you've had considerable experience with the methods police use. In what way?"

"I've lived in some rough and tumble communities, where the young people have less to occupy them, more peer pressure to do anti-social things, and often a poor example from their parents. I've been called any number of times to go to the police station to help get some youth out of jail. Usually it was some kid who had never been picked up before, whose parents were either appalled by what their child had done or furious with the police for suggesting that their child had committed an illegal act. The youth was often really frightened, and I've seen compassion as well as toughness from the police who brought them in. Some of these kids would never end up there again, but there were others, too many of them, who thought that free will meant they were free to do what they will."

I laughed. Then another thought came to my mind. "You mentioned free will. I've had a question about that. I was going to ask Martin, but he became too sick to carry on, and I never did develop much of a relationship with Philip Eccles— not that I didn't like him very much."

"He was in a difficult position here."

"I know. The congregation looks to the incumbent for direction, but since he was just temporary, he didn't want to put his stamp on things."

"Exactly. We had a long talk about it last spring while I was here. What was your question?"

"Well, last winter, I came to an organ recital in the church. There were a lot of people, many of them not members of our congregation. As we were leaving, I saw this one man, wearing a sweatshirt that caught my attention. I didn't know the man, and I've never seen him since.

"In the first place, the sweatshirt showed a crazy-looking kid flying an airplane and heading straight for the ground. That made me angry. It's a stereotype of aviation that has no basis in fact. I was annoyed, but wouldn't have said anything to him if the message on the sweatshirt hadn't also caught my attention. It said, 'If God is your co-pilot, you'd better change seats.' Well, I didn't agree with that either and I went up and spoke to him about it. It was an immediate reaction, and I hadn't organized my thoughts, so I didn't present them very well. But instead of discussing it with me, this man sort of closed his face, made it into a rigid mask, and you could see him pull down the shutters on his mind. Bang! Bang! All he would say to me was, 'God is always in control.'"

Douglas nodded but said nothing.

"I went home and thought about it, and sort of organized my argument."

"I'd like to hear it."

"Okay. Here it is. If God gave man free will, I assume that He intended man to exercise control over his life."

Douglas gave a brief nod, more to encourage me to continue than to agree with me.

"Let's look at the duties of a co-pilot. The pilot is in command of the flight. The co-pilot does the following things: reads the checklist, brings it to the attention of the pilot if he strays off course, calls out his airspeeds, and warns him if he gets too low on his approach. Now isn't that what God does with men's lives?"

"Hmm. I see I'm going to have to be careful how I answer this." He thought for a minute. "First, I assume that you are accurate about the duties of the pilot and co-pilot. That's your field. Your analogy is a good one. I can take it a bit farther.

For example, you could relate the reading of the checklist to one's indoctrination in the faith. God certainly will give you guidance if you stray off course. The speed analogy can represent one living in the fast lane, or alternately being lazy and not meeting one's obligations. And the business of being too low on the approach could be made to represent someone descending into sin in a serious way."

He paused a moment and I waited for the rest.

"However, though the man wearing the sweatshirt did not seem to have the ability to discuss it with you, he was, in the end, correct."

"Oh?"

"God *is* always in control. Now I think the maker of the sweatshirt used a poor analogy. Obviously, he got your dander up, since you know more about aviation than he, but think about what he intended to do with that sweatshirt."

I was silent, so Douglas continued, "What did the wild picture do?"

"It got my attention, that's for sure."

"Exactly. Don't you think that's what it was intended to do? So then, when you looked at it, you read the message. Do you think the sweatshirt manufacturer was trying to make you climb into the other seat the next time you flew your plane?"

I laughed. "No, I don't think so."

"Of course not. So what did he intend? He intended for you to stop and think about your relationship with God."

"I see."

"So, do you think it served its purpose?"

"Well, yes."

"Of course it did. It got you to go up to the wearer and discuss it with him, and it has occupied your mind for several months so that you mentioned it to me. It is not intended to express any profound truths. It is meant to set you on a course of thinking about God's role in your life. Am I making myself clear?"

"Very."

We walked along in silence for a few paces before I got up the nerve to ask-no, to issue the challenge-that had formed in my mind.

"Then if God is always in control. . ."

Before I could continue, we heard ourselves being hailed, and looking up, saw that we were passing the RCMP headquarters. In the parking lot, calling to us, was Sgt. Jameson. He came over.

"I thought you would like to know that Frank Corrigan's son, Brett, will be arriving on the bus from Georgetown at about five o'clock. I thought you would probably want to see him."

"Of course."

"We will meet him and talk to him for awhile. We'll let you know when we're through."

"Thank you. I'll be at the rectory, or if he doesn't have transportation to get there, I can meet him at some other place."

"We'll tell him. I'd better warn you though, the Georgetown police told us that Brett Corrigan went out to find solace after hearing of his father's death, but he didn't do it in a church."

"I understand."

"In fact, that's why he's so late getting here today. They couldn't roust him out of bed before nine o'clock and by the time they had interviewed him, an eleven o'clock bus was the earliest he could catch. It takes six hours to get here, even though it's not all that far."

"I remember driving down. It's at least a four and a half hour drive because the road winds all over the place. Wouldn't it be faster to fly?"

"Yes. A little. Also a lot more expensive. It

doesn't save much time though, because you have to go east to Calgary or west to Vancouver and change planes. There's no direct flight. It still takes four hours."

"What sort of person is this son? He must be young."

"Mid-twenties. Other than that, he's an assistant manager at a supermarket, so he hasn't done too bad for a person his age. He's divorced and has one child."

I asked tentatively, "I don't suppose he could have been down here yesterday afternoon?"

"Forget it!" Jameson replied. "When the Georgetown police went to his home to advise him of his father's death, they clocked the time at seven-thirty-five. He was at home. There's no way he could have driven it in that time and no scheduled bus or plane would have gotten him there. Anyway, his landlady said he came in about seven-fifteen, and his co-workers at the store say that he left for his afternoon off at one o'clock exactly. By the way, the pathologist puts the time of death at some time between four-thirty and five."

"The Georgetown police couldn't be mistaken?"

"No way. We asked them to verify the details of his whereabouts and they say he was there at one p.m. and home by seven-fifteen. We were interested also, because he is the heir, and because he has a record."

"Oh?"

"I can't say anything about it, but it did make us look at him closely. But I'm afraid he's squeaky clean on this one."

We took our leave and walked on toward the church. I stated, "I'm afraid I was thinking a very sinful thought."

"That you wish this son could be shown to be Frank's killer?"

"Yes."

"The thought entered my mind also, I'm ashamed to say. It would be so convenient."

"I wonder what sort of crime he committed?"

"From Jameson's reaction, I would imagine that it was some crime involving violence. I don't think they would get so interested if he had only stolen a twenty out of the till."

"Um. You're probably right. By the way, where were you between four-thirty and five yesterday? I doubt if even you are exempt from their scrutiny."

Douglas laughed delightedly. "You're right. It's rather interesting being a suspect, but I was at the Golden Age Retirement Home and if old Mrs. Bell and George Tregassen can't remember who called on them, at least the staff, to whom I introduced myself, will."

"Good. I'm glad you have an alibi. We had a hard enough time finding you, and we wouldn't want to start looking all over again."

Out of the corner of my eye, I saw Douglas turn his head and give me a thoughtful look. I wondered what he was thinking. Remembering the discussion between Douglas and Betty that I had overheard that morning, my anxiety level escalated a few notches, and I found myself amazed that this should be so. Surely if this man didn't have what it took to stick it out through our current troubles, we'd be better off with someone else.

I felt the first skip in my heart's rhythm as I realized that it was not just for the congregation that I felt anxious, but for myself personally. In the short time I had known him, he had become someone who could be very important to me, and that raised danger flags in another area. I was an impostor, a non-believer masquerading as a church member. I'd have to watch myself. I'd almost opened my big mouth once too often already.

Chapter 11

At the church, the temporary secretary, Ethel Fuller, trying to catch up on her work, was constantly interrupted by people calling to ask questions or express opinions on the murder or on Frank's character. Ethel grimaced as she hung up for the umpteenth time. "If I were keeping score, it would be about zero to fifty, Frank versus everybody who has called. He's not very popular, but I don't like people calling, to the church especially, and saying it serves him right."

"Is that what people are saying?" I asked. "I don't believe it!"

"Actually, only a few have said anything like that, but nobody seems to be grieving." Ethel's voice was heavy with censure.

She had brought sandwiches and fruit. The coffee maker had been rescued from the office, and as Douglas and Ethel tried to get some of the routine work of the church done, we munched on the food and sipped hot coffee from styrofoam cups.

"Let's go talk to Albert," Douglas suggested.

"Right. Shall we go in my car? It's a bit far to walk."

We threaded our way through the downtown traffic in my old Malibu station wagon, and found a place in the crowded parking lot of a large hardware store. To get in the door, we had to run an obstacle course composed of piles of bagged potting soil, garden hoses, wheelbarrows, and carts. Inside, we weaved through a maze of aisles piled high with merchandise on sale, sidestepping heavily laden shoppers carrying precarious piles of purchases, flattening ourselves against the shelves to avoid being run down by shopping carts with protruding broom handles and fluorescent tubes, driven by raving maniacs, and tripping over hyperactive children. One table, covered by a jumbled heap of knickknacks, some of which had fallen to the floor, was being pawed over by impatient customers. It carried a sign showing a ten-sided gold coin with a bird that more nearly resembled a duck than a loon, holding a fish in its beak. Above the fishy loon, a slogan proclaimed, *You'd be loony not to snap up these bargains!* As an icon for this type of store, it was perfect.

Finally arriving at a half-flight of stairs ascending to where Albert Wallace's office overlooked the sales floor was like surviving the charge of the Light Brigade. We had to shout to each other over the din.

"He seems to be doing well. Half the town must be here," I boomed at the top of my lungs.

"It seems so. Is it always this busy?"

"I don't know. I usually shop at Lakeside Lumber or Gordon's Hardware, or if it's garden supplies, at the Plant House."

"Are they down in your end of town?"

"Yes. Also things are less frantic than here and the service is better. This is one of those discount outfits with low prices, lots of merchandise and next to no service. Albert seems to do well at it, though. I personally am willing to pay more for service and a quieter atmosphere."

We reached the top of the stairs and entered the office. A young secretary with bleached blonde hair in one of the modern frizzy hairstyles, and wearing one of the minutest of mini-skirts, looked up at us with curiosity. Douglas asked if we could speak to Albert, and without getting up or turning her head, the blonde creature called out, "Al, it's not the cops this time—it's someone a lot more holy."

Albert Wallace came to the door of his office, beamed his welcome, and exclaimed, "Come in, come in. Take a load off your feet." He held a chair for me and waved Douglas to another before moving around his desk and sitting portentously in his large swivel chair. "What brings you here?"

"We are concerned about all the suspicion that is being directed at members of the church over Frank Corrigan's death, and have decided to get everyone's story so that unsubstantiated rumours don't get started," Douglas explained smoothly.

Albert looked appraisingly at me but said nothing.

"Robin has volunteered to come as a representative of the church, because I don't know the people as well. Most of you have businesses or jobs, and Robin felt that she could get away from hers."

Albert nodded. In the outer office, the blonde secretary was lapping it up.

"What was it that you wanted?" Albert still seemed to be holding back, perhaps remembering how he had been raked over the coals in committee meetings.

"We are trying to find out where everyone was yesterday afternoon so that we can counter any rumours that people might not be able to account for their time. Do you mind telling us where you were?"

Albert seemed to relax and became quite loquacious. "Wednesday is my afternoon off and I chauffeur Cleo around to do her shopping. First we went to the Super Drug Mart to get our prescriptions refilled. I've got my ulcer medicine and my blood pressure medicine, and Cleo would positively fall apart if she didn't have all her pill and potions. We both take vitamins and I take ASA to prevent strokes. They say you should take one every other day, but I figure I'd be better off to take it every day. In fact, I take two a day."

And hope you don't cut yourself with a knife and can't stop the bleeding, I thought acidly, knowing from my university training in biology that aspirin reduces blood clotting. Why can't people follow their doctor's advice?

"After the drug store, we went to the Smoke Shop to get our week's supply of lottery tickets and check on our old ones. We didn't win anything." He made a face. "We never do. We've won two dollars a few times, and occasionally five or ten. Maybe someday we'll hit the jackpot."

If they ever did, I wondered if they would give ten percent of it to the church.

"Then we went to the Exeter Mall, and Cleo spent most of the afternoon in the dress shops. As if she doesn't have anything to wear! I just followed along behind her to carry things and pay the bills. We ended up going to the Farmer's Market in the mall parking lot. Their produce is a lot fresher than in the stores and if you haggle enough, some of those guys will lower their prices and you can get a pretty good deal. Then we went home and had dinner. Is that what you wanted to know?"

"Did you see anyone you knew?"

"I don't think so. Cleo might remember."

"What time did you get home?"

"Um. I'm not sure. Five thirty or thereabouts. Ask Cleo."

"Did you go out again before the meeting?"

"No. Let's see. After dinner some neighbours came over. They're non-stop talkers, so I had to call Jean to open up. I had a hard time getting away."

Somehow, this last sounded a bit contrived. Maybe it was the defensive way Albert told it. I didn't know Albert well enough to decide whether to believe him. I did know that the police would want someone other than a wife to verify his alibi.

"You don't think it was just some burglar that Frank surprised in the office?" Albert was still riding that hobby horse.

Douglas shook his head.

"It's terrible what people think they can get away with," Albert pontificated, glancing out over the sales floor. "They just pick stuff up and put it in their pockets and if you try to stop them, they threaten to sue you. Someone ought to put the fear of God into some of these young punks. Not that older people don't do it, too. We've even had little old white-haired ladies who, when you stop them, turn into really mean, nasty bitches. You wouldn't believe some of the language!"

"I think the police are looking for a somewhat different sort of person than that," Douglas explained.

"I don't see why. Some young punk probably thought he could walk in and take some stuff, and Frank caught him."

"And locked the door behind him with a key?"

"Oh, I didn't know that."

Trust Albert to miss an essential point that everyone else picked up right away.

Albert then started on his next grievance. "I don't see why they won't let us use the office. I was down there today, and some young kid who thought he owned the world because he was wearing a uniform, stood in my way and wouldn't let me in."

"They have a lot to do. They were still collecting evidence when we were there at noon. As soon as they are done, they will let us back in our office. Actually, I have found them very considerate."

Albert had to have something to complain about—his way of asserting authority where he had none. "You'd think someone in the church had killed Frank, the way they act."

I commented sarcastically, "*That* is exactly what they *do* think."

"That's what I mean. You'd think they'd send someone with a bit more sense than that James character."

"Jameson," I corrected him.

"It's a damn shame the way they hound us. They should be out trying to find out who had it in for Frank."

"I am under the impression that is exactly what they are doing." I said it slowly, emphasizing each word. Albert was beginning to get under my skin. I found myself siding with the police even though earlier in the day, I had been critical of them.

Douglas gave me a meaningful look and suggested firmly, "I think we had better be on our way. We have other people to see."

We got to our feet and Albert again became the genial host as he ushered us out. The secretary was sitting at her desk, legs twined around each other, repairing her nail polish. She watched us with avid curiosity as we left the office. I had a strong urge to get out of the whole place—office, store, everything—and never come back.

Outside, I apologized to Douglas. "I'm sorry. I shouldn't have let him get to me like that. I can't stand to talk to that man for more than two minutes."

"That's all right, Robin. We got the information we needed. One does have to realize, though, that he probably does have a point about the shoplifting."

I sighed. "Yes, he does. The way that store is

crammed with stuff, I suspect that a lot of it does go missing, even with his one-way-glass office and the surveillance cameras. I could understand that, but his attitude toward the murder investigation irritates me. None of us like it, but at least most of us realize that it has to be done."

"Yes, and I find that the police are being very professional, even if I did have a bit of a stand-off with them last night."

I grinned, remembering the scene. "We were all about to break into cheers for you." Douglas, for once, looked flustered.

"Another thing about Albert's store," I continued, "I suspect that he has a lot of theft by employees. He pays minimum wage and the turnover is very rapid. Did Nick suggest to you that the church keys be stamped, 'Do not copy?'"

"Yes, he did."

"Well, do you think that if someone brought one of those keys to this store that the teenage clerk who makes duplicate keys would pay any attention? If he could even read, that is?"

"Possibly not, especially if someone offered him a ten to make a copy."

I grinned at him. "What sinners we are!"

"No worse than people have been for thousands of years."

"You think so?" There was skepticism in my voice. "The general consensus seems to be that crime is on the rise."

Douglas climbed into the passenger seat of my car, wincing as he sat on a spot where the sun had hit the dark blue vinyl upholstery. He rolled down the window and reached for the seat belt. "I think that conception is probably because of better record-keeping by the police and because the news media inundate us with news about crime."

"They do, don't they? I wish they didn't concentrate on it so much. The news is always so depressing, I don't even watch it on TV. I listen to the six o'clock news on CBC and read the *Globe and Mail*, but I don't listen to or watch the late news or I'd never get to sleep. Why can't the media give us a little peace?"

"Because most people would miss their daily dose of scandal and violence if they did." Douglas voice grated with barely controlled anger. I risked a quick glance at his firmly set jaw, and thought that for the first time I was seeing this priest with his mask off. There was indeed a man with ordinary emotions in there somewhere.

Douglas went on, "People are shocked when they hear of flagellation, of violent sex, and various forms of physical self-mutilation, yet a majority of people mentally torture themselves every day. The media bring them news of war, conflict, murder, violence, sex, and sadism because they would miss it if they didn't get their daily fix."

I reached for the key and started the car, using the mundane activity of worming my way out of the parking lot to cover my discomfort. I brought the conversation down to a more neutral level. "You don't think crime is all that pervasive?"

"No. Compared with nearly every age in history, we here in Canada at least, are no worse, probably better."

"Everyone thinks things were better in their childhood or in their parent' or grandparent' time."

"It wasn't though, was it? People got away with more, and some things that now are considered quite terrible, were not even considered crimes. I'm sure there was just as much child abuse, but it either wasn't talked about or was considered normal. It is only because our attitudes have changed that all these revelations of systematic abuse in residential schools are coming to light.

That happened in the good old days, but is only now being recognized. Women used to be considered property, so crimes against women were not thought of as such."

"It's the violence of it now that bothers people." I steered the car through the traffic of the downtown area, annoyingly hitting every red light.

"If I related to you the story of a man being mugged, his clothes torn off him, and being left in a ditch beside the road, while passersby deliberately avoided him, until finally one of them picked him up and gave him aid, would you think I got it out of yesterday's paper?"

"Probably."

"I didn't. It's the parable of the Good Samaritan."

"So we're not sinners?"

"Everyone sins. That's why confession is a part of the service every Sunday."

"That's something I have wondered about. Where to next, by the way?"

"To Layton Nathanson's office. I told him I'd like to talk to him in more detail and he said he would be in all afternoon. After that, we might catch Sue Ambler as she leaves the school."

"No, I think that on Thursdays, she has drama club after school."

"That's out, then. Perhaps we could catch Gretchen Schmidt at the hospital. I need to make some hospital visits anyway. You could leave me there and I'll walk home."

"Sounds like a good plan."

"What were you wondering about? In relation to sin, that is," Douglas asked, trying to make the question sound casual.

"What I was wondering about is that you think of sinners as murderers and rapists and so forth. But we are all told that we sin constantly."

"You have a rather secular version of what sin is. You relate it to crime, which is of course sinful, but there are many other things we do, or don't do, that also are sinful. And yes, we all sin. The only person who has ever lived without sin was Jesus."

"Just what is sin then?" I worked my way into a parking space and fished into the container on the dash for parking meter change.

Douglas turned toward me, propping his left arm on the back of the car seat. "To sin is to fall short, to not measure up to what God expects of us."

"What about disobeying one of the Ten Commandments? Would that be sin?"

"Definitely."

"Even the first?"

"'Thou shalt love the Lord thy God with all thy heart and all thy soul and all thy mind and all thy strength.' How can you possibly live up to God's expectations if you don't love Him?"

"But aren't some sins worse than others?" I ventured hesitantly.

"No. Sin is sin." I could see him watching me, waiting for the reaction he knew would come.

"Are you saying that Frank's murderer can get absolution just as easily as someone who forgets to give their spouse an anniversary gift?"

"Yes, if he or she truly repents."

"But they've committed a really terrible crime. Surely they aren't considered the same as someone who has always led a good life."

"The person who killed Frank may very likely be urgently and frantically in anguish over his or her act. I wouldn't be surprised if that person isn't the most earnestly repentant sinner in this whole town right now. If this person is truly repentant, then absolution is assured."

"Then someone could live a life of crime and repent on his deathbed and you say his sins can be absolved, just like anyone else's."

"Yes."

"That doesn't seem fair!"

"That person has probably had friends, family and God Himself after him all his life to repent his life of crime, return to God, and live the good life. So, if he finally does it, do you think God is going to say to him, 'You certainly waited a long time to repent your sins. I'll let you have absolution, but only on alternate Wednesdays?'" Douglas warm brown eyes were laughing as he continued, "Read the parable of the workers in the vineyard."

How did I ever let myself get caught in this corner? Douglas was getting uncomfortably close to the carefully guarded secret of my non-belief. My hands clutching the steering wheel, I stared out through the windshield at the sun glaring relentlessly off the dull blue surface of the Malibu's hood. I thought idly that I needed to wax the car and wondered why such an irrelevant thought had strayed into my mind. I tried to sort out the implications of what Douglas was saying. How, I wondered, could someone who did not believe in God be guilty of committing the sin of non-belief, when that sin was dependent on a belief in God? No God, no sin! But if there was such a thing as sin, by some other definition, I was guilty of it every time I recited the Confession, or the Creed for that matter. And here I thought I was doing such a nice thing.

"But suppose this habitual criminal goes to church every Sunday and recites the Confession, thinking he can put one over on God, as well as fooling other people, but has no intention of reforming?"

"Then he might as well walk out before the Absolution. It is not intended for him."

"But. . ."

"Do you ever go to the early service on Sunday, or on Wednesday morning, when we use the Prayer Book?"

"Occasionally. Why?"

"Then, Robin," the laughing eyes belied the stern tone of voice, "you haven't been listening."

I raised my eyebrows in interrogation. He shifted into the stained-glass voice I had heard him use in church and recited: "'Ye that do truly and earnestly repent you of your sins, and are in love and charity with your neighbours, and intend to lead the new life, following the commandments of God, and walking from henceforth in His holy ways: Draw near with faith, and take this holy Sacrament to your comfort; and make your humble confession to Almighty God....'"

I sat silently for several moments, letting those mighty words hang in the air.

"That's powerful stuff!"

"It is, isn't it? It's called the Invitation and comes just before the Confession. So if you get down on your knees and say the Confession, you'd better mean it, or the Absolution is meaningless."

It was like a blow to the pit of the stomach. I hoped my reaction wasn't too obvious. I passed a hand over my face to hide my emotions as I asked weakly, "How do you know whether someone really means it or whether they're only saying the words?"

Douglas opened the door, slid out of the seat, then bent over and looked across at me as I still sat behind the wheel.

"I don't have to know," he said. "God does." Then he added in a gentle voice, "Remember, the invitation is always open. God never gives up."

Chapter 12

Layton had a small office in a professional building just off Main Street. We found him at his desk, surrounded by papers, file folders, a computer, and a calculator. A cup of cold coffee sat by his elbow. There was no one at the secretary's desk. His shirt-sleeves were rolled up, his tie loosened. He seemed hot and flustered, wiping sweat from his brow with his handkerchief, then fiddling with it rather than putting it in his pocket.

If you sat still and relaxed, I thought, you wouldn't get so hot under the collar.

"Working alone? Is it convenient to talk to you?" Douglas asked.

"That's okay," Layton replied. "Yes, I'm alone, but I'm not that busy. I've given my secretary some afternoons off this week to make up for extra time she put in the first half of the month. We were quite busy up to the fifteenth when the tax installments had to be in."

"Was she off yesterday?"

Layton smiled ruefully. "Yes, unfortunately she was. I think the police are questioning everyone in the building to see if anyone noticed whether I was here. I think it's terrible that Frank was murdered, especially in the church, but I didn't do it so I wish they'd leave me alone. It has my daughter all upset, and we've been trying not to do that. She's having a bad enough time." He didn't elaborate, probably assuming we knew what he was talking about.

He kept looking at me quizzically, but since Douglas did not explain my presence and Layton apparently did not want to question it in front of Douglas, he didn't say anything. I was sure that

Douglas realized that the soft soap he had used on Albert would not work on Layton.

"You said the police have questioned you about an incident when you worked for Revenue Canada."

"Yes, but it doesn't mean anything."

"How is that?"

"I checked over the income tax return that Frank submitted, about three years ago, I think, and I found some discrepancies. Actually, the computer kicked it out because some of the deductions seemed abnormally high."

"How does that work?"

"The computer has a profile for each occupation, and if a return didn't fit the norm, it kicked it out. I was a group head, and had the authority to make the decision on whether to investigate a return further. I had a lot of experience and had a feel for what made sense and what didn't. You have to realize that not all returns that don't fit the norm are fraudulent. I would go over them to see if there was something else in another part of the return that explained the discrepancy. If not, I'd pass it along to the auditors, who would ask to see the records the person had to support his claim. Frank's return was obviously fraudulent, kind of amateurish, actually."

"What happened then?"

"He had to pay the extra tax plus a penalty. The penalty used to be twenty-five percent; now it's fifty percent of the tax owed."

"Did he try to fight it?"

"By the time I got all the information and checked it against other sources, nobody fought it! Anyway, it would have hurt his business more for it to be known that he was being investigated. He didn't want publicity, so he paid up."

"He had the money to pay it with?"

"Oh, sure."

"He had no idea you were responsible for his troubles?"

Layton shook his head. "No. I wasn't the auditor who went over his books. Frank would never have known I was the one who uncovered his little fiddle."

"Had he ever mentioned it to you while he was in the church?"

"No. I'm sure he didn't know me from Adam before he joined the church," Layton declared, too vehemently, I thought.

"If he knew that you had worked for Revenue Canada until recently, he might have complained to you about official harassment or something, in order to justify himself."

Layton shook his head. "He wasn't the type."

"How do you know?"

"He just didn't seem that type, that's all," Layton countered, fiddling with a pen on his desk and shifting his position. "He seemed really tight-lipped. I never really got to know him, anyway."

Douglas sat back, his arm casually draped over the back of an adjacent chair, his brow creased in thought. During the ensuing silence, Layton continued to frown and fidget. I decided to stay in the background.

"I am wondering," Douglas went on quietly, "why, as treasurer of the church, you didn't object to Frank being hired."

Layton shrugged. "Why would I?" he challenged.

Douglas raised his eyebrows. "I would think that you would worry about the possibility he would steal from the church."

"He didn't."

"I assumed as much. But you must have been concerned."

"I just decided to keep an eye on him. I've watched the books very closely for unusual expenditures. There haven't been any discrepancies. He didn't actually handle any of the finances and couldn't sign cheques."

"But you must have wondered whether he'd be a competent person for the job."

"I don't see why. The guy makes money. He's a good businessman." After a pause, Layton proceeded to demolish the argument he had been making by adding, "His kind of job didn't require very much, anyway."

"I have gotten the impression that Frank wasn't a good businessman, that he was just on the fringe of respectability."

"Maybe so. But he could still make money. You can't deny that. Some of his income tax returns showed his gross in six figures and he worked out of his apartment with very low overhead."

I finally felt I had to ask the question Douglas did not seem to want to put directly to Layton. "Is making money your main criterion for success, for respectability?"

Layton gave me a look as if he wondered when I had crawled out from under a log. "What else is there?" he asked.

Douglas gave a weary sigh. He changed the subject.

"Was there anyone else here yesterday who could vouch for your presence?"

"One or two people dropped in and I got a few phone calls, but I can't think of anyone who could definitely give me an alibi. But I don't think the police will seriously consider me a suspect. I'm a respectable businessman." The over-assertive tone of voice gave the lie to this statement. Bully for you, I thought. I'm a respectable businesswoman, but I'm sure they would have been delighted to have hung it on me.

"I hope you are right," Douglas stated blandly. "Why did you leave Revenue Canada, by the way?"

"I retired. I'd have stayed longer, but Felicity, my wife, wanted to be near our daughter. She's been having a rough time. She's had two miscarriages, so my wife thought we ought to be nearby to take as much of the physical strain off her as possible and give her support. I found I didn't want to be retired, so I started this little income tax business. It's about right for me. Not too much pressure, except at tax time."

"The Revenue Canada office is in Georgetown, isn't it?"

"That's right. We miss the bigger city, but Exeter isn't too bad."

We got up and prepared to take our leave. Douglas shook Layton's hand and asked, "Would you like to put your daughter on the prayer list?"

Flustered, Layton protested, "She isn't a church member."

"That's all right. She doesn't need to be."

"Yes, we'd like that. Thank you."

Once outside, I turned to Douglas and asked, "Don't you think some of that sounds a bit fishy?"

"I don't know. It bothers me."

"I can't imagine him being so dumb."

"How do you mean?"

"What I mean is that Layton is a pretty intelligent person, with a lot of business smarts. I can't see him being taken in by Frank."

"I see what you mean. I'm not sure I believe in this 'money is the only thing that is important' idea."

"Is it that you don't believe it, or you don't think Layton does?"

"Both."

"Um, yes. I got the same impression. Also, he stressed what a good businessman Frank was, after having told us that Frank's attempt to cheat on his income tax was amateurish. He keeps contradicting himself."

"I'm afraid Layton's statements don't add up. I hope there isn't something a great deal more serious behind them."

* * * *

As we walked out of the building, deep in conversation, we quite literally ran into Tom and Polly Holmes. Tom was a big, lumbering, silent man; Polly was the exact opposite. Small, bird-like, quick-moving, and incessantly talking, she was a person I tended to avoid at church social gatherings because she was so hard to get away from once she had you cornered. She literally held onto you, grasping your hand, arm, or sleeve as she talked—and talked and talked. Both Tom and Polly were clad in tennis attire. I had heard that Polly was quite good, but couldn't imagine Tom on the tennis court. They were retired and spent most of the winter in Palm Springs, looking down with disdain on those who wintered in Yuma, Arizona.

"Oh, *hello* there," Polly gushed to Douglas. "I've been hoping to meet you. Imagine bumping into you here. I just *loved* the service last Sunday, and you gave *such* a wonderful sermon. Isn't it *terrible* about Frank Corrigan? Whoever would have thought it. And in the church, too, though it wasn't really in the church was it, but in the office. That's not really part of the church, is it? Have they figured out who killed him yet?"

While Polly paused to draw breath, I managed

to break into the stream of words. "This is Polly Holmes and Tom Holmes," I said hastily before Polly could get underway again.

Douglas shook Tom's hand. The latter acknowledged the introduction with a grunt. I suspected that he suffered from atrophied vocal cords as a result of never being able to get a word in edgeways. For once, Douglas did not offer his hand to Polly, probably fearing the consequences, but Polly already had a grip on his sleeve.

"I'm not surprised that someone killed him. There are probably all kinds of people who would liked to have. I'd have liked to myself, after what he did to us."

In the silence that followed this bombshell, even Polly seemed to realize what she had said. I asked weakly, "What did he do to you?"

Suddenly sober, Polly lowered her voice a fair number of decibels. "He cheated us out of thousands and thousands of dollars, that's what! Didn't he, Tom?"

Tom merely grunted. Polly was in full swing again, her voice rising as she chattered away. "It was when we lived up in Neeceville, that's up near Georgetown, you know. We wanted to sell our house there and move into a condo down here where the weather is better in the winter and where we could be near our grandchildren."

What difference would it make? I wondered. They weren't here to enjoy either one in the winter anyway.

"We had a big place; swimming pool, tennis court, view. A really lovely place. But it was too much for us anymore. We had it listed for *ages* with an agency Frank worked for, but it didn't sell and we were getting desperate. Frank kept saying that big places like ours weren't selling at the time.

Everyone was counting their money and not putting it into big houses. Anyway, that agency had picked up a gimmick from some big American outfit, that if they couldn't sell your house, they would buy it from you."

"That sounds like some sort of con game," I commented.

"Well, actually, this big American chain did it, and I think they did all right with it. Anyway, when Frank couldn't sell our house, the company had to buy it from us, and of course, they paid next to nothing. You know, just the bare minimum they could get away with. So we took what they offered us, and just a few days later, we met these people at the tennis club who said they had heard that we finally sold our house. They said some friends of theirs had bought it and were complaining about how much it cost. These people we were talking to teased us about making a killing. We found out their friends had paid over a hundred thousand dollars more than we had gotten for it. This couple thought their friends had been trying to buy the house for months, but they weren't sure it was the same house, and we could never prove it. We sure didn't see any offers from them.

"We were absolutely furious, but the agency backed Frank up and their lawyer and ours both said there was no way we could get back at them, so we just had to take our loss and leave town with our tails between our legs. We did make a big stink to the real estate board, and the agency fired Frank. We didn't know he had come down here until he popped up in church as our administrator or director or something; I never did figure out just what. We were horrified, but everything was in turmoil with Martin leaving and no one seemed to pay much attention to us."

"Did Frank know that you were members of the church?" I asked.

"I don't know. We started going to early service to avoid him. You know, he even took communion, and I doubt if he was even baptized."

"Do you know that he wasn't?" Douglas inquired.

"No, but he didn't seem like a person who came from a religious background."

"However, in the Anglican Church, a person who has been baptized anywhere is entitled to take communion. He may well have been."

"I think he only took the job because it would give him status and he probably only came to church as a way to impress people. I think he just did it so that he could tell his clients that he was a church administrator, or whatever he was called, so they would have faith in him." Polly was in full flight again and since her high-pitched voice carried well, I looked about nervously to see if anyone else on the street was taking notice. No one seemed to pay the slightest attention. They were used to getting their fix of scandal and violence on the tube, not in real life, I assumed. Look what they were missing!

"Do you *know* that he did this?" Douglas persisted.

"I couldn't prove it in court, if that's what you mean, but you can bet that's why he took the job."

"It may be so," Douglas cautioned, "but I wouldn't go around saying so if I were you."

"Also," I added, "I don't think you should talk at all about your problems with him, especially not to the police."

"Oh!" Polly gasped. Her eyes widened. "You don't think they'd suspect *us* do you?"

"I think they would be very happy to suspect you,

if they found out you have such an excellent motive."
I glanced at Tom, who stood like a pillar of stone, not
saying a word, not registering an emotion.

"But we wouldn't *kill* Frank because of it."

"Try telling that to the police! On second thought,
don't try telling it to the police, or to anyone else."

"Where were you yesterday between four-thirty
and five, by the way?"

"Is that when it happened?"

I nodded.

"Let's see. At home I think. We have so many
social engagements, but I'm pretty sure we were
home."

"Did you see anyone or talk to anyone on the
phone?"

"Oh, we must have done."

"Do you remember anyone you might have seen
or talked to during that time period?"

"Oh dear, no. I'd have to think about it and try
to remember."

"Do that. You might need to. In the meantime,
keep mum."

"But don't lie to the police," Douglas cautioned.
"They may get onto it if they start looking into his
past."

"Oh no. We won't lie. But I see your point,
Robin, about not running out and telling the police about it."

"Don't tell *anyone*," I warned.

We parted, and as I looked back at them walking down the street, I could see Polly in an animated and one-sided conversation with Tom. I
wondered whether she would really be able to control herself. Now there was someone who could
spread gossip! She was better than Internet. The
only way I could squelch the cold shiver I felt was
to remind myself that Polly had no access to the
information that had been broadcast last night.

Chapter 13

We stopped by the shop on Main Street where Marcia Chancellor worked, noting the Alternative Lifestyle store next door. Its door stood open and I gazed into the interior with curiosity. I had expected it to be old, cobweb-bedewed, and dimly lit. It wasn't. It was fairly plain, with merchandise unimaginatively displayed on plain tables, but it was well enough lighted and not a bit spooky. I didn't see the Swan of Tuonela.

Jacqueline's, the dress shop, was anything but plain. Newly remodeled, it showed a glittering face to the public. Window displays of dazzling elegance never failed to arrest me in my tracks when I walked down Main Street, even though it was a place I never shopped.

The owner of the shop offered us the use of her office, with the same grace and charm displayed by the entire place. I eyed the chairs, which looked too elegant and fragile to sit on, and eased myself tentatively down onto the velvet-cushioned seat of the nearest one. Marcia was agitated and flustered, sitting on the edge of her chair and alternately wringing her hands and twisting the fabric of her skirt between shaking fingers.

"This is terrible. I can't imagine anyone murdering someone in our church. I didn't like him, but I never expected that anyone would get mad enough to kill him."

"The police think it was an unpremeditated act, done on the spur of the moment," Douglas commented.

"He could get people very mad at him. Oh! I probably shouldn't have said that. I didn't say it to the police, but they got me so flustered, I don't know what I said. I'm sorry I ever got myself involved in this business. I never realized it would turn into something like this."

"None of us did," I affirmed soothingly. "Where were you yesterday afternoon?"

"Fortunately, I was here working."

"Then you have nothing to worry about. Are the police satisfied that you were here?"

"I think so. The owner of the shop told them so, very firmly, I might add. She also told them it didn't do her business any good to have the police tramping in and out."

I saw Douglas raise his hand to his mouth to hide a smile. As for the police, I'm sure they meet that sort of attitude quite regularly and don't pay any attention to it.

"Well, we won't keep you." Douglas rose and extended his hand. "Thanks for your help and don't worry about things."

"I'll try, but it's most upsetting." She gave the impression that she wouldn't try very hard. She seemed a chronic worrier, and having never had such a whale of a worry before, would probably milk the last bit of angst out of it.

* * * *

We pulled into the hospital parking lot about four-thirty, hoping to catch Gretchen Schmidt at the end of her day's work in the medical records office. I think there must be a conspiracy among architects of large hospitals. I have never been in one you could find your way around in. Medical records? That's down the west corridor, beyond the administrator's office and the accounting department, just before Nuclear Medicine. The trouble was that beyond the administrator and the accounting office, the west corridor ended. One could go right or left. The left branch led off into a more poorly lit, deserted section, just right, or so we thought, for such a sinister sounding place as Nuclear Medicine. Instead, it led eventually to the laundry room. Retracing our steps, we tried the right-hand branch and found that it led us to another west-leading corridor, full of bustling people pushing gurneys or rushing about carrying large, tan manila envelopes. Radiology, a sign divulged. Stymied, we were about to beat a retreat, when Douglas spotted the directory of the Radiology Department, and found Nuclear Medicine tacked to the bottom. An arrow pointed the way, and after a short search, we found Nuclear Medicine and beside it, Medical Records.

We entered a door; a cheerful face popped around a stack of files, saying, "Be with you in a mo." Soon the body that went with the face appeared, and we asked for Gretchen.

"Too bad, you missed her. She left about fifteen minutes ago." While we were lost somewhere between laundry and the nukes no doubt.

We backtracked to the lobby without too much difficulty and went to the information desk. Douglas pulled out a list of parishioners who were currently patients at the hospital or the attached extended care facility. Since he did not yet know these people, or know his way around the hospital, he introduced himself to the receptionist and started jotting down room numbers.

I was about to take my leave when the outer door opened and Dr. Alan Gotfriedson hurried in. He spotted us and veered in our direction. I introduced him to Douglas, who said, "Ah, yes. You are the doctor who has taken so much interest in the Meachams' problems."

"That's right. And now they have this suspicion of murder hanging over their heads."

"They seem to be holding up quite well. We visited them this morning."

"That's good to hear. I was going to call them this evening, will anyway. I was going to call you as well, to fill you in on the problem Shirley had with Frank Corrigan."

"Robin has done that already."

"Good." Alan smiled at me. "Robin is one of the few who seemed to understand what was going on."

Douglas shifted uncomfortably and asked, "You said something about the Meachams having suspicion hanging over them. How did you know about that?"

"My receptionist has heard the gossip around town."

Douglas sighed resignedly. I would have liked to use some language not fit for the ears of one's clergyman.

"Our rumour-monger again," I muttered.

"Apparently so," Alan agreed. "I'd like to know who it is."

"So would we all," Douglas affirmed. "By the way, have the police questioned you? They seem to have gotten around to quite a few people."

"Yes. I was in my office in the late afternoon yesterday, which is when, I gather, the murder was committed. We were quite busy. My staff and my patients can vouch for me. I don't like to give out the names of my patients, but my staff were questioned, and the sergeant seemed satisfied."

"Good. Robin and I are getting everyone's stories in order to squelch rumours as best we can."

"Good for you. Well, I've got to run. I enjoyed your sermon Sunday, by the way."

Alan took off at a fast lope, and I remarked to

Douglas, "I sometimes wonder whether it's his patients who are in danger of heart attacks, or Alan himself."

* * * *

I went directly to the flying school, which I had neglected all day. Things were running well, better probably than if I had stayed there. Everyone wanted the latest scoop on the murder—the last thing, at that time, that I wanted to talk about. A couple of reporters tracked me down and I had to deal with them firmly.

"Ask the RCMP," was my stock answer.

"Hell, they won't tell us anything," was their reply.

"Then you're out of luck."

Our last meeting before the open house was scheduled for seven o'clock, and by six-thirty, students and pilots began to drift in. It looked as if the entire school was going to be there. I'd have been delighted if I thought they were coming because of a commitment to the success of the open house. Their presence, I realized sourly, was more out of curiosity about the murder. They'd get put to work anyway, even if I had to lock the doors to keep them in.

We cleaned and scrubbed and put things neatly away in the hangar, lounge, and ground school room. We were to rent tables and chairs, and members who were bringing their own home videos or slide shows of flying trips were to bring their own equipment for showing them. I assigned locations to each and we made sure that there was either an outlet or an extension cord handy to each location. We would use the school's own training materials. We set these up and put signs on them threatening dire consequences to anyone who removed or changed anything.

"Remember," I told the assembled aviators, "always project a positive image. No war stories. We want to leave people with the impression that flying is an enjoyable and safe pastime. If anyone asks about airplane crashes, answer with the information you have already been given about our school's safety program, our perfect record, and strict safety guidelines.

"Don't overlook the children. They are our future customers. Many of you can remember, as a child, wanting to be a pilot. Those of you here are the ones who hung onto that dream. So treat these children in a way that will make them remember the experience and long for the day when they can take flying lessons.

"Finally—absolutely *no* booze. Not even a beer." This elicited a good-natured groan from the assemblage. "This is a family affair and we need to set a good example. Any questions?"

One young wag in the back waved his hand excitedly.

"Yes?"

"Who killed the guy in the church?"

I pointed my finger at him and spluttered, "You're out of order. That's a war story."

We ironed out the last of the minor problems. I dithered around, realizing that I had planned to do a lot in preparation for the open house, only to leave to go to the church.

"Don't worry," Gayla assured me. "We have everything in hand. You gave us good directions earlier."

As I continued to check and recheck, Jan, my only female flight instructor, said to me, "Give us a break! We've got everything under control. Trust us." She tried to sound exasperated, but her voice was light, and I knew that though I was being a nuisance, my staff understood and were trying to take some of the strain off me. I'd have to throw them a party after this was over. I wouldn't commit the sin of leaving that undone, I told myself, amused at my newfound piety.

I finally made my weary way home, ate a skimpy meal, and fed my cat who protested vociferously about the lateness of his evening meal, diving into his dish and gulping his food as if he feared I would yank the dish out from under his nose or forget to ever feed him again. I mulled over the events of the day. For the first time, I had the vexing thought that I had not shed a tear or considered the waste of Frank Corrigan's sudden and early death. I may not have liked him, but a life cut short was a life wasted nonetheless. If I had believed in it, I would have prayed for his soul.

I dropped into bed and slept the sleep of exhaustion.

Chapter 14

In the morning I got to the church about nine o'clock, just after morning prayer. I found Douglas in the office talking to Sgt. Jameson. Douglas motioned me in and told me we had our office back. Standing to the side, looking ill at ease, was a young man of medium height and build, with dark brown, uncombed hair and dark, troubled eyes. His chin showed a stubble of beard and his faded jeans and chambray shirt looked as if they had been slept in. He appeared distinctly hung over.

"Good morning, Mrs. Carruthers," Jameson said pleasantly, then indicated the young man. "This is Brett Corrigan."

"Hello, Brett," I greeted him. "It's a shame we have to meet under such sad circumstances. You have our sympathy."

"Thanks," the young man mumbled. He turned to Douglas and said in a voice that was vaguely surly, "The cops said you wanted to see me."

"I wanted to meet you, Brett, and tell you that you are in our prayers, and that if I can be of any help to you, you need only ask. If you want to go into the church and pray, you are welcome to do so."

Brett looked startled. "Uh, no thanks."

"Also, when you feel up to it, we should sit down and talk about funeral arrangements."

"Say again?"

"The funeral. We need to make arrangements."

"Oh. I never thought about that."

"I don't want to pressure you. Come in when you feel like it. Where are you staying?"

"At the Lake City Motel."

"Is that nearby?"

"Yeah. I walked over."

"Good. Any time you want, I'll be here to talk to you. You had better call first, however."

"Okay, thanks." Brett shuffled off and walked disconsolately out the door, where he paused and turned back. As soon as the men's backs were turned, his facial expression changed from one of hang-dog grief to the type of insolent sneer of youths who defy authority. I saw him ever so casually give Douglas the finger, turn and walk away.

"Not your most upstanding specimen of young manhood," I heard Jameson saying, contempt in his voice. "At least he spared you the obscenities he used in every sentence when he was talking to us last night."

My rage welled up, surprisingly, at both of them. At Jameson for judging Brett so harshly and failing to take into account the young man's grief; at Brett for taking his frustration at authority out on Douglas. I hurried to the outer door and caught up with Brett on the sidewalk. He turned as I hailed him, the insolent facial expression still in place, impatience obvious. I wondered whether the sloppy clothes were an act, a kind of defiance at our staid, do-good attitude.

"You don't need to treat our priest with disrespect, you know. He's trying to help you."

"What's bugging you, lady? Fuck off."

"I saw you give him the finger. There was no call for that. He's trying to help you."

"A fucking lot of help your type is to me."

"What do you mean?"

"Hell, isn't it obvious? You assholes are too high and mighty to care about me. You'd just like to dump this murder charge on me to get yourselves out from under. Fuck you."

I felt my face flame brick red and my mouth

open to release an angry torrent. *No*, I thought, *I'm not going to give it back in kind.* Controlling my anger with considerable difficulty, I replied as calmly as I could. I reached out to touch him, but he twitched away as if I might contaminate him. "You're wrong, Brett. We know that you didn't kill your father. Can't you accept the sincere act of a compassionate priest? He really cares, you know."

"Shit!"

"He does. Whether you are willing to accept his help or not, he will be there to offer it. He means what he says."

Brett looked away, then down at his feet. He kicked idly at a loose stone, his hands bunched into fists in the pockets of his rumpled jeans. He said nothing.

"No one is trying to frame you. Everyone who knew that Frank had a son is praying for you."

"Praying?" he spat out.

"Yes, praying."

He lifted a face distorted with anguish. "Well, you can forget it. My dad never belonged to your church anyway. It was just a job. He was a Roman Catholic."

"We can pray for Roman Catholics, too." I felt a distinct sense of guilt at talking like this about prayer. I'd never prayed in my life. Furthermore, I had the uncomfortable memory that only yesterday I had been wishing that this young man would turn out to be his father's killer.

Brett was staring at the sidewalk again, restlessly scuffing the toe of his well-worn loafers. His blustering outburst had not hidden the pain in his voice.

"Douglas can put you in touch with the Roman Catholic church here in town, if you'd like. He would be happy to do so. Or help make arrangements to have your father's body taken to Georgetown if you'd rather have the funeral there."

Brett had raised his head and was staring skyward, his entire body tense, like a deer ready to spring away at the first indication of danger.

"Are there any other family members who can help? We didn't know of any others."

Brett shook his head.

"Is your mother dead also?"

"No, but she won't care."

"Are you sure?"

"Shit. She couldn't split fast enough as soon as I was out of school and she didn't have to look after me."

"Where does she live? Do you know?"

"Toronto somewhere, I think. I get a Christmas card every year. She's remarried, I guess. Or maybe not, but she's living with another fucking guy."

"Are you married?"

"We're split up." The reply was quick and defensive. His body became taut.

"I'm sorry."

"Why should you be?"

"Brett. Give us a chance."

"Oh, shit!"

What could I say? He seemed angry when I scolded him, resentful when I sympathized. I wanted to react in some useful way to his misery, but he seemed like a wounded animal, in need of help but alert with fear of anyone who tried to touch him.

"Look, I gotta go." He seemed to be waiting for my permission.

"Just don't go away mad."

"Okay. Well, be seeing ya." He turned hesitantly and with back hunched and hands in pockets, he slouched off down the street.

Jameson was still in the office. "Anything new?" I asked.

"We're still digging," he replied.

"Did you take his prints and look at his shoes?" I asked, jerking my head in the direction Brett had gone.

"Didn't have to print him. His are on file. There's no blood on those shoes."

"Are you comparing his prints to those in the office, even if he has an alibi?"

"Yes, we are. Have to nail everything down, you know."

"I assume you haven't found any of his?"

"Not yet. We lifted literally hundreds from the office, the corridor, and the outside door, and it will take some time to classify and compare them all."

"You found ours in a big hurry." *And the Meachams,* I added silently.

"Yours were all over the place."

Jameson's attitude was decidedly different now, light and almost bantering, but I could still see those eagle eyes darting about, taking everything in. I assumed that I was now numbered among the good guys, and would no longer be subjected to the derisive interrogation of yesterday.

When Jameson had left, Douglas suggested that we go see Jean Givens at her real estate agency. Paul St. Cyr had called and had made arrangements to meet us for lunch at the Brown Jug, a pub with an excellent luncheon menu. I called Penny and asked her to join us. I had not talked to her since we had gone home Wednesday night. That seemed a week ago and I was startled when I realized it was only a day and a half.

At the real estate agency we asked for Jean and were directed to her office. A tall, willowy blonde woman of about thirty, elegantly dressed, rose from her desk to greet us.

"I'm Allison Kaminski, Jean's secretary," she introduced herself. "Jean isn't here today. She had a district meeting in Georgetown so she left last night. She said you might be along and asked me to give you all the help I can."

"That's very good of you, and of Jean. I'm the new incumbent at St. Matthew's, Douglas Forsythe, and this is Robin Carruthers."

"I'm very glad to meet you. Jean has spoken highly of you and feels her church is in good hands. I'm not a member, but I've helped her do several things for the church, and I feel some kinship in that way. I'm sorry you are having all this trouble."

"You would be very welcome to come to our church any time. We like having visitors."

"Maybe I will. Now, how can I help you?"

We all sat down and Douglas continued, "We are trying to determine where everyone was during the late afternoon Wednesday. Can you tell us where Jean was?"

"She left here about three-thirty to pick up a couple who wanted to see a house out in the Fairview area. I don't believe she came back here at all, at least not before I left shortly after five."

"How long would you say it would take Jean to show the house?"

"Probably not over an hour."

"I see. That still leaves some time," Douglas murmured thoughtfully and Allison Kaminski cocked her head inquisitively.

"When was the murder committed?" she asked.

"Between four-thirty and five, they think."

"I'm sure she can account for her time." Allison did not seem worried about her employer. "In fact,

I think she told the police that she dropped into a coffee shop after leaving the potential buyers. I don't know which one."

"She has talked to the police then?"

"Yes. They were here yesterday."

"Good. We won't have to follow it up. We are trying to get everyone's story so we can keep unfounded rumours from developing in the church. We don't expect to solve the crime, you understand. I'm quite sure the police can do that in time."

"I understand."

"How long have you worked for Jean?" I asked.

"Nearly five years. She is a wonderful person to work for—very thoughtful and considerate. I am one of those fortunate people who really like their jobs."

"That's wonderful. I think Jean is fortunate to have you."

"Thank you." Allison smiled, showing perfect white teeth. Truly a beautiful woman, Jean was indeed fortunate to have her, not only for her looks but for her personality and cool efficiency. I could imagine the positive impression she would make on potential clients. What a contrast with Albert Wallace's secretary.

Douglas took up the theme again. "We need to know something about Jean's relationship with Frank Corrigan."

Allison smiled. "Yes, I expected that you would. Jean said to tell all, so here is the story."

Allison leaned back in her chair, crossed shapely ankles, and thought for a moment. "Frank Corrigan apparently came to Exeter about two years ago after being fired by an agency in Neeceville. At around the time he came to Exeter, Jean had lined up a buyer for a large, quite expensive property. Actually, it had come about as a

result of her going out to look for something specific that this buyer wanted. The property was not
actually listed as being for sale, but Jean found
that the owners would be willing to sell if the price
was right, and Jean's buyer was willing to pay.
The sellers were reluctant to list the property, and
were only agreeing to this specific sale. Jean went
to the sellers' home to get a contract signed, only
to find Frank there. The sellers told Jean that
Frank had offered them a deal with a lower fee,
which would still have amounted to a tidy sum for
him after Jean had done all the work. Frank had
found out the potential buyer's name also, and
the sale went through. Jean did all the work and
Frank got all the money."

"Why didn't the people who were selling the
house realize that it was Jean who had done the
work and tell Frank to get lost?" I wanted to know.

"Unfortunately, people are greedy. If it takes a
long time to sell a house and they know you are
working hard, they usually don't complain much,
but if you sell one quickly, they resent paying the
percentage. That's the cause of most complaints.
They don't realize that the agency's fee went to
support the resources that allowed the quick sale
to occur. Also, Jean does a lot of work that she
doesn't get paid for, and the easy sales make up
for the difficult ones. These particular owners probably didn't realize that Jean had put in a lot of
time trying to find what the buyer wanted."

"Didn't she say so right there on the spot?"

"They were talking to her through a crack in
the door. She never got in the house."

"That makes me think they knew they were
cheating her."

"Perhaps."

"Do people ever back out completely?"

"All the time. We had a situation recently where the buyer kept making offers and our client kept turning them down, until finally the buyer offered to pay the asking price. Then our client suddenly decided not to sell. There was Jean, the buyer's agent and the buyer, all standing in the yard with their mouths hanging open, while the seller, ex-seller that is, walked back into the house and shut the door."

"Frustrating," Douglas commented.

"Very. Jean wouldn't have gotten a lot out of it at best because the fee would be split with the other agency, and our agency's part doesn't all go to the agent who makes the sale. So you have to take the easy ones when you can. But Frank was very adept at nosing out that kind of thing and getting in there with his offer."

"Good grief," I exclaimed. "I think I would have punched his lights out!"

"Unfortunately, the police think Jean may have done just that."

"Do you?"

"No, I don't. Jean was upset, but remember that this was two years ago, and Jean has done well since then and hasn't held a grudge."

"But I can see the police looking at it as a good motive," Douglas mused.

"Yes, unfortunately. But I don't believe it for a moment. Besides, right now she had every reason to want Frank alive."

"Why is that?"

"We have a large rural property listed and it just hasn't sold. It isn't what people are looking for right now and our client is firm about the asking price. On Monday, Frank called Jean and told her he might have a buyer for it. Jean suspects that Frank was going to take a commission from the buyer, which would be unethical, but as long as we did things at our end in an ethical fashion, Jean saw no reason not to make the sale. It seemed to be on the verge of being finalized, and Frank was going to come in yesterday with the papers that would have made it binding. Of course, by then he was dead, and we don't even have the buyer's name."

"The buyer hasn't come forward?" I asked.

"No. Possibly he doesn't want to become involved in a murder investigation, or possibly he doesn't know who is representing the seller. We're trying to find out, and have asked the police to let us know if they find anything among Frank's papers, but they won't promise. Our contract is about to run out, and if our client can find out who Frank was dealing with, they might bypass us."

"So you may have lost another big sale."

"Yes, and this time, we needed Frank in order to pull it off."

Chapter 15

We stopped by the hospital and, having taken only one wrong turn in wending our way through the maze of corridors, found Gretchen at work. She apologized for having missed us the previous afternoon, explaining that she had been leaving an hour early each day to make up for extra time she had worked when another woman was off on maternity leave.

To our question, Gretchen replied that she had gone straight home, changed into shorts, and worked in her garden. She lived in a small house on the hillside on the eastern edge of town. She thought that one or more of her neighbours may have noted her arrival at home or seen her in the garden, but she didn't know for certain. She had not spoken to anyone or noticed who was about. There were always children playing in the area— you could hear them as a constant background noise—so presumably there were parents at home who might have noticed. She did not know her neighbours well. One had a Rottweiler, which snapped at her through the chain link fence, but the husband took the dog to work with him, and it had not been there. Gretchen thought the wife worked also, but didn't know what hours she worked. She tended to avoid them. Other neighbours were less objectionable, but she didn't think any of them were out in their yards. If they hadn't cut down the shade trees, they wouldn't have to lock themselves up in their houses with the air conditioners on. Still, they might have seen her from their houses.

"Have the police asked you about this?" I queried.

"Yes, they have. I don't think it's any of their business to pry into my private life and question my neighbours, but they were insistent and I don't have anything to hide. But I can imagine that guy next door with the obnoxious dog chortling over the fact that the police are investigating me in connection with a murder."

"I don't think you have anything to worry about," Douglas said in a soothing voice.

Gretchen snorted, "Of course not."

"How well did you know Frank?"

"Not very well, but that was too much."

"Were the police interested in your relationship with him?"

"There wasn't any relationship. They tried to make a big deal out of the fact that I'd told him off a time or two. I didn't like him. He was the typical male chauvinist. Also, I didn't think he did enough work to justify what we were paying him, but a lot of others felt that way also. I wasn't at the church Wednesday. I didn't have a fight with him. I didn't hit him over the head."

End of story.

One thing about Gretchen, she was very straightforward and never tried to obscure her thoughts in vague words. She could be blunt and her feminism sometimes wore on the nerves, but I had also seen her perform acts of incredible kindness and compassion.

Go figure!

* * * *

Betty met us at the church. We decided to walk to the Brown Jug and spent a companionable twenty minutes in the warm sunshine with a fresh breeze blowing off the lake, talking about anything but the murder. I listed some of the good restaurants and some of the sights the Forsythes ought to see. I extolled our excellent library and told them that if they were musically inclined, the Georgetown Symphony gave three concerts in Exeter each winter and they should talk to Paul St. Cyr about subscribing. They were interested and each asked the other to remind them to talk to Paul.

"We tend to get talking and forget things like that," Betty explained, squeezing Douglas' hand. They were holding hands like young lovers as we strolled along.

We were early at the pub and chose a booth near an open window, having cool drinks as we waited for Paul and Penny. After a few minutes, we noticed a man at the far end of the bar staring morosely into a glass of beer.

"I'm afraid that young man has subscribed to the hair-of-the-dog theory," Douglas said, rising and walking over to the bar. When the man turned his head as Douglas laid a hand on his shoulder, I recognized him as Brett Corrigan. The two talked for a few moments, then I saw Brett shake his head. Douglas came back to our booth, a worried frown creasing his brow. "I asked him to come join us. I'd like a chance to talk to him."

"Let me give it a go." I slid out of the booth and went over to Brett. He looked at me for a few moments, trying to place me, then a look of annoyed recognition passed over his face, to be replaced by one of slack-jawed non-interest.

"C'mon over," I said. "We'll buy you lunch."

He looked at me speculatively for a long moment, his dark eyes narrowing.

"We won't make you say grace."

That got a smile out of him, and he heaved

himself off his stool and followed me to the booth, beer glass in hand. Douglas rose, and Betty introduced herself in sympathetic tones.

The hang-dog look was firmly in place on the young man's face, and I had the same feeling that had occasionally overcome me when dealing with his father—that he was putting on an act, using us for some means of personal gain. I was certain that his grief was genuine, but he seemed to be able to turn it off and step into another role. What that role was intended to accomplish, I had no idea.

"It must have been a terrible shock to you to hear of your father's death," Betty said. "Sudden death is always a blow, but murder must be far more so. I don't know how we can help you, but if there is anything, please tell us."

Brett bent his head and rested his forehead on his hand. Sitting beside him, I could see the look of pain and watch his efforts to control it. I wanted to put my arm around him, but knew he would shrink from it. I could see that Douglas also was looking for a useful way to intervene. His previous offer, a straightforward Christian one, had certainly fallen on stony ground.

Brett took a deep breath and raised his head. "He wasn't much of a father, but he was all the family I had."

"In what way was he not much of a father?" Douglas voice was kindly.

"He didn't think much of me. He was always off on some scheme to make money and when I went out and got a plain old McJob and stuck with it, he said I didn't have any ambition. He thought I was lazy, but I wasn't. I got a job in a supermarket when I was fifteen, and when I got my driver's license, I transferred up to the store in Georgetown. We were living in Neeceville then. I worked up to cashier, then got put in charge of the dairy department. Now I'm assistant manager. I've always worked hard and tried to learn the trade. But it doesn't pay real well and Dad didn't think much of it—said if I had any ambition, I'd get ahead a lot faster."

"I don't see anything wrong with what you're doing," Betty exclaimed. "Most parents would be delighted if their kids got a good job and stuck to it. I think that being an assistant manager at your age is great."

"Yeah, that's what I think, but Dad never saw it that way. He was always on me to get with it, get out and make some money. Especially if I tried to borrow some from him. He was a real tightwad. He never gave me nothing."

I hid a smile behind my hand. I could imagine it. Wheeler-dealer dad closing the bankbook when plodding son wants to live a bit higher on the hog. I wondered what Brett had wanted to borrow money for.

"He got my wife thinking the same way. She was always on me to make more dough. She wanted me to get out of my blah job and get into something where we could have fancy vacations and stuff. But I could remember the times when Dad's schemes fell through, back before he got into real estate which he did pretty good at. He'd promise me things when the dough was rolling in, then he'd hit a rough patch, and I wouldn't get what he'd promised me. Shit—oops, sorry!—I just wanted to have a job I knew would be there the next day, and a steady income, and someday work up to manager maybe, when the boss retired, and live comfortable."

"There's nothing wrong with that," Douglas encouraged him.

Was it my imagination, or was there an undercurrent of something else? Why was Brett playing on our sympathy this way? Where was the surly youth with his obscene gestures?

"Did your wife work?" I asked.

"Yeah. She's a dental tech. She always made more than me. She and Dad both thought that proved there was something wrong with me."

"Are you paying alimony or child support?"

"Hell, no!" The answer was quick and violent. Better stay away from that subject.

I had noticed Douglas in frowning thought. Now he seemed to have reached a decision. "Brett, I think you should. . . ."

Before he could expound on whatever plan he had devised, the door opened and Penny and Paul came in. Following behind them was Albert. My hopes fell to the floor with a dull thud and lay there. Penny would have been instantly helpful and sympathetic, and Paul was a gentleman, but what Albert would do to our fragile hold on Brett's confidence, I shuddered to think. Like an adolescent puppy, he could be counted on to knock over the vase, spill the water, and strew the flowers on the floor to be trampled on.

He wasted no time in making a clairvoyant out of me. As soon as introductions had been made, he pumped Brett's hand and propounded ponderously, "So sorry about your father, young man. The person who killed him ought to be hanged."

"Albert!" I exclaimed sharply, as people at neighboring tables craned their necks and all conversation ceased.

Brett, looking numb, stumbled to his feet and muttered, "I'd better go."

"No don't. Sit down." Penny put an arm firmly around his shoulders and pushed him back into his seat. "Move over." She slid into the booth beside him, and I scrunched into the corner to make room. Douglas and Betty moved over to make room for Albert as the waitress arrived bearing a chair and an additional place setting which she laid at the end of the table for Paul.

As she took our orders, the intensity level of the atmosphere subsided and the other diners returned to their own concerns. Brett gave Penny a once-over with eyes that virtually undressed her, and perked up noticeably. The chitchat flowed around him, but he seemed not to mind. Occasionally Albert would clumsily bring the conversation back to the murder and would receive a swift kick under the table from Penny. He finally got the point and changed his tack.

"By the way, Penny, you are going to be dead yourself if you keep riding your bike the way you do."

"Me? What did I do?"

"Cleo, my wife, and I saw you ride like a bat out of hell into the Farmer's Market the other day and slam on your brakes and skid to a stop. You're a menace on that thing."

"What day? Wednesday?"

"Yes. That's our shopping day."

"Oh that. I was in a hurry to get some tomatoes before the stall that has those ripe hot-house ones closed for the night. They close at five, but if things are slow, they sometimes close earlier. Don't worry. I don't usually ride like that."

"You'd better not. If you rode a motorcycle, you'd be the terror of the highways."

"I would not! I do ride a motorcycle, or used to when I could afford one, before I bought the condo. It was a nice quiet one, and I rode it carefully and adhered to all the safety regulations."

"You rode a motorcycle?" Incredulity registered in Albert's voice.

"Sure. Why not?"

"It doesn't seem very ladylike."

Penny, on the verge of unleashing a distinctly unladylike broadside at him, glanced around at the company she was in, and held her tongue. The broth of discontent bubbled and seethed. Brett shifted his gaze from one to the other in wide-eyed amazement.

But what neither Albert nor Penny had caught onto yet, as wrapped up in their argument as they were, was that they had each given the other an alibi for the time of the murder. I sighed with relief for my friend, Penny. It was good to know that she was out of the running for the role of murderer.

Albert, whose every remark seemed to land him in hot water, switched his attention to me. "How's business?" he asked neutrally.

"Fine, as long as the weather holds," I quipped.

Turning to Brett, Albert explained, "Would you believe it? This lady runs Carruther's Aviation." Trust Albert to be twenty years behind the times. He went on, "I think I ought to charter a plane from you when I have to fly to Vancouver. I bet it wouldn't be any more expensive than these airlines. It's a crime what they charge."

"It depends on what kind of a plane you want to charter."

"A nice big one with a bar and a hostess. Maybe you'd pour me a drink personally."

"If I were flying, I'd be in the cockpit," I stated firmly and added, "with the door locked."

"Ho, ho! Listen to her. She knows me."

"The trouble with you, Albert, is that you have 441 tastes and a 150 budget."

Everyone looked perplexed. That's the trouble

with telling flying jokes to people who don't fly. No one understands them. Then Brett laughed and my heart warmed to him. At least he had the good manners to try to help me save face after I had dropped a brick.

Albert excused himself and took his leave, and Brett who had been making surreptitious glances toward the bar, leaned close to Penny's ear and murmured, "How about a beer?"

"No thanks. I'm working." Her voice was friendly. Seeing that he wanted out, she slid over and got to her feet. When he jerked his head toward the bar and grinned hopefully, she shook her head, but gave him a smile full of gleaming white teeth. Reluctantly realizing that he wouldn't get anywhere with her, he thanked us politely for his lunch and tottered off to the bar for some more hair-of-the-dog.

"I'm worried about that young man," Douglas mused.

"Yes," Betty replied. "I think he has really had the props knocked out from under him."

What had Douglas been planning to do for Brett? And what had been Brett's purpose in playing the role of bereaved son of ungrateful father? Albert had blundered clumsily into both plans, leaving the wreckage behind. Brett, I knew, was lost to us now.

Chapter 16

With Albert and Brett gone, we could finally get to the business that had brought us there. I asked Paul where he had been on Wednesday afternoon.

"I was at home, phoning people about their Symphony renewals. I talked to several people, but can't remember when. You know, I think my memory is failing me. When I was a reporter, I had to remember a lot of things and do it under pressure. I had to be sure of my facts. Now that I'm retired, I can't seem to be bothered any more."

"What did the police think?"

"They were interested, and they took a copy of my list, so I guess they were going to contact the people I had called. I had ticked off the ones I talked to, but I don't remember what time I talked to them. I've been doing it all week. A lot of people aren't home in the daytime, so I made calls Wednesday where I didn't talk to anyone. I left messages on answering machines, but there's no way to verify the times."

"I expect they will sort it out."

Paul gazed out the window and continued wistfully, "You know, I've reported on a lot of murder investigations in my life. I never quite realized how frightening it can be to an innocent person until now."

"I daresay it's pretty frightening to the guilty person as well," I quipped.

"Were they interested in the article you wrote for the *Chronicle*?" Douglas asked.

"Oh, yes. We had a real free-for-all discussing that. I tried to tell them that Frank should have been hitting me over the head, not the other way around."

"We've been through this with several other people. But I expect that they will find someone you were talking to at the critical time."

"I hope so." He sounded dejected. "Excuse me." He got up and headed for the washroom. Penny's eyes followed him, concern on her face.

"You know, he really is failing."

"You think so?" I asked.

"He used to be quite a vivacious person. Now he just shuffles around."

"Perhaps he needs something challenging to do," Douglas suggested. "What might he be interested in?"

"I don't know. I expect I could find out, though." She brightened. "He has always taken a sort of fatherly interest in me, so I guess it's time I should take a daughterly interest in him. He's really a sweet man."

"I think you should do that."

I was amazed and amused that Penny, who had caught on to Brett instantly, had not noticed the kind of interest Paul showed toward her. It wasn't fatherly.

In the past few weeks, he had shaved off his skimpy goatee, had his scraggly, white hair neatly trimmed, and replaced his rumpled shorts, faded shirts, and sandals with neatly pressed slacks and coordinated shirts or sweaters. His eyes brightened when she entered the room, his gait accelerated to open doors for her, he bent his head to listen to her every remark. If she started to take an interest in him, it could do nothing but improve his life. Lucky old goat!

I knew that there had been a man somewhere in Penny's background, and that the experience had not been a successful one. I didn't know the details and never pressed her for information. She held men at arm's length. It was going to be interesting watching this relationship. But back to the present.

"I'm glad Albert can give you an alibi," I told her.

"He can?"

"Remember what he said about seeing you at the Farmer's Market?"

"Robin! You didn't think I needed an alibi, did you?"

I could feel my face flush. "Penny, I didn't. But Sergeant Jameson has a suspicious little mind."

Penny howled with laughter. "Oh, Robin. Can you just see me being hauled away in chains? Where were you at the time of the murder? Me? Out riding my bike. Very suspicious. Take her away."

"Don't joke about it."

"Why not? It's a lot more fun that worrying."

Paul came back and Betty remembered the Symphony subscription. Paul perked up and for the next five minutes they discussed the Symphony and Paul jotted things down in his notebook. We got up, paid our bill, and left.

"No bike?"

"Not this time," Penny responded. "Paul will very sedately drive me back to work."

* * * *

Betty took the bus back to the rectory, leaving the Jeep back at the church for Douglas. He and I detoured to the high school. Sue Ambler had an hour free between two and three and had agreed to meet us.

She told us that on Wednesday she had gone to the supermarket on her way home and had probably been there from about four-fifteen to four-forty-five or so. It had been right on five o'clock when she got home, and her husband had arrived about five minutes later. That's odd. I had never noticed her wedding ring before. There was no Mr. Ambler in the church, but when she called him by name, Lesley, the penny dropped. Come to think about it, I had always seen Sue and Lesley Randall-Jones sitting together. High school boys, eat your hearts out!

"I don't remember seeing anyone I knew at the store," she said. "However, I am always being hailed by people I don't know from Adam, who regale me with tales of their precocious offspring's doings. I suppose most students remember their teachers...."

You bet! I thought. No student of yours would ever forget *you.*

". . .and even their parents do, but I can't possibly recall all of them. So someone may have noticed me there."

"Did you use a credit card?" I asked.

"Yes, I did."

"At that store, the clerks always look at the name on the card and call you by name."

"That's right. They always call me Mrs. Ambler. I doubt, though, that they would remember one name among hundreds."

"You never know. One might."

"Maybe there's hope for me yet." Her laughter tinkled in the empty classroom.

* * * *

At the church, Ethel Fuller looked up from her desk as we entered. "Brett Corrigan just called."

"Oh?" Douglas perked up with interest.

"He said he forgot to tell you when he saw you

at lunch. He doesn't want a funeral for his father. He claims that his father told him that when he died, he just wanted to be cremated, without a funeral."

Douglas looked deflated. "Do you think that's true?"

"I doubt it," Ethel replied with acerbity. "Personally, I think he made it up. And I think he was drunk."

As we sat down in his inner office, Douglas said wryly, "At least it solves one problem."

"What's that?"

"I've never officiated at a funeral for a murder victim. I was rather agonizing over what to say."

"I can see that would have been a problem." Especially, I added to myself, when dying was the most popular thing he had ever done. "By the way, Brett told me this morning that his father was a Roman Catholic, so he probably was baptized. I think we'd better tell Polly Holmes so she doesn't say too much about his taking communion."

"Good. I'm glad that is cleared up. Incidentally, while you were chasing off after Brett, and thank you for doing that, Jameson filled me in on his background. He said that since the entire story had been in the news, they decided it wasn't confidential."

I expressed my interest.

"Jameson told me that about a year and a half ago, Brett was arrested for assaulting his wife. I gather that she was somewhat of a shrew and had been verbally abusing him. He backed her into a corner and slapped her several times, hard enough to bruise her face, until she crouched down and covered her face. He was very contrite afterward, and apologized profusely, but she wasn't having any of it and called the police. He was given probation, but his wife got a restraining order to keep him away from her and the baby girl."

"Is he supposed to be paying child support?"

"Apparently their lawyers hatched up an agreement that he wouldn't have to pay, but in exchange, he was not to have any visitation rights."

"That's odd."

"The thinking was that if he was supporting the child, he would be able to demand visitation rights. He didn't like it, but was forced to go along. One day, he was spotted outside the daycare watching his daughter in the playground. The police were called and he was told to stay away."

"Hmm. You don't know whether to feel sorry for him or not. I can't quite figure him out."

We sat in silence for a while, then Douglas said wonderingly, "I can hardly believe what a bunch of predictable old fogies we all are. Everyone was doing perfectly normal, ordinary things on Wednesday—shopping, gardening, working, napping, cooking, telephoning, drinking beer in the back yard."

"All except one of us."

Douglas gave me a sharp look. "You're right. All except one of us. I wish it wasn't so. Did any of them seem out of character to you? You know them better than I."

"No. They didn't. They all acted perfectly normal."

"What about Albert Wallace? He seems all hyped up."

"That's just Albert. He's like that. At least we've been spared the lodge-brother routine. I presume Frank wasn't a Mason, and I don't think any of the other men are."

"He seems so inconsistent. First he intimates that Frank had it coming to him and now he is all for having Frank's killer hanged."

I laughed. "He's not inconsistent at all. He is one of those people who spout off the appropriate platitude or remark for the given occasion. I doubt if he ever thinks about what he says."

"I see."

"When he talks about fear of God, I'm sure he is not really thinking about that, but is thinking of young punks as he calls them, getting cornered in a back alley by someone who would delight in breaking a few of their bones."

"Unfortunately, that is what a lot of people think when they talk about the fear of God."

"I've been wondering," I mused. "Perhaps you would answer a question for me."

Douglas viewed me with interest. "What is it?"

"Well, you talk about God's love for His people, and that we can always be sure of His love. So where does this fear of God come in? Isn't that contradictory?"

Douglas grinned broadly. He leaned back in his chair, clasped his hands behind his head, and remarked, "Ah! Now we're back on my turf."

He paused for a moment as if marshaling his thoughts.

"God loves us. Of that we can be certain. He loves us, even with all our sins and our inadequacies. Never doubt that.

"We also find references in scripture to the fear of God, even to fear and trembling, but that certainly does not mean we should live in abject terror if we think we might have offended Him. Our God is also a forgiving God, because He loves us.

"Did you ever fear that your father might take away the car keys if he ever learned about the warning you got for some minor traffic infraction, back when you were a teenager?"

"Not exactly that, but similar things. I get your point."

"Did you ever doubt when your parents did something like that, that they still loved you?"

"No. Of course not."

"So you can both love and fear someone at the same time, and you can feel loved by someone you fear."

'The person I used to fear most was a professor at university. I was really impressed by her, and wanted very much to do well in her course. She had a reputation for being tough, and I went into exams with a feeling of dread, but I went prepared, because I didn't want to fail her. I always did well. There were other courses where I sort of slouched along thinking I could breeze through the exams, and I often didn't do as well as I should have."

"I've had that experience myself. That is a good illustration of how your fear of your favourite professor could make you really work and do well in her course. But you didn't have any real physical fear, did you? It was more a desire to measure up."

"That's right."

"People do fear the final judgment, which is of course, God's alone. In a way, it is the fear of the unknown. I think it can be constructive if it keeps them from wallowing in sin, for instance, but it can be destructive if carried too far and one loses sight of God's love."

Douglas leaned forward and eyed me intently. "Robin, I think there is something else you want to ask about, isn't there?"

I opened my mouth to speak, but no words came out. The question—no, the challenge—that I had intended to issue the day before, stuck in my throat and I found I couldn't bring it forth. I had been going to ask why, if God was in control of people's lives, if God so loved his people, He let such horrible things happen to them. Yesterday, I could have asked it, defying Douglas to prove it, but today the words wouldn't come. There were other things I would have liked to talk about as well, things that, to me, defied understanding. But I couldn't talk about them either. Not to Douglas, I couldn't.

As I sat there trying to figure out what to say, a commotion erupted in the office, the door to Douglas office was flung open, and an angry man hurled himself through it, with Ethel Fuller right behind, looking helpless. For the first time since I had met him, I saw a fleeting look of annoyance pass over Douglas' face.

"This is Guy LaRoche," Ethel said hastily. "I told him you were busy."

"Come in, Guy." Douglas used the French pronunciation of the name, which Ethel had not. "You look upset. How can I help you?"

"You can call off the fuckin' cops, that's what you can do," Guy shouted.

"I beg your pardon?"

"You sicked the cops on me. You think that 'cause I'm not one of your crowd, and I'm French, and I'm a working man, you can make me out to be your fuckin' murderer."

"None of those things is true."

"I'm no murderer. I do my job. I lock up after me. I wasn't here Wednesday, I work here Friday."

"I'm sure you weren't here Wednesday. No one has accused you of being here."

"The cops have. I know they'd like to let all you rich creeps off and pin it on someone like me."

"No one in the church has done that."

"Then why the fuckin' cops come to me and wanna know where is my key and what the hell I think I was doin' Wednesday?"

"Guy, they are questioning everyone who had anything to do with the church. Just because they have come to you to ask you questions doesn't mean they suspect you."

"The hell it don't!"

"No it doesn't. They have questioned everyone, from me on through our parishioners, and I presume they are starting on people outside the church. They are merely trying to gather information."

"They question you? They make you tell what the hell you were doin' ?"

"Yes."

"What the fuckin' hell they think they doin' accusing a padre?"

"Their job," Douglas replied with some acidity.

"Oh."

"I assume they are satisfied with what you were doing at the time?"

"Hell, yes. I was cleanin' a bank and was locked in it, with the assistant manager right there with me."

"So you are in the clear. Rest assured that no one in the church sent them after you or accused you of murder."

"Well, okay." Guy sounded mollified. "Guess I'd better get to work."

Most of this tirade flowed over me without fully entering my consciousness. Sunk in thought, I wrestled with the problem of what had come over me. I sensed a major change, but could not define it.

Yesterday, I had been about to openly challenge Douglas with the crucial question that keeps a lot of non-believers confirmed in that stance. Today, I couldn't even ask the question. Why?

Because I wasn't prepared to accept the answer I would get. Call it intellectual integrity or something, it did not seem proper to ask a question whose answer you were not going to believe. I had a vision of my cat's vet ranting about people who brought their animals to her, then totally disregarded her advice. I didn't want to put myself in that category. Then why had I been willing to ask it yesterday? If yesterday, why not today?

Because I didn't want to embarrass Douglas.

Nonsense! He probably gets asked that question, in one form or another, all the time. He probably knew what I was about to ask and was prepared to answer it. It would not embarrass him.

Then because I felt I had to play fair with him. Why today? Why not yesterday?

Because it might trigger his rejection of me. *Now we're getting there*, I thought. Why did this bother me? Because—because I had fallen in love with him.

The realization hit me like a physical blow. Immediately behind it was the additional realization of the utter futility of it. I, Robin Carruthers, who had sworn adamantly that I would never again enter any relationship with another man, had fallen hopelessly in love. Yeah, hopeless, that was the word for it. I couldn't think of anyone on God's green earth that I had less hope of being able to enter a romantic relationship with than my priest, who incidentally had a wife I had come to adore and a relationship with her that I would have given anything in the world to have with some other person.

"Excuse me a minute," Douglas was saying. "I want to go over something with Guy." He got up and left the office, and I took the opportunity to resort to cowardly flight. I was out of the church like a shot, in my car and driving home.

* * * *

My cat, Cloud Nine, was waiting for me at the door, yowling for his supper. He got his name because he looks like a big puffy cumulus cloud. I didn't think Fair Weather Cumulus quite befitted a cat, and casting about for some other way to say it, I thought of nine as a number associated with cats, and Cloud Nine popped into my head.

He had been skinny when I took him in as a starving waif, but my vet had put him on a special, very nutritious diet which he loved. I had been busy, and didn't think to stop filling his bowl to the brim every time it was empty, and to start rationing his food, until one day I looked at him and realized he resembled a blimp. As anyone who has ever tried to diet will tell you, it's easier to put it on than to take it off, so there he was, all fifteen pounds of him.

He gobbled his food while I paced the floor trying to work out my problems. He gave me an occasional wary glance, as if wondering whether my nervousness had any implications for him. Then he sat and fastidiously washed his face with a paw, after which he stared at me through slitty eyes, a smirk on his face.

"Laugh at me, you dumb cat," I growled. But when I sat down, he jumped onto my lap, turned on his purr motor, and bumped me under the chin with his head.

At least one creature loves me, I thought, as I stroked his sleek, fat back. We sat in companionable silence for a long time before I dumped him off and made myself a sketchy supper.

Soul check time, I told myself. *I've got to work this out.*

Did I really love Douglas? Yes, probably, in a way. It wasn't a firm yes. Or was it perhaps an infatuation brought on by close contact in a highly charged emotional atmosphere? Perhaps partly, I admitted, but it was more than that.

Or was I in love with love? Was I envious of the obvious deep and comfortable love that Douglas and Betty showed for each other? I realized that their love was based on years of meeting life's problems togethere—of starting out on a small salary, with debts to pay, children to raise; of making a success in each parish they served; of seeing the kids grow up, leave home, get an education, marry; of having grandchildren to spoil; of having worked out the roles each would play in the relationship; of other factors I could not even imagine.

I certainly envied them. I had realized too late that I had not really loved Dale, that it had been merely an infatuation, cemented feebly by a shared interest in flying. Dale's idea of love was what you did in bed at night, and other than that, about all I got from him was an occasional "Hi, hon" when he had come back from a flight.

My parents had loved me, I was sure. I had been an only child, born late in their lives, after they had all but given up hope of having a child. I had never doubted that I had been wanted and loved, but both my parents had died when I was in my twenties. Before that, I had been able to call them and discuss my problems, and had gotten sound, common-sense advice, a lot of which I rejected as young people often do. I missed this steady base to my life after they were gone, but gradually had grown to accept it and to develop the feeling that I was self-sufficient and could handle any problems that came up without too much wear and tear on my emotional system.

Until now. Now I was helplessly at sea.

Where could I go for help? People often go to their clergyman for help in time of stress. Ha! That was a good one. Douglas was absolutely the last person I could go to with this problem. Besides, he probably had female parishioners falling in love with him all the time. I wondered if they had lectures in seminary on how to escape the clutches of predatory females.

Added to my problem was the ongoing one of not wanting to let Douglas know that I did not believe in God. This deception had become an even more acute problem. Douglas seemed to sense that I needed to talk about my spiritual life, but now more than ever I knew I could not talk to him about it. I dared not risk triggering his displeasure or non-acceptance.

No, if I wanted to have any kind of a relationship at all with Douglas, I would have to keep this problem strictly to myself.

As usual.

Chapter 17

I awoke early Saturday morning with the summer sun streaming in the open window. I had the urge to go flying, to get away from the worldly problems that were weighing me down.

I put on a light-weight flight suit over shorts and a T-shirt, and drove to the airport. Opening the hangar, I pulled out my pride and joy, a DeHaviland Chipmunk military trainer. There were only a few people I let fly it, though we did occasionally use it for tail dragger training or aerobatics. It gleamed in the sun, its yellow paint with the orange, red and brown trim reflecting the light.

As always, doing the pre-flight, strapping myself in the cockpit, and firing it up were accompanied by a rising tide of excitement, which calmed to a relaxed enjoyment when the take-off roll began. The tower wasn't open yet, no one was in the air and I had the world to myself.

The Chipmunk is a real stick and rudder airplane, making no pretense of being a car with wings as many civilian planes do. This morning, however, was not a time for aerobatics. That requires a high state of excitement, is vigourous exercise and leaves me wrung out, drained dry. Today I wanted to fly low in the slanting early morning sunlight and enjoy the gifts of nature (of course abiding by the legal five hundred feet above the ground rule—as a flight instructor, I had to set a good example). I left the city and headed for the surrounding hills, rolling to mimic the curving slope, watching my shadow rise up to meet me as I cleared a hilltop only to fall away into the abyss on the other side. Trees stood sharply outlined in the slanting sunlight, casting long shadows westward. A herd of grazing sheep, startled when I swept over a ridge above them, took off in a woolly waterfall down the hillside. Sorry that I had startled them, I turned back, climbing, and saw them stop their flight and settle down again to graze.

I chased my shadow up the hay meadows in the valley, rolled the wings from side to side to feel the smooth, easy response of the controls, and headed out over the lake. On the near shore, the water stood calm and glassy. Farther out, puffs of wind rippled the surface. I circled a becalmed sailboat, waggled my wings at the waving sailors, and headed back toward shore. I set myself up for a long, straight-in approach. The tower was open and I was cleared to land. No other traffic was in the air.

When I was two miles out, I already knew I had this one nailed. Flying hands-off, perfectly trimmed in the still, calm air, I was sliding down an invisible wire that would take me right to the runway threshold. I pulled the nose up and eased the power off and felt the moment when the wing gives up the effort to keep the plane airborne and loses its lift. It coincided exactly with the moment the wheels touched the runway, all three of them, the two mains and the tail wheel, simultaneously. So smooth was it that I could not feel the moment of touchdown. I had made a perfect landing, something that even highly skilled and experienced pilots only manage to do a few times in their lifetime. A feeling of great joy welled up within me. Then the earphones crackled and a voice came over the radio. "Only angels land like that."

Angels! As if it were a code word, I came crashing back to reality. I'm supposed to be an avenging angel in search of truth and justice. I wondered how an avenging angel might land. Sort of like a carrier jet, I thought. Tonnes of screaming metal thudding onto the carrier deck in a highly controlled crash, full power on so if the tail hook misses the wires you can go around again. Yeah, that's about right, I thought. That's what I should be doing.

* * * *

I changed and went to the church. When Douglas saw me, he looked pleasantly surprised and remarked, "You have a lot of spring in your step this morning. What's up?"

"I've been up," I quipped, pointing skyward. I told him about the flight; about the beauty of the landscape in the early morning sun, the smooth ease of the control response of my plane, of the perfect landing. I omitted the part about angels.

"It's been a long time since I've made a perfect landing. I'm really proud of it. Oops! That's a bad word, isn't it?"

"Pride?" he laughed.

"Yes. Isn't that supposed to be a sin?"

"Many people think it is the most important of the sins, the one that leads to all the others."

"Oh, oh. I'm in trouble."

He smiled. "I don't think anyone is going to deny you your moment of pride. We can have pride in doing something well, as long as we don't let pride rule our lives, as long as we don't become so self-centred that we feel we are better than everyone else, as long as we humbly realize that without God's help, we can accomplish nothing. You might think of your perfect landing as a gift from God, a realization, in the ability you show, of God working through you to help you make the most of that talent."

Now I was floundering again. I hadn't even been thinking of God when I was out flying that morning. I sat there in confusion, unable to put anything into words. Why hadn't I kept my mouth shut in the first place?

Douglas went on, "I think that if I had an experience such as you describe, not just the landing, the entire flight, I might think that I was in the presence of God. You know, you don't have to see some majestic figure appear out of a thundercloud to feel God's presence. It can be a quiet, peaceful thing. I felt it in this church that night you people first showed it to me. Betty did, too."

I thought back to that night and found that I could recall an aura in the church that had seemed to hold all of us spellbound. Was that really what God was like? Could I ever feel that way?

"Was that when you decided you wanted to come here?"

"I had a pretty good idea before, but that was when I knew for certain I wanted to come, and when I also knew you wanted me."

"We knew it, too."

"There. You see! God was speaking to all of us. You asked me yesterday about God's love. Have you any doubt that He was speaking to us in terms of great love?"

Why do I get so tongue-tied when I am asked a direct question about God? What a pickle I'm in now, I thought. Here I have truly fallen in love for the first time in my life, and the man I have fallen in love with is offering me the perfect love I so deeply desire, not with himself, but with his God.

But was I really in love? I was aware that something had changed. Perhaps being made to think about God's love had made me realize that there is another kind of love than a physical, sexual one.

Did I love my parents? Of course I did. Did I love my grandmother, whose home I used to visit every Sunday? I loved her very much. Just because I love a man who is near my own age, does that mean that my love must be of the physical-sexual type?

There is another kind of love that can be directed toward a person of either sex and any age, a person who enriches your life, who you feel you cannot do without; someone who gives you something you cherish.

What then did this man I had hardly known up until a few days ago, give to me that I felt I could not do without? That was a tough one. Perhaps it was that he always seemed to know what I needed. He knew it even to the point where I found myself hiding it from him. Now, because of my feelings toward him, his importance to me, I had to withdraw from him or, I felt, I would lose him forever.

I don't know whether Douglas sensed my confusion and discomfort. I think he did. He sort of came down to earth and changed the subject.

"Did you see the letter in the *Chronicle* this morning?"

"No. What was it about?"

"Someone who seems to have a vindictive dislike of organized religion is suggesting that now that we have experienced murder in our church, ritual sacrifice can't be far behind."

"What? That's outrageous."

"It is, isn't it? Paul says this fellow is a persistent writer of letters to the editor, and is a confirmed atheist."

"Lots of people are atheists without being mean about it," I muttered defensively.

"I know. One wonders about people who have

to continually defend their stance. It gives the impression they aren't really sure."

Some recollection stirred in the back of my mind. "What's this man's name?"

Douglas turned to his desk, adjusted his reading glasses, found the paper, and opened it to the editorial page. "Elwood Twombley. Do you know anything about him?" At my snort of derision, he inspected me over the top of his glasses.

"Oh, him! He's always writing drivel. I doubt if anyone really pays attention. People used to write answers to his letters, but now they don't bother."

"That's what Paul says. The editors consider him comic."

"I hope they're right."

He put down the paper. "Anyway, I think we ought to call on Shirley and Harry again, to see how they are getting along."

* * * *

The Meachams were delighted to see us, and I couldn't help noticing how good they looked. They were calm and relaxed, and made me feel like a tightly stretched spring.

"Have the police been back?" I asked.

"They were here once more to ask us a few more questions. Don't worry, Robin, they are not harassing us or anything like that. We still don't have an alibi, but I'm sure they will eventually find the culprit." Shirley looked as easy in her mind as her words sounded. "Oh! And the letter arrived," she exclaimed.

"The letter from Albert?"

"Yes. I'll go get it." She bustled off into an adjacent room.

Harry remarked, "It was just a brief, utterly

cold communication, but it doesn't seem to bother Shirley at all."

She returned with the letter, removing it from a rumpled, battered envelope. "It came just like that," she said, making a face at the soiled envelope. "It's postmarked yesterday."

"We think someone was carrying it around in a pocket or purse and only just discovered they hadn't mailed it," Harry theorized.

Shirley handed it over and Douglas and I read it together. It was brief and totally devoid of any sympathy or emotion, but it was the bottom of the letter that caught my attention.

"Look at that." I stabbed the paper with a forefinger. Beneath Albert's signature, which was unreadable, was the notation AW:mm. "He didn't write it like he said. He dictated it to a secretary, and not one at the church, either."

Harry craned his neck over Douglas's shoulder. "Don't tell me Albert still has Marlie Merkle for a secretary? I thought Cleo would have gotten rid of her long ago."

Shirley giggled. "I never had to worry about Harry's secretaries. He always got ones with at least thirty years practical experience, didn't you, dear?" She dug an elbow playfully into Harry's ribs.

"Those were only the ones you knew about."

They laughed.

"Does this Marlie Merkle have frizzy blonde hair and wear mini-skirts?"

"That's her," Harry answered. "Say, you know, I bet that's where a lot of the gossip comes from. Albert sits in his office and calls everyone on the phone. He talks in that loud voice, the door is always open, and that Marlie has a mouth on her. I never realized she still worked there or I'd have thought of her before."

"Why would she get things so inaccurate?" Douglas queried.

"Probably because she only hears half of each conversation. She takes what she hears and embellishes it, and as you know, that's how rumours get going."

"You're right, dear. She's not a bad girl actually. We know her. She lives down the street a ways, with her folks. But I still don't know what that young man of hers sees in her. She doesn't seem his type. Nice young man—Roberts or Robertson or something. He's a constable in the RCMP."

"*What* did you say?" I almost shouted.

Douglas and I exchanged glances. "No wonder they had the lowdown on us so soon," he said. "They had only to get this constable to call his girlfriend. He was there that night, the young one at the door to the meeting room. I remember his name from his name tag."

Shirley gasped. "And here we've been wondering who in the church would do that to us!"

"It is a relief," Douglas remarked. "I was not looking forward to finding someone in the parish who was actively sabotaging you, Shirley."

Shirley answered weakly, "I wasn't either."

I gave the letter back to Shirley and told her, "I think that you personally should give this to Sergeant Jameson, and in that nice sweet motherly way you have, tell him that you realize where he got his gossip from and that you forgive him. That ought to make him feel like a heel."

* * * *

When I got home, Cloud Nine met me at the door, and twining around my legs, tried to convince me that I had forgotten to feed him that morning.

"Go away, Fatso. I know you. I also distinctly remember feeding you."

When I sat down, he instantly leapt into my lap and made himself comfortable, wriggling contentedly when I ruffled the fur on his back.

Why, I wondered, can't I find someone to love me that is somewhere between this big fat white cat and a God I don't believe in?

The answer to my question seemed both simple and incredibly difficult. Why not love God? Because I really don't believe in Him, I told myself with finality, and that was that.

Chapter 18

In the early afternoon, I arrived at the flying school to make final preparations for the open house. The place was neat and clean. An assortment of audio-visual equipment was already in place. Some of the students were busy washing the planes, vacuuming their interiors, and removing stray charts and candy wrappers. Some flying was still going on, so the cleaning crew had to snatch planes as they came in.

The newest planes, with the most modern equipment, were to be displayed most prominently. With the 150's, it made little difference, but the 172's were ten years apart in age and the newer one had the latest in navigation equipment, a Global Positioning Satellite receiver, installed in it. We planned to show that off. It would tell anyone wanting to fiddle with it that we were four-tenths of a nautical mile south of the centre of the airport, ten feet below the elevation at the centre (the runway sloped up slightly toward the far end), and would give all the relevant communication and navigation frequencies as well as direction and distance to all the navigation aids. Great stuff! Expensive also. In addition, the Automatic Direction Finder would swing around to point to the non-directional beacon four miles off the far end of the runway. The Instrument Landing System receiver would tell them that the plane was to the right of the course centre-line. The VOR wouldn't tell them much, since we were sitting in a valley and the nearest station was forty miles away.

The Bonanza had all the equipment except the GPS, which I hoped to add as soon as I could afford it. It also had even more fancy stuff: a flight director, an autopilot, and a stormscope which, I hoped, would not be pointing out any thunderstorms that night.

All seemed in order, until I got to the front office.

"Gayla, you'd better get out some more T-shirts."

"Oh, are they all gone? We ran out of polo shirts and some of the guys bought T-shirts instead." Everyone was to wear a red shirt with the school logo. We would also sell them to people who came to the open house. Gayla went off to the storeroom, but came back empty-handed. "We're all out."

"Out? I hope you ordered more. We'll have to pick them up before the T-shirt shop closes."

Gayla's face was downcast. "I didn't realize we were out."

I stared at her. Controlling my temper with some difficulty, I said, "When we get low on things, they need to be re-ordered. We have to have those tonight. We always sell at least a dozen."

"I'm sorry."

"Well, call the shop and see if they can do some for us in a hurry. Get two dozen, all sizes."

A few minutes later, Gayla hailed me. "They don't have that many red T-shirts on hand. All they have in that quantity is white."

"Then get white, with the logo in red. And make arrangements to get them picked up. Be sure they know we need them tonight."

Gayla went back to the phone. When she was through, I asked her, "Are the *Chronicle* and the TV station going to send reporters?"

"Oh, I forgot."

Not another oversight! I should have kept better track of what was going on. It required constant vigilance to make the place run smoothly, to notice when things needed ordering. No one else paid that much attention, but I had built up this business by keeping on top of things. This was our busiest time of year. The open house was our opportunity to increase our business. I shouldn't have dropped everything and gone running over to the church like I did.

Or should I? Yes, I decided, I'd done the right thing. That was where I had been needed. If it affected my business, I'd have to accept that. I'd have to make do the best I could.

Jan came over to me. "Gayla's all upset about forgetting to call the paper and the TV station, but don't worry. All those reporters who were trailing around after you Thursday night got an earful from us about the open house. They'll be back."

Maybe there's something to the Hollywood adage that 'all publicity is good publicity if you want to sell something.'

I busied myself with a myriad of other matters until it was time to move the planes up to the hangar door for display. The Bonanza would rest in state between a 150 and a 172, their wings overlapping. The Chipmunk had been moved out of the hangar, surrounded by a fence on which were signs telling people to stay off. I didn't want people tramping all over it.

The Bonanza was there, as was the 150, but the 172 was not.

"Where's Five?" I asked Joyce.

"Out on a flight."

"What? That's the one that has to be in the display."

"Can't you use Four?"

"No. We need Five. When's it coming back?"

"I blocked it out for a two-hour segment at four o'clock."

I strode to the nearest phone and called the

tower. The 172 was on a local flight, they told me. Did I want it called in? I did. I could hear the controller over the receiver we always had on in the office.

"Robin Five, tower." Pause. "Robin Five, tower."

The tower phoned me back and reported no contact. I drew a blank from Flight Service, also. To both, I ordered, "When you get in touch with them, tell them to get back on the double."

About twenty-five minutes later, the plane rolled up to the door. I booted the occupants out, bawled them out for turning the radio down so they couldn't hear the tower, told my clean-up crew to give it a quick once-over and put it in place. What next?

I didn't have long to wait. A dull, shabby, beat-up looking Cessna 152 pulled up to our tie-down area. The tail was nearly dragging on the ground, the nose-wheel strut fully extended, revealing dirt-caked grease streaks on the under side of the cowling. I recognized it as one owned by a small flying club at the far end of the field. I went out to talk to the pilot, who appeared to be a young woman in shorts and a halter top.

"Hello," I greeted her. "You're from the Valley Flying Club, aren't you?"

The girl shifted her gaze from me to the hulking young man squeezing out of the right seat.

"Yeah," he replied.

"I know we advertised free tie-down space, but I didn't mean for other people who have tie-downs on the airport to use them. It's for people flying in. Could you please take your plane down to your club? You are welcome to come back and join the festivities." And move it quick, I thought, before someone thinks it's mine.

"Yeah, I guess," said the big youth. He leaned

into the plane and called out, "Hey, you getting out here or going down to the club with us?" For the first time, I noticed the third person in the plane, sitting sideways in the baggage compartment. No wonder the tail was dragging with all that extra weight back there.

"Get out!" I demanded.

The man unfolded himself, half-rolled over the back of the seats, and wriggled out of the tight confines of the cockpit. To my consternation, I found myself looking into the face of Lance Brock.

"You know better than that," I told him bitterly. I turned to the girl. "Aren't you aware that putting three people in a two-place airplane is both illegal and highly unsafe? You're way over gross weight, and your centre of gravity is way aft of safe limits."

She shrugged. "I don't know anything. I'm not a pilot."

"What were you doing in the left seat of this plane?"

"I'm teaching her to fly," the large youth replied. "Want to make something of it?"

"Shut up," Lance hissed anxiously.

"Are you a flight instructor?" I asked the youth, thinking he looked too young.

"What's it to you?"

"I'm in charge of general aviation safety at this airport. I can find out who you are and what licenses you have."

"Okay, okay. We'll take the plane down to the club. Let's unload the beer here, though." He leaned into the back and pulled out two six-packs of Molson. Lance moved away, trying to dissociate himself from the other two. *I really don't know this guy*, his actions said louder than words.

I took a deep breath and counted to five.

"You," I pointed to the large youth, "I presume, have a pilot's license."

"Yeah. What of it?"

"Get in your plane, in the left seat, take your girlfriend, and taxi slowly and carefully back to your club. Leave the booze and leave Lance here. Lance can take the beer out the exit gate and wait for you by the road. If you do one single thing other than what I've just told you, I'll call the MOT and report you for every violation I can think of.

"And you," I whirled and addressed the girl, "if you're interested in learning to fly, go to a real school and take lessons from a real instructor. These clowns could have killed you out there."

I watched them leave and escorted Lance to the gate. In defiance, he popped the top on a can of beer and started guzzling it.

"Don't throw your empty on the ground," I told him. He turned to face me, trying hard to think of a handy-dandy come-back and not succeeding. He turned and walked away. I watched him stand by the road until a Toyota Four-Runner came screaming up and slewed to a stop. Lance and the booze disappeared inside, the vehicle took off, and almost immediately a truck from the TV station pulled in.

Close timing!

Jan had been right. The reporters were out in force, with TV and still cameras, extra lights and millions of questions.

* * * *

The guests began to arrive. We let the early birds tour the exhibits and view the planes, waiting for a large enough crowd to accumulate. A flight instructor sat in each plane, while spectators ei-

ther climbed into the other seat or peered inside.
The instructor demonstrated what the controls do
and explained what all those funny clocks on the
instrument panel were all about. It was interesting in this day of digital clocks that people still
related anything round, with numbers and point-
ers on it, to clocks. Did they ever look at the oil
pressure gauge on their car and wonder what that
clock was for?

There would be a spaghetti feed, but first everyone was invited to the awards ceremony. We had
gotten some trumpeters, a snare drummer and a
small choir from among the high school's music
students. We gave each of them a club T-shirt and
offered them all the spaghetti they could eat.

After the early birds had circulated around the
exhibits, and a sizable crowd had gathered, we
ushered them into the hangar where chairs had
been set up. At one end were risers for the pilots
being honored to stand on. On a higher platform,
the choir took its place, and at the four corners of
the hangar stood the trumpeters and drummer.

"Let the ceremony begin," said Jan into the
rented PA system. The trumpets sounded a fanfare and the snare drummer added a drum roll.
"We are here to honor the intrepid aviators of Red
Robin Flying School." Another flourish from the
trumpets and drum.

"First, let us honor all the pilots who have flown
for the last year without an accident or violation
of the law. That includes... *everybody!*"

Great applause, as various pilots clasped their
hands above their heads, or gave the V or thumbs-
up sign.

Well, not everybody, I brooded, remembering
Lance and wondering whether I should work with
him to try to change his ways or just kick him out.

Jan went on to list pilots who had been members and had not been involved in an accident for two, three, four, and more years. Finally, she called upon our oldest member and presented him with a plaque for twenty years of safe flying.

"Now for our 'All the Way to the Top' award. This man started out here washing airplanes, then pumping fuel. Finally, he had accumulated enough money to take flying lessons, which most of us didn't bother doing before we started ours." Laughter. "He got his private, then his commercial, instrument rating and, finally, his flight instructor license. He has gone all the way from being called *Hey, you* to being called *Sir*." More laughter, and as Jan introduced my newest flight instructor, the man who had started here as a teenager doing odd jobs, a great cheer arose from the other pilots and was picked up by the spectators. The trumpets and drum added to the din. I had told them to give us a flourish whenever it seemed appropriate, and they were following those instructions with gusto.

The excitement and joy were catching. The spectators were no longer sitting still and clapping politely, but had gotten into the spirit and were shouting and cheering.

"Now we come to the part so many of you have worked so hard for," Jan exclaimed. "These are students who have reached landmarks during the year. First, those who have soloed."

A shouting group of young men and women, wearing T-shirts that said, *I Did It! I Soloed!* ran, leaped, and pranced to the front and clambered up onto the risers, where they stood at attention. As Jan read their names, I hung a medal around the neck of each one. Each student had his or her group of friends cheering, and at the end, there was a mad session of high-fiving among them.

"Now, the students who have passed flight tests for licenses or ratings." Trumpet fanfare. "First, the private pilots." Drum roll. As Jan read the names, each man or woman dashed to the front, hopped up onto the risers, and bowed to allow me to hang even larger medals around their necks. The last was Peter Trask, and as he bent his head, I congratulated him and whispered in his ear, "Thanks for the alibi." He grinned at me, then waved his hand high in the air, while Lisa and her retinue cheered wildly.

"Finally," intoned Jan, "we honor a student who has gone from private pilot last year, to obtaining an instrument rating, commercial license and flight instructor license, all in one year."

This student was a middle-aged man who had finally last year realized a lifelong dream to learn to fly, and found he couldn't stop learning. He didn't live anywhere near Exeter, but had heard about the school from a former student and would come to Exeter for a concentrated course in each of the areas of flight experience. He had finished his instructor course last week, and would soon be heading home, but had stayed on for the ceremony. He was tall and lean with kinky hair that was starting to turn grey, a leathery face and an unusually sober, formal manner. Instead of running to the front, we had planned that he would march there solemnly, to the accompaniment of the choir, the trumpets and the drum.

"See our conquering hero comes.
Sound the trumpets, beat the
drums.
Sports prepare, the laurel bring.
Songs of triumph to him sing."

He bent his head, and I placed on his brow a laurel wreath fashioned by one of the city's florists, then he stepped onto the highest riser, to the shouts of the throng, and the blaring music. No returning war hero could ask for a better reception.

After the ceremony, the chairs were moved aside and folding tables set up. Huge kettles of spaghetti, bowls of salad, and trays of garlic bread, courtesy of a local caterer, were set out, and everyone made a mad rush for the food line. After the feast, the video tapes and slides again began to roll. The students, still draped with medals, and the honoured pilot, still wearing his laurel wreath, circulated among the guests, receiving congratulations and answering questions. The reporters had filmed the ceremony and were now interviewing anyone they could get their hands on.

I spotted Nick Valutin in the crowd, shepherding two boys of about eight and ten years of age. They were round-eyed and awestruck. They sucked in huge mounds of spaghetti and went to all the airplanes and film presentations. Future customers, I was sure.

"Enjoying yourself?" I asked Nick, having to shout to make myself heard.

"We certainly are," he shouted back. "The boys are absolutely thrilled."

"Your grandsons?"

"That's right. I think this is a wonderful idea. It puts a whole different perspective on flying than the usual air show."

"That's the idea. This is what flying is really about. Air shows dramatize the macho and dangerous aspects of flying. We want to show that it can be a safe, pleasant, fun-filled, family-oriented pursuit."

"Well, you're doing a good job," Nick assured me. He worked his way to the edge of the throng, where it was marginally quieter. "Have you and the rector figured out where everybody was on Wednesday afternoon?"

I groaned and made an elaborate display of consternation at having the conversation brought back to the murder, to Nick's amusement.

"Pretty much. We found out where the rumours are coming from, and Douglas is going to politely but firmly put a stop to it."

"Something tells me I'd better not ask who." He frowned and lowered his voice so I had to bend close to him to hear. "I can't understand why so many people hated Frank. He did my son and daughter-in-law a good deed."

"What did he do?"

"They had to sell their house when my son was transferred to Vancouver. Not the father of these kids, my other son. They couldn't afford to pay a big fee to a realtor. They needed everything they could get so they could buy a house in Vancouver where the prices are a lot higher. They had it advertised on that do-it-yourself real estate bulletin board in the Exeter Mall. They hadn't had any luck yet and were getting desperate. They thought they'd have to list it with a realtor, because it was almost time to move. Then Frank came along and told them he thought he had a buyer and offered to handle it for only about three percent, a lot lower than anyone else. Sure enough, it sold right away.

"You know, I think he performed a real service that a lot of people needed. I can't see why everybody was so down on him."

I wondered what Jean, or her secretary, Allison, would think of that.

"Well, anyway," Nick cheered up. "I enjoyed the party."

"Thanks. I'm glad you did. It looks like the boys did also."

"I'm going to have trouble dragging them home. That reminds me, are you going to the rector's induction?"

"I wouldn't miss it."

"Different type of celebration, but very impressive in its own way. You'll find that there's no one like Anglicans to put on a good bash."

Chapter 19

I was unlocking the door of the house about eleven o'clock when I heard the phone ring and scrambled to answer it.

"Robin? This is Penny. Come over to my place quick. I've called Douglas, too. Don't come to the front or you'll never get in. Come through the parking lot in the back. I'll be at the back door."

Before I could ask what was up, she had disconnected. I hopped back into the car and made time over to Penny's condo. It was a good thing that Penny had told us to come to the back. The street in front was choked with traffic, and several police cars with red and blue lights flashing lit up the scene. Douglas and Betty arrived at the same time I did and Penny let us in.

"What's happening?" we all wanted to know.

"Come up front." Penny led us along the corridor, through a couple of fire doors, finally opening the last one only a crack, just enough so we could all get a look. A small, white-haired man in trousers, slippers and undershirt was screaming at two large Mounties who were gently trying to restrain him.

"Calm down, Mr. Twombley. Take it easy. Let's go inside and talk about it."

"We can't go inside," the man yelled. "It's all full of glass! Why don't you go arrest all those bastards and throw them in jail and throw away the key?"

"Who are you talking about?"

"Those fanatics at that church. Use your head man! You know they're out to get me."

"What church, Mr. Twombley?"

"That god-damned Anglican church. They're the ones that did this."

The policemen exchanged knowing looks over the little man's head, gently grasped him by the arms, and steered him through a door. Others crowded into the hallway.

"Twombley?" I mouthed to Douglas over the din.

"I don't believe this," Betty exclaimed in dismay. "Penny, what happened?"

"You'd think someone attacked him with a submachine gun for all the commotion, but actually all that happened is that someone threw a rock through his living room window. He's been ranting and raving to everyone who would listen ever since."

"Any idea who did it?"

"I don't. He does."

"I didn't know you lived in the same building as that guy," I remarked.

"I didn't either, until tonight. I only moved in a couple of months ago. I don't know many of my neighbors. Come on up. Let's have some tea."

We trooped up a flight of stairs to Penny's apartment and she busied herself with tea-making chores. Douglas, in jeans and a T-shirt, dropped heavily onto a couch, looking stunned. Betty didn't look much happier. They'll pull out now, for sure, I thought, even if God did talk to them in the church that night.

Penny brought the tea tray, and even after all the spaghetti and cold drinks I'd consumed earlier in the evening, the tea hit the spot.

"I called Shirley and Harry after I called you," she chattered idly, "because they know Elwood Twombley. I think they belong to some club that he does. But they weren't in."

Conversation stopped, tea cups clattered into saucers, and Penny, realizing the implication of what she had just said, murmured, "Oh, oh."

"Why would they throw a rock through his window?" Betty voiced the concern of all of us. "They probably went to a movie or something."

I rubbed my face with my hands. "*We* know that it doesn't make sense, but consider what other people might think. Here is Shirley, so upset with Frank that she quits her job; then when he turns up dead, murdered, they are cool as cucumbers and cite their faith in God. Now a church detractor is attacked. I can see someone coming up with the theory that they are religious lunatics. I'm sure that throwing a rock through a window is a fairly minor misdemeanor, and normally wouldn't have attracted all this police attention, but now that Twombley has gotten the cops out in force, they might actually consider that his accusation might be true, especially if they weren't convinced of the Meachams' faith. If he screams loudly enough and often enough, he might get them to consider that he has a point."

"Let me call them again." Penny got up and went to the phone. She pushed the re-dial button and in seconds was saying, "Shirley. I'm glad I got hold of you. Where have you been?"

She listened for a minute, then cried in an anguished voice, "From now on, hire a detective agency and don't do anything without their knowing exactly where you are."

Excited noises came from the phone. "Why? I'll tell you why. Yes I'll hold for a minute." There was a pause. "The police? They were fast. Yes, good-bye."

Alarm was written all over Penny's face. "She says they were out walking in the moonlight. And the police just got there."

Douglas rose. "I think I'd better go over."

"Honey, you have to get some sleep. You have to get up for the early service tomorrow." Betty's face wore a worried frown.

"You don't think I could sleep, do you? Are you coming, or do you want Robin to drop you off at home?"

"I think I'd better come."

* * * *

I called the rectory the next morning, and Betty, sounding tired, answered the phone.

"What happened with the Meachams last night?"

"The police were gone when we got there. They hadn't stayed long, only asked where Shirley and Harry had been. They told the police the same thing they told us; that it was a beautiful moonlit night and didn't get dark until about ten-thirty, so they went for a stroll in the moonlight after it finally got dark. I didn't realize how close their house is to where Penny lives. It's farther to drive because her condo is on the hillside and the road doesn't go straight down, but there's a path that does."

"How did Shirley and Harry take it? The police coming again, I mean."

"For once, they seemed pretty shook up. It seemed to bother them more than the murder did."

"I don't know whether the police will consider that good or bad."

"I don't either."

On my way into the church, I caught up with Jean Givens and related Nick's story to her. Jean greeted it derisively. "There's a gimmick somewhere. He used to hang around that bulletin board, and he also kept track of all the homes for sale by owners and managed to talk to most of those people. He also knew who in business or government was being transferred, and who was taking their place. You can bet he had some shady little scheme."

Was it sour grapes on Jean's part, or another of Frank's underhanded deals?

"I don't think we need tell the Valutins, though. Let them stay happy."

Jean frowned. "I guess so. At least now that he's dead."

* * * *

The church was jammed with people again. There were even more than the previous week. I leaned over to whisper in Penny's ear, "Ghouls. I know how to get people to come back to church. Have a murder every week."

Penny replied, "It is disgusting, isn't it? I never thought I'd want to see fewer people in church."

Before the service began, Douglas walked out to the front of the congregation, spread his hands and said in a cheerful voice," 'This is the day that the Lord has made. Let us rejoice and be glad in it.'" He welcomed visitors and gave a few announcements, then, speaking in a more serious tone, addressed us. "As you know, one of our parishioners was killed in the church office on Wednesday."

A stir spread through the assembly, especially those in the back. I saw one, who I recognized as a reporter who had been outside the church on several occasions this week, pull out a notebook and hold his pen poised over it.

"I would like to ask you to cooperate with the police, who have a large and difficult task to perform in trying to resolve this matter. They can do it much better if we give them all the help we can.

"Furthermore, I would like to ask you all to be careful what you say. We have had wild rumours circulating around the church and the community for over a month now, and we have seen what damage they can do. The source of these rumours was an innocent one, not at all malicious, but nonetheless it caused a very unfortunate situation. I ask you all not to talk about anything unless you know the facts, then stick to those facts. Thank you." He turned and walked away.

I gave Penny a surreptitious thumbs up and she said softly but with conviction, "Right on!"

The hangers-on began to drift quietly out of the church, the reporter looked chagrined, and everyone realized there would be no scandal during the service that day.

The Processional began and we rose to sing. In the choir was the tenor Betty had enlisted the previous Sunday. The choir had increased by several members. Betty's recruiting campaign must be in full swing.

A few die-hard scandal-mongers were still present when Douglas gave his sermon, which was all about God's love, a theme I didn't seem to be able to get away from. It had no sinister overtones of murder and scandal. I presumed that it was the sermon he had planned all along and he showed no inclination to change it. The last of the hangers-on gave up in disgust and slipped out of the church—before the collection was taken.

We used Eucharistic Prayer Number 5 from the *Book of Alternative Services*, and I do think that when Douglas came to the line," but we rebel against you by the evil that we do," he emphasized it a bit more than one would expect. However, I still didn't know his oratorical style very well, so was not sure of this.

* * * *

As I moved with the stream of parishioners out of the church after the service, Tom and Polly Holmes caught up with me. She squirmed her way between bodies, dragging Tom, whose progress was more like that of a bulldozer, behind her. Others had to press themselves against walls in order to avoid being flattened.

"Robin, I have such good news," Polly bubbled. "We have an alibi."

"That's great. What is it?"

At least two dozen parishioners who had undoubtedly had no inkling that the Holmeses were even involved, must have overheard and slowed their progress toward the door, their ears flapping. The reporters should have stayed!

"We remembered that Paul had called about renewing our Symphony subscription, so we called him to ask what time he had called us. Yoo-hoo, Paul. Come over here." She waved frantically and Paul St. Cyr made his way through the crush of the departing crowd to where we were standing. He was neatly dressed in coat and tie, and had managed to pick up Penny on his way out.

"I was just telling Robin that we figured out that you called us about a quarter to five."

"Are you sure?" I asked.

"That's right," Paul answered. "We started putting things together and realized that it must have been at that time."

"Good. Did you talk to both Polly and Tom?"

"Yes. Tom answered the phone, then Polly got on the line."

Amazing! I'd known them for two years and had never heard Tom say a word. Paul, it would seem, had been privileged to experience a rare phenomenon. I stifled the impulse to ask Paul how he could possibly have recognized Tom's voice.

"That's great," I said. "Let's go tell Douglas."

Douglas was delighted at the news, but had difficulty freeing himself from Polly's clutches so that he could greet the remaining parishioners. Paul, Penny and I moved to the side and waited until the others had left, then Paul asked Douglas, "Do you think I should call the police and let them know?"

Douglas frowned and thought for a minute. "I'm hesitant about advising you to do that. If they come back to question you again, you should tell them, but when you do, it will involve the Holmeses in the murder investigation in a way that might be unpleasant for them."

"Oh, do you mean their trouble over the real estate sale?"

"Yes. How did you know?"

Paul laughed, "Polly told me, at great length and in great detail. When I was a reporter, I'd have loved getting onto something like that."

So much for her promise to keep mum.

When Paul and Penny had left, Douglas turned to me. "Come over to the rectory for lunch, Robin, and let's coordinate all our information."

All right, I thought. This will be a safe sort of conversation, and Betty will be there as a buffer. Nothing much can happen.

Chapter 20

We ate a delicious meal of cold meats and salad accompanied by light conversation with no mention of murder. Then we went into the living room and Douglas picked up a pad on which he had made some notes. He adjusted his reading glasses and started down the list.

"I can fill in more gaps as a result of conversations I had at the church this morning. Jean Givens says that the police called her and reported that the potential buyers and the seller of the house she was showing Wednesday afternoon think she must have left them after four-thirty, and a waitress at the coffee shop remembers her because of her red blazer with the agency logo. So, although she may have had the best motive, discounting the possible counter-motive, she now can be shown to have an alibi."

"That's wonderful," Betty and I chorused in unison.

"Now the others. Albert and Penny give each other alibis, as do Paul and the Holmeses. Nick was drinking beer with the RCMP Inspector. Layton, by the way, had his presence in his office verified by a man with an office across the corridor. He called to tell me this and spent what seemed like half an hour complaining about police harassment. Frankly, I can't see why he feels that way. They questioned him, as they did all of us, but when they found evidence that seemed to exonerate him, they had the courtesy to call and tell him so. They had a few more questions about what he knew of Frank's business affairs, and that seems to have soured an otherwise positive contact."

"It probably has to do with not wanting clients

to know he had been suspected," I said. "Actually, I've found the publicity, even if it's negative, to be helpful. We've had a lot more interest in the school than I can ever remember."

"Good for business, eh?" He gave me an amused smile.

"It certainly is."

"I spoke to both Gretchen and Sue this morning. Two of Gretchen's neighbours saw her in her garden at the critical time. The clerk at the checkout counter at the supermarket was a former student of Sue's, but was too shy to strike up a conversation. Anyway, she vouches for Sue. You were giving a flight test. I was at Golden Age, and most of the others were not suspected at all."

"What about me?" Betty giggled. "I feel left out."

Douglas grinned at her. "We'll have to see if we can dig up some deep, dark, sinister past for you, then scramble frantically to find you an alibi."

Betty aimed a playful kick in his direction, deliberately missing.

Douglas continued, "Alan Gotfriedson and Marcia Chancellor were at work, and Guy LaRoche was cleaning a bank. We don't know where Anders Olafson was, but the police seem satisfied. Now, who have we left?"

"The Meachams."

There was a long pause. "Yes, the Meachams."

"And they were also out last night when someone threw a rock at Elwood Twombley's window."

* * * *

Into the ensuing silence came a knock at the door. Betty went to open it.

"Hello, Sergeant Jameson," we heard her say. "Come on in."

The tall policeman came in. Douglas extended his hand. Jameson nodded to me.

"I thought I'd come along, and sort of give you a progress report. Also to tell you that we picked up three juveniles in that rock-throwing incident last night."

We all perked up at this news. I asked, "Why did they do it? Was it just random vandalism or was Twombley the target?"

"He was the target. The kids live in the neighborhood and have had run-ins with him. Like the time one was out walking the family dog and let it pee on Twombley's shrubs and he came charging out of his house and let the kid have it with both barrels, so to speak."

"So it didn't have anything to do with the church?"

"It did in a way. They heard about the letter and thought it would be fun to stir things up and watch the reaction. It worked out even better than they planned. They were having great fun watching all the commotion, but someone overheard them and tipped us off."

"Good. That's out of the way." Douglas heaved a sigh of relief. "We were just now going over the whereabouts of everyone. We can update one thing for you. Paul St. Cyr called some other parishioners named Holmes at about a quarter to five and talked to them for ten minutes. The Holmeses verify this."

Jameson pulled out a notebook and made a note. He showed no special interest in the Holmeses.

"We are expanding our inquiries to people who had real estate contacts with him recently. There are a lot of them, but we are trying to find ones who feel they were cheated in some way. By the way, one of the other tenants in Corrigan's apartment house saw him leave his second floor apartment at five past four and walk down the stairs. This tenant heard Corrigan greet someone, but didn't hear that person speak and doesn't know whether it was a man or woman."

"Cherchez la femme?" I asked.

Jameson laughed." We have *cherched*, but we haven't found any *femme*. There didn't seem to be much activity in that direction.

I'm not surprised, I thought. Frank had always impressed me as an exceptionally cold fish.

"So we are still doing a lot of slogging, asking a lot of questions."

"Are you sure Brett Corrigan is out of the picture? He certainly seems to fit the bill. He reacts violently to being thwarted, he didn't care much for his father, and he's a schemer."

"Sounds like you've had a run-in with him," Mrs. Carruthers."

"I've talked to him. Also, he had lunch with several of us. He's obviously grieving, but I still think he might have hit his father in a fit of anger and regretted it later."

Jameson sighed. "You're right. He does seem like an obvious suspect. He's one of those guys you get a gut feeling about and keep looking at over and over. But he's clean as a whistle, unless he grew wings and could fly."

Fly! Suddenly, several things snapped into place. I sat bolt upright and exclaimed, "I think he could!"

The other three looked at me open-mouthed, obviously thinking I had flipped.

"May I use the phone?"

"By all means," Douglas replied.

I dialed the flight school and heard Gayla's

cheery voice. "Gayla, do you remember the Cherokee Arrow that was parked where it was blocking the Medevac and we couldn't move it?"

"I sure do."

"What time did he come in?"

"He must have got there about three-fifteen. He came into the office at three-twenty and asked about rides to town. I told him where he could catch the bus and he went off to the bus stop."

"When did he come back?"

"It must have been about five-forty-five. He probably came back on the five-thirty-five bus. Rod had been going to move the plane before he left at six, but it was gone. Don't worry. Joyce sent a bill."

"Are you sure it was five-forty-five, not six-forty-five? Rod didn't go home at six."

"Yes he did. He came back later. I'm sure it was five-forty-five."

"What did the pilot look like? What was he wearing?"

"Let's see. He was young, medium height and build, sort of ordinary looking. He had dark, brown hair. He had on stone-washed jeans and a blue plaid shirt. And he had old, dirty grey Nikes," she laughed, "with the laces untied. That's why I noticed them."

I asked, through a rising tide of excitement, "Would you look up who that Arrow was registered to?"

There was a long pause, filled, for me, with agonizing suspense. Gayla came back on the line. "It belongs to the Georgetown Flying Club."

I let out my breath. Half way home, I thought. I got the aircraft ID and the Georgetown Flying Club's number from Gayla and hung up. Three faces were turned toward me, taut with suspense.

"On Wednesday, a dark-haired young man of

medium height and build, wearing stone-washed jeans, a blue plaid shirt, and old grey Nikes, parked a plane belonging to the Georgetown Flying Club on our ramp, took the three-thirty-five bus into town, returned to the airport at about five-forty-five, and took off without doing a pre-flight or run-up. We've said a lot about how long it would take to get to Georgetown from here, but in that plane, which is a small, four-place retractable, he could have gotten to Georgetown in an hour's flying time if he went direct and pushed it. That gives him just about the right amount of time to get back to his home by seven-fifteen, if it was Brett Corrigan flying it. Do you mind if I make a long-distance call?"

"No. Go right ahead."

I started to dial the number, paused for thought, then turned to Douglas.

"Douglas, I'm going to commit a sin."

"What kind of sin? I'll think up a suitable penance."

"I'm going to tell a fib. Otherwise, I'm not sure I'll be able to get an answer without Brett finding out about it." I finished dialing the number.

A bored voice answered the phone, "Geo-tun Flyn Club," followed by the loud pop of a gum bubble bursting. If she had been my receptionist, I'd have fired her on the spot. I put on my most charming manner.

"Hello there. I wonder if you could help me. We asked everyone around here and nobody claims them, and so we thought the pilot of your plane that was here might have." I didn't explain where here was. "You see, someone dropped some really expensive sunglasses on our ramp, and I'm sure he's looking for them. Could you tell me who was flying Echo Uniform Oscar on Wednesday afternoon?"

"Just a minute. I'll look."

My hand was sweating so much I could hardly hold the receiver, which I gripped in a white-knuckle vise. It seemed an eternity before the bored girl got back on the line.

"That was Brett Corrigan. Want me to tell him?"

"Oh, no! You see, we'll have to make sure they're his, so we'll have to ask him if he lost anything and have him describe them. Could you give me his phone number, and don't tell him. If they're his glasses, he'll get them back."

"Yeah, I guess you're right. Just a sec. I'll get his number."

I noticed that Jameson was in the kitchen and had quietly lifted the receiver on the extension phone. I hadn't even heard it click. The girl in Georgetown came back with the phone number, which we really didn't need, but I had to keep up the pretense. I dropped the receiver back in its cradle as if it had turned and attacked me, my hand shaking.

In the kitchen, I saw Bruce Jameson make a motion like Wayne Gretzky makes after he has scored a goal and I heard him whisper, "Gotcha, you son of a bitch!"

* * * *

Jameson called the RCMP detachment and issued orders in a low voice we could barely hear. We could make out the words *clothing*, *airport*, and *bus driver*. There was a pause while Jameson waited impatiently, then he gave out an exclamation, "That does it! We've really got him now." He came back into the living room, barely able to control his excitement.

"Corporal Smith, who took your prints the other night, has found a perfect match for Brett

Corrigan's right thumb on the underside of the lip of the countertop in your office. Before I go, though," he looked at me, "I'd like to know what made you think he was a pilot."

"Because of something he said, and because he laughed at a joke."

"That joke you told at lunch that nobody understood?" Betty asked.

"Nobody but Brett. I thought at the time that he was just laughing to be polite, but it seemed out of character. If someone had laughed just to keep me from being embarrassed because my aviation joke was a dud, it would have been one of you, or Penny or Paul, but you were all still trying to figure it out."

"What was the joke?" Jameson wanted to know.

"Albert Wallace was there and was trying to pretend he wanted to charter planes from me. He wanted a big one with a bar and a hostess, but he wanted to pay less than the airlines. There was a provincial air ambulance parked on our ramp. In fact, Brett's plane was blocking it. It was a Cessna 441, a medium-sized, pressurized, turbo-prop twin, which would have been a very expensive type of plane to charter. A Cessna 150 is a small, two-place trainer. I told Albert he had 441 tastes on a 150 budget."

"Now I get it," Betty laughed.

"You know, it was Brett's lack of manners that created the situation where I would remember his airplane. He carelessly parked where he was blocking the Medevac 441. If he had parked in a proper spot, I would never have noticed the plane."

"You said something Corrigan said tipped you off?"

"Remember when we met him in the church office on Friday morning? Douglas said something to him about funeral arrangements and he replied, 'Say again?' That is an aviation term meaning exactly what it says, but I can't think of any time I have ever heard someone who wasn't a pilot use it. For example, on that flight test I was giving on Wednesday, the student didn't hear the altimeter setting at Pine Hill and asked for it again using ordinary, conversational language. I had to get after him about it, so he came back with, 'Say again altimeter setting'. I think I would have noticed it Friday morning if I hadn't had a lot else on my mind."

Douglas ran a hand over his hair. "I wonder why, when Albert told him you ran an aviation company, he didn't get the connection and become alarmed about it."

"Think back to what was said. Sergeant Jameson here introduced me to Brett as Mrs. Carruthers. At lunch, I can't recall anyone calling me Robin, and when Albert started talking about chartering airplanes, he told Brett that I ran Carruthers Aviation. The business hasn't been called that for years. There was a faded sign on the old hangar with that name on it up to about eight years ago, when our new hangar was built, but most people would have noticed our large red and white sign saying Red Robin which has been there since I changed the name twenty years ago. Trust Albert not to. If anyone had called me Robin, or had given the correct name of the business, I suspect that Brett would have been out of there in a flash. But Carruthers Aviation meant nothing to him."

"Well, I've got to go." Jameson started toward the door, but turned and retraced his steps. He impaled me with his beady eyes and said, "That was a good bit of acting you put on. I'll remember that if I ever have to question you again." I didn't know whether to be intimidated, amused, or flattered.

Jameson bounded down the steps two at a time. We watched him swerve the cruiser into traffic and speed away. A knot formed in my stomach as I visualized the net tightening around Brett Corrigan and realized my role in it.

"I feel guilty now, thinking back on the time I said I wished it would be Brett so our church members would be off the hook."

"Yes, I know", Douglas replied, placing an arm around each of us and pulling us close to him. "That was before he became a flesh and blood person we were trying to help."

All the sunshine seemed to have gone out of the day.

Chapter 21

How right Nick Valutin had been I found out as the night of Douglas' induction rolled around. I had known nothing of such things until a few weeks before, when I had learned that a new priest is treated to a ceremony affirming his new covenant with his parish. The bishop would officiate. There would be visiting clergy, choirs, and local dignitaries to mark the occasion. Everyone who had been to one before had told me how thrilling it could be.

On the night of the induction, I heeded the advice of older parishioners and arrived a half hour early. Already there was a line-up to sign the guest book and the pews were filling up. The first few rows were reserved for family, clergy and honoured guests.

The golden rays of the early evening sun lit up the west window and sent sparkles of coloured light over the interior of the church. At the end of the service, we would make our way around to the hall for the reception in a rose-gold twilight. Douglas' children and their families were there. They stood behind him as he greeted people leaving the church after the service. Betty snatched me out of line and introduced me as "our super-sleuth."

It was one of the few occasions when I could be persuaded to wear a dress and jewelry, and I even tottered along on high heels.

* * * *

A feeling of excitement hung in the air. John Vieth was giving a splendid organ recital—Bach, Handel and Widor.

The music stopped. A hush fell over the church,

and looking to the rear, I could see Jeremy Givens holding the cross with much more confidence than he had shown before. Behind him and out the door, the massed choirs of several local churches, each in their own robes, with our choir members interspersed among them, were forming themselves into a double line.

John Vieth struck up the opening notes of the processional hymn and the massed choir began to move toward the altar behind Jeremy, the crucifer. Behind the choir came clergy members from other local churches and from other Anglican churches in the diocese. Some wore albs and stoles; some from less ritualistic churches wore business suits and ties. Two were women. Then came members of the judiciary in black robes, trimmed in red, and our mayor, Victoria Bainbridge, wearing her chain of office. Behind them came Douglas, a white cope of patterned brocade richly embroidered along its borders and on the shield that hung down the back, draped over his shoulders. Last in line came the Bishop, the Right Reverend Michael Staines, in an even more richly embroidered cope. The lace-edged cuffs of his white rochet, held in place by broad red bands, showed beneath the edge of his cope: his left hand holding his staff or crozier, in the shape of a shepherds crook; his right, on which he wore a ring with a purple stone that sparkled in the brilliant light, holding a hymn book from which he sang in a clear tenor voice. He was a tall man, and with the added height of his tall white mitre, he towered over everyone else.

The old church seemed filled with the joyful sound of music, and as the procession moved toward the altar in stately pomp, the bears, foxes, geese, and beavers carved into the rood beam seemed to awaken and look down in awe at the ancient ritual unfolding beneath their feet with such jubilant sound.

The familiar ritual of the Eucharist flowed through the church. It was different in subtle ways, with mention by Bishop Michael that Douglas had been chosen to be priest and pastor of this parish of St. Matthew. This time, Douglas was not leading the service, but was occupying the frontmost pew, in front of his congregation, facing the altar.

"As we stand in God's presence," intoned the bishop, "let us pray that grace will be given to Douglas, and to all of us in this ministry, that we may fulfill the responsibilities which are ours."

The sermon was given by one of the visiting Anglican priests. Then came the Covenant in Ministry, during which Douglas was presented to the bishop by the regional dean and the church wardens and installed as the incumbent. Then came the presentation of the symbols of ministry. Individuals and families from the parish presented Douglas with a Bible, a prayer book, a *Book of Alternative Services*, and a book of Canon Law, as well as symbolic gifts of bread, wine, water, and oil.

After the gifts had been given and received, Douglas stood before the altar and, for the first time, turned to face his new congregation, a look on his face that seemed to combine awe and joy and wonder, as the weight of all the history and majesty of the Church through all the ages was brought to bear on this man, in this church, before this congregation, at this one special time.

As Bishop Michael stood one pace behind, and one step above, he proclaimed, "I present Douglas as the priest among you. . ." The shutter of my mind clicked the moment into timelessness, and imprinted it forever on my memory.

Chapter 22

The summer days passed swiftly, long days full of heat and haze, with hardly a cloud in the sky and hardly a breath of wind. We opened early, as many pilots learned that the cool morning air provides more lift for the airplane's wings as well as for the human spirit. We stayed open late and flew well into the long summer evenings. Our two instructors who were teachers in regular schools were now able to instruct full-time. Even with six instructors on the staff, their schedules were full. They happily worked overtime, and I had to watch that they didn't exceed their limits. They still hung around the school, eager to talk to anyone about flying, anxious to sign up new students. The enthusiasm of the instructors was one of my best advertisements.

One nice thing about running a flight school is that your employees are eager to come to work. All of mine had some other connection with flying besides their work. The instructors flew for fun, or did charter work. The line boys and girls were taking their pay in flying lessons. Gayla was a pilot herself, and Joyce an eager navigator for her pilot husband. We hired an extra dispatcher during the busy season. This year, we hired one of our students.

This gave me an excuse not to hang around the church. I came just as services started and left immediately after. As there were no Church Committee meetings in July and August, my contact with the church was minimal. I did not plan this deliberately, but found that it suited my purposes. I felt that I could not have close contact with Douglas, and my busy schedule gave me a good excuse to stay away from him.

I went home evenings feeling a pleasant tiredness and fell asleep as soon as I dropped into bed, arising about five a.m. to get ready for each new day. I seldom took a day off. That could come during the long winter season when flying is at a minimum.

When I did think about the changes in my spiritual life, it was more in the way of an intellectual exercise, and when, after about two months, I realized that I had been thinking about it, I found I had developed a theory or a means by which I might be able to believe in God. It was still quite insubstantial and would depend a great deal on whether I received any encouragement from some knowledgeable person.

Someone like Douglas. But, of course, I couldn't ask him.

My problems with organized religions sprang mainly from two things: the common notion of what God is, and the belief in the Biblical versions of creation.

I could not possibly believe in God as a white-bearded old man sitting on a throne on top of the clouds. I had flown up there many times and had never seen Him. I had the feeling that if there was a God, He (or She or It)—I couldn't really conceive of It as having gender—must be a great deal more remote, even nebulous, perhaps some sort of energy rather than a solid thing. This didn't really work for me either. God would have to be Something that could understand the human mind. I wondered whether the idea of being created in God's image might only apply to man's soul and mind, not to his body. But without some concrete idea of what God might be, I couldn't bring myself to believe in His existence.

I had never had much trouble with the creation versus evolution debate. Evolution has occurred and is occurring all around us all the time. No sane, educated, and at least reasonably intelligent person can deny that fact without going through mental gymnastics of denial that would leave me exhausted.

Why, I wondered, couldn't people just believe that God created evolution? That God, for some unfathomable reason, decided to create a universe that would contain a planet, Earth, on which God could somehow control the evolution of plants and animals so that one form would emerge all-powerful and be capable of reasoning and acting in ways that would be pleasing to Him?

In fact, one can see in what is known of the formation of the world, a parallel to the Biblical story of creation having occurred in seven days. You just have to imagine God's day as one covering eons of human time. The day and the night were created by setting the earth in rotation. Gradually, dry lands separated from the oceans and lifted up. Primitive life forms began to develop: plants, then animals, developing together, and only in the last tiny portion of time (the sixth day) did man, the vehicle of God's mind and soul, appear. On the seventh day God rested, and everything went to hell.

If this did occur, I thought, it didn't turn out too well. While some of us live good lives, as God wanted us to, at least part of the time, others do not, and almost no one consistently lives up to God's ideal all of their lives. What went wrong?

I was back to my previous idea that God is either not all-knowing or not all-loving. I think I'd rather have the loving God than the all-knowing one, and it would seem that this is what we got.

The only way I can square a loving God with the things that happen on earth to good people, is to believe that God only created us to live our lives as we devise them and does not control everything we do. In other words, He gave us free will. Perhaps He has the ability to do anything He wants with us, but chooses not to.

Why would He not want to? Possibly because if He interfered every time we had a problem, we'd never learn to take care of ourselves. We would remain as helpless as babies all our lives. We would never develop character, never solve problems, never have to make choices. In giving us free will, He would be allowing terrible things to happen, but the alternative would negate His entire plan in creating us.

I have trouble with the usual concept of heaven. I think I'd be bored stiff. But if I could go from this life to another where there were exciting things to do, challenges to accept, difficulties to overcome, and triumphs and rewards in the end, I'd be willing to go any time.

But what is this God that can manipulate the most intimate details of human life, who may have watched over me, led me on, and chosen the precise moment when I would be most receptive in order to get through to me? I needed a handle to get hold of the concept of God. I found it in the spectacular advancements in the field of science.

In Biblical days, people were very ignorant. I wondered if God had appeared to some of the more intelligent or the best storytellers, with some sort of manifestation of what He wanted of man, and these prophets relayed the message to the people of their times in terms that those people knew. God would have used simple means and His word would be interpreted in the light of the times and cultures in which the people lived. It would have been like a parent whose three-year-old had asked, "Where did I come from?" The parent would not have gotten out a book on human reproduction, but would have told a simple story in language a three-year-old could understand. I had the idea that we were now figuratively at the age to be university students, and religious fundamentalists were still trying to teach us out of a kindergarten text.

If this were so, then the Incarnation, Crucifixion, Resurrection, and Ascension began to make sense. God must have seen that humans were not interpreting His word in the way He had intended. When I am giving flight instruction, and a student doesn't seem to get the point of an exercise, I will say, "Let me show you." I will take over, do the manoeuvre, explaining as I go, then give the controls back to the student. Perhaps this is what God did. He created a person to be His representative, to live among us, and to be and do exactly what God wanted of us. Then to show us that there is life after death, God would have contrived a situation in which Jesus, His representative, would die in unquestionable and very public fashion, so there would be no doubt that He was dead. Then God would resurrect Him, making Him appear in the flesh to people who knew Him and would spread the word. The last act would be what we would now call a media event, a spectacular ascension. Indeed, if this was God's plan, it worked. The stories are as alive today as they were nearly two thousand years ago, and God's word has spread all over the world.

So, I wondered, what would happen if I looked for God in the light of modern knowledge?

Astronomers and physicists are making spectacular advances in the understanding of the universe. They are looking farther into space and seeing stars and galaxies in terms of their structure. They know that the universe is not bounded by what they can see, as every new advancement in telescopes allows them to look farther into space and see it in greater detail.

At the same time, other scientists are probing deeper and deeper into the makeup of molecules, atoms and subatomic particles. It is now known that tiny particles of matter constantly bombard this planet, and that many pass completely through it. In other words, the earth and everything on it is composed of particles held together by various forces, with a lot of space between. So when we look out into the heavens, are we not seeing much more massive things from the inside? I wondered if the earth is not a tiny particle in some massive table leg or cat's whisker or flu virus. If this is so, might there not be some cosmic being who is highly intelligent, extremely well-equipped, with the capability of looking deep into the things around it and of manipulating very tiny parts of them at its will?

Our God.

If this God does exist, and if He allows our world to exist long enough, one wonders if His existence might actually be proven by science. I hope not. I'm afraid that the reality might be a letdown compared with the mystery, and I'm sure there would be people who would complain that He was not what they had envisioned. On the other hand, He might be infinitely better than the human mind can imagine.

How could I find out whether this thinking would be acceptable? The Church has its structured ideas about the worship of God. Might this

THE EVIL THAT WE DO   257

be too far-out? They couldn't possibly just say, "Think what you want, as long as you believe in some form of god." In fact, every Sunday in church, we recite a Creed, which someone described as a long list of things we believe in. Looking at it more clearly, it is not long; it is not precise, even though it covers a lot of ground:

"We believe in one God, the Father, the Almighty, maker of heaven and earth, of all that is, seen and unseen. . . " It requires us to believe in the Incarnation, the Crucifixion, the Resurrection and the Ascension; that God, through Jesus, will be our judge; that God is the giver of life and that there is life after death. It doesn't say that God is a white-bearded old man sitting on a throne on top of the clouds or that when we go to Heaven, we will wear white gowns and sandals, sprout wings and a halo, and play the harp.

I could not think of this God as having human form or gender, but could call it God and refer to it as Him for the sake of simplicity. This God would have to be formless and unknowable in my mind, and I could not conceive of Him speaking to me in my language. But perhaps, on the occasions when I had a feeling that something special had happened, such as that moment during Douglas induction, it had been a manifestation of God's presence among us.

I tucked these thoughts neatly into a back corner of my mind and purposefully busied myself with the problems and pleasures of a long, successful season of flying, avoiding the thought that the winter lay ahead, when there would be too much time for unbidden thoughts about my spirituality to come to me. That was another time. I would not think about it now.

* * * *

It was a Sunday in late September. Clouds began to mass in the west, and a restless wind pushed the falling leaves along before it. For the first time in months, we needed the lights on in the church for a daytime service.

We had enjoyed a long, sun-filled summer, and on the feast day of our patron saint, St. Matthew, on September twenty-first, we had held a special service on a clear, warm evening. Now Mother Nature seemed to be warning us that such things don't last forever, that we had better prepare for change. I knew that there could still be periods of good flying weather well into October, but with a feeling of regret, I realized that the enjoyably hectic life was soon to end, and bleak winter was on the way, when there would be little flying and far too much time to reflect on things I'd rather shove into my subconscious.

The church had settled into a routine, with a happy buzz of activity. New groups had formed, an active stewardship campaign was underway, and the September Church Committee meeting had been as dull as an old black cassock.

As the procession to the altar began, I recognized the hymn as one with a catchy tune and a long vocal line and reminded myself to take a deep breath.

> "Praise to the Lord, the Almighty,
> the King of creation;
> O my soul, praise Him, for He is
> thy health and salvation."

Then I heard treble voices raised:

> "All ye who hear,
> Now to His temple draw near."

All the voices joined for the last line of the verse:

"Joining in glad adoration."

Children looking angelic in their homemade gowns walked side by side with the now large adult choir. It was amusing to see their scrubbed faces above the little red gowns. I was used to seeing them in cut-off shorts and black Vancouver Canucks T-shirts, but now the only hint that such attire was still to be found underneath the gowns was that ragged sneakers of varied hues stuck out from under the hems.

I said to Penny, "I see they have gotten the children's choir going now that Sunday School has started up again."

"Yes. I hear that they pay them a loony every time they show up."

"Loony tunes," I remarked.

We giggled like a couple of naughty school girls, and an elderly lady in the pew in front of us turned around and gave us a withering glare.

At the end of the service, before the Dismissal, Douglas announced, "I wanted you all to know that Brett Corrigan has confessed to killing his father and has agreed to plead guilty to second degree murder. Let us pray."

There was a rustle as two hundred people got down on their knees.

"Heavenly Father, we pray for the soul of Frank Corrigan. We also pray for his son, Brett, that in his years in prison, he will come to accept Jesus as his Saviour, that he will accept You into his life. We pray that he will be cured of his dependence on alcohol, that he will learn to accept responsibility for his actions, and that when he is released from prison, he will make a life for himself that is free from greed and violence. We ask this in the name of Jesus Christ, our Lord. Amen."

"Amen," said we all.

Douglas asked me to come to the office after the service. He and Betty greeted me as Douglas removed his long, white alb and hung it in the closet. The short-sleeved grey or white shirts he had worn during the heat of the summer had given way to a long-sleeved black one, and he pulled on a jacket over it.

He said, "We haven't seen much of you lately. You don't need to leave just because the investigation is over."

That was one of the reasons, I acknowledged to myself. I would never, never, ever admit to the other reason I had steered clear of Douglas for the last three months.

"You are always welcome at the rectory," Betty added. "We will have to have you come to dinner one of these days."

"Anyway, I wanted to fill you in on Brett Corrigan," Douglas continued. "Sergeant Jameson came to see me yesterday and gave me all the details."

I expressed my interest.

"As you know, in spite of the evidence that he had rented the plane, the positive identification by the bus driver who noticed him because he seemed so much more upset when he went back to the airport than he had coming in, the identification by your dispatcher, the fingerprint in the office, and the fact that blood on his shoe was of his father's blood type, Brett continued to deny having killed his father. His lawyer planned to bring up as many technicalities as possible in order to raise the question of reasonable doubt. Then, just this last week, the police got the results back from the DNA tests, and can prove without a doubt that the blood on his shoe was his father's. Apparently he put his clothes through the washer several times to remove blood stains from them, but didn't real-

THE EVIL THAT WE DO 261

ize he had stepped in the pool of blood.

"Anyway, when confronted with the DNA evidence, his lawyer told him it was all up and he caved in and confessed. He said he flew down here to ask his father for a loan to buy an airplane, a request which Frank greeted with scorn and contempt. When Frank turned his back on Brett and scolded him for swearing in church, Brett lost control, picked up the rock and hit Frank with it. He was horrified at what he had done and fled in panic."

"How did he lock the door?"

"He didn't go out it. He said he met his father coming out of the apartment house, they walked to the church and Frank locked the door after them so they could have a private conversation without being interrupted. When Brett ran out of the office, he saw two women standing on the sidewalk talking, so he ran through the church and out the door of the sacristy, which by the way, has the kind of lock that doesn't come unlocked when you open it from the inside. So when he pulled the door shut behind him, it was still locked. I know. I went out it the other day, shut the door behind me and found myself locked out. I had to go clear around to the other side of the church. Brett tried to get himself under control, went back to the bus stop, and caught the bus to the airport. The driver remembered him because he had asked for directions on the way in, and noticed the change in his demeanor. He then hurried to his plane and took off as quickly as he could. He got home just in time to change clothes before the police arrived to tell him about his father's death."

"Did the bus driver notice the blood?"

"There apparently wasn't that much. Just a fine spray."

"Still, he seems to have left a pretty broad back trail. The police would have gotten onto him before long."

"They would have, but they still appreciated your shortcutting the process. Apparently the bus driver was considering going to the police and telling them about Brett after hearing about the murder, but his wife persuaded him to clam up. She didn't want him to get involved with the police."

I grimaced. "I daresay a lot more crimes would be cleared up if witnesses were willing to come forward."

"Probably so. Of course, when they asked the bus driver, he came across with the information. I visited Brett at the RCMP lock-up. He is pretty despondent. I think it is a mixture of genuine regret at killing his father, and his realization that he faces twenty years or so in prison. There is self-pity there, but also an awful awareness that in one thoughtless moment, he brought his whole world crashing down around him.

"He did have some concern for others as well. He is dismayed that his little daughter is going to grow up having to cope with being the daughter of a murderer. His ex-wife hasn't come to see him, nor has his mother. He says that, even though he performed an unspeakable act in our church, we are the only people who have shown him any compassion. Incidentally, he singles you out as the one who responded the most to his needs."

"Oh, no!" I wailed. "That makes me feel terrible. I'm the one who put the finger on him. Does he know that?"

"No, I don't think so."

"I'm glad he pleaded guilty so I don't have to testify against him."

"So far, he doesn't seem to have connected you with your dispatcher who identified him."

I groaned, "And I'm the one who kept asking Sergeant Jameson if he was sure Brett had an alibi because he seemed the most likely person to have done it. I feel awful!"

"But you were correct, weren't you? It wasn't as if you were trying to frame him. I remember once we were talking about pride as a sin. Give it the name self-centredness and you will see that it was behind this crime. Both the perpetrator and the victim were acting out of selfishness, roles that were customary in their lives."

Douglas reached out and laid a hand over mine. After a long reflective pause, I heaved a deep sigh and remarked, "You were right when you said that the killer was the one going through the ordeal."

"Yes." Douglas smiled and looked out the open door of his office into the main church office, where Shirley Meacham in her role as church secretary was helping count the money in the collection plates. "I think the experience gave strength to Shirley and Harry."

"I agree."

"Anyway, back to you, Robin. We do miss you."

"I didn't want to be a nuisance," I stammered.

"You are no nuisance. We love you."

Pulling myself together, I blurted out, "I can't associate with you on false pretenses. I have to tell you something."

Douglas had risen to go to his desk. He turned, smiling. "That you don't believe in God?"

I gasped. "How did you know?"

"Oh, Robin. It shows all the time. You are not a natural liar, in spite of the sergeant's remarks, and you don't try to disguise your feelings. Working as closely with you as I did, I couldn't help but notice that you feel awkward and show reticence whenever you are asked something that directly relates to God. You can talk about God on an impersonal level, but not on a personal one."

I asked weakly, "Then why do you put up with me? Why do you still welcome me in the church?"

"Because I think you are looking for God." He made an expansive gesture that included the whole church. "Where better to look for Him than in His house?"

"I still don't understand what you see in me."

"What I see in you is a person with great moral integrity, one who values justice and will not stand by when someone near her is threatened. People like you are rare."

"Really? I don't think I'm exceptional."

"I remember that morning you stormed in here. Everyone else had said to me, 'Do something!' You came in and said, 'What can we do?'

"Look back to Biblical times. Think of the events of Jesus' crucifixion. When Jesus was arrested, except for a brief show of defiance, all His followers melted away. Even His disciples abandoned Him. Not one person came to speak up for Him.

"Robin, I think that if you had been there, you would have marched into Pontius Pilate's residence, shaken your finger under his nose, and said, 'How dare you? Let this man go!'

We all broke out laughing at the vision Douglas had created.

"Seriously, Robin, I miss the discussions we used to have. They kept me on my toes. Come back again and talk some more."

I sat there, doubt sticking out all over me, and Douglas said with the serene assurance of the true believer, "Give it time, Robin. It will come."

I knew then that the door that had been closed to me three months ago was now open again and I could confidently walk through it. Perhaps I would never come to a true belief in Douglas' God, or perhaps I would. The prospect excited me.

Douglas was holding out a hand to me, both physically and spiritually. I reached out and took it.

About The Author

Like the narrator of *The Evil That We Do*, author Anne Barton is a flight instructor and a church committee member, flies a military trainer and has a cat named Cloud Nine. She does not have red hair.

WATCH FOR THESE NEW COMMONWEALTH BOOKS

	ISBN #	U.S.	Can
❑ **EPITAPH FOR A CLICHÉ,** Susan L. Zimmerman	1-55197-012-0	$4.99	$6.99
❑ **SAND DREAMS,** William Allen	1-55197-002-3	$4.99	$6.99
❑ **DEATH BY CHARITY,** Carol Ann Owen	1-55197-020-4	$4.99	$6.99
❑ **DAYS OF THE MESSIAH: PHARAOH,** Ehab Abunuwara	1-55197-004-X	$5.99	$7.99
❑ **POOLS OF ANCIENT EVIL,** Eric E. Little	1-55197-008-2	$4.99	$6.99
❑ **DEMANITY DEMANDS,** Eric Tate	1-55197-018-X	$5.99	$7.99
❑ **NO TIME CLOCKS ON TREES,** Gary Lilley	1-55197-020-1	$4.99	$6.99
❑ **FOR YOU, FATHER,** Jennifer Goodhand	1-55197-016-3	$4.99	$6.99
❑ **JOURNEY TO SPLENDOURLAND,** L. J. London	1-55197-024-4	$4.99	$6.99
❑ **I.R.S. TERMINATED,** Charles Steffes	1-55197-137-2	$4.99	$6.99

Available at your local bookstore or use this page to order.

Send to: COMMONWEALTH PUBLICATIONS INC.
9764 - 45th Avenue
Edmonton, Alberta, CANADA T6E 5C5

Please send me the items I have checked above. I am enclosing $_____$ (please add $2.50 per book to cover postage and handling). Send check or money order, no cash or C.O.D.'s, please.

Mr./Mrs./Ms._____

Address_____

City/State_____ Zip_____

Please allow four to six weeks for delivery.
Prices and availability subject to change without notice.

WATCH FOR THESE NEW COMMONWEALTH BOOKS

WATCH FOR THESE NEW COMMONWEALTH BOOKS

Robin Carruthers runs a flight school, and is a member of St. Matthew's Anglican Church, though ambivalent about her belief in God. When one church member is murdered and another suspected of the killing, she teams up with new priest Douglas Forsythe to quell the rampant rumors by finding the real murderer. In the process, Robin finds the answers to questions much closer to home.

The Evil That We Do

by
Anne Barton

"All in favour?"

"Wait a minute," Sue Ambler interjected firmly. She pulled out a soft-bound book. "I have here a copy of Canon Law and it says. . ."

"I don't think we need to refer to diocesan canons for a simple committee decision that's purely local." Albert betrayed unusual defensiveness.

My ears pricked up. What decision, I wondered, is Albert so sensitive about? What's been going on?

"Let me have my say," Sue looked around defiantly.

"Go ahead," Albert conceded.

"Canon Law governs all phases of the operation of the church. It is generalized in many cases, allowing us some leeway, but what the Maintenance Committee did is obviously contradictory to Canon Law." She waved the book in the air.

"We only agreed to pay a bunch of bills," Frank muttered.

"No you didn't. Bills, yes. The routine bills that came in, and you replaced a broken window pane in the garage at the rectory. That's okay. That's what the committee is for. But you also accepted the resignation of a salaried employee, and that's way beyond the scope of the Maintenance Committee."

"We didn't actually do that," Layton said. He as treasurer, Nick as rector's warden and also representing Buildings and Grounds, Frank, Albert, Gretchen, who was the people's warden, and the rector comprised the committee in question. Layton continued, "We just okayed the answer to Shirley's letter."

"What letter?" Sue demanded.

"The letter Shirley wrote resigning her job."

"Who was the letter sent to?" Sue's look in in

Frank's direction plainly said that she didn't believe it was sent to him.

"To the Church Committee," Albert answered.

"So why didn't you bring it to this full Church Committee meeting before acting on it?"

"I'm the *chairman*." Albert was now definitely on the run. "I thought I should make the decisions."

"You're the chairman, not the commanding officer." Paul's acerbic reply sparked a flicker of alarm that momentarily passed across Albert's face. Almost instantly, his mask of suavity flooded back. "I had no intention of offending any of you."

Gretchen was the one looking offended. Every time one of the men used the term chairman I saw her open her mouth to voice a correction, but the action was too fast-paced for her to get a word in edgeways.

Penny got in on the act. "It says in the minutes that the committee wrote a letter accepting Shirley's resignation. Who wrote it, and what does it say?"

"I wrote it myself. It was just an acceptance."

"Where is the letter Shirley wrote?" I asked. "And a copy of the letter you wrote back? I think we should see them."

Albert looked uncomfortable. "I've got them."

"May we see them?"

"Well, I don't have them with me, but she very specifically said she was resigning." Anxiety registered in Albert's voice again.

"I don't see what we're arguing about," Myrtle declared. "She told me herself she was going to resign." A few others nodded in assent.

"That's not the point," I explained. "The point is that the Maintenance Committee didn't have the authority to make the decision they did."

"What difference would it make?" Myrtle in-